PRAISE FOR LAURA MARNEY'S NOVELS:

"A gently humorous ... West Highlands."
GUARDIAN

"A shot of adrenalin... Hard-core romance for the bitter and twisted." *INDEPENDENT, 50 BEST SUMMER READS*

"At last, a funny novelist with guts." HENRY SUTTON, *MIRROR*

"Biting wit, brilliant characterisation and hilarious antics – whether you are 16 or 60, you'll be rocking in your chair." *DAILY RECORD*

"Endlessly witty and good-natured... Marney has introduced a darker tinge to her writing without relinquishing an ounce of her charm Do not miss out on Laura Marney." *GLASGOW HERALD*

"Marney shows rare insight into the human condition, and her unique style and wit have the reader laughing out loud one moment and incredibly sad the next. She manages to offset the gruesome reality with some sparkling banter. A real breath of fresh air." JACQUELINE WILSON, *BRISTOL EVENING POST*

"Laura Marney in dizzying form. Effortless prose and solid characterisation... an honest, rounded and enviably simple novel that feels wholly organic in its unfolding." *THE LIST*

"Divine comedy... a joyous celebration of human imperfection." LOUISE WELSH

"The writing has an engaging confidence, a comic brio which comes ... ly inhabiting her narrator's character... She's a natural " *SCOTSMAN*

"... Laura Marney is that she's Scotland's best-kept literary secret and for once, the goods live up to the fanfare... A sparkling black comedy with guaranteed out-loud laughs." *YORK EVENING PRESS*

"Insight, compassion and a rollicking, earthy humour... If you suffer from giggle incontinence, beware!" ZOË STRACHAN

Also by Laura Marney

NO WONDER I TAKE A DRINK

NOBODY LOVES A GINGER BABY

ONLY STRANGE PEOPLE GO TO CHURCH

MY BEST FRIEND HAS ISSUES

Published by Saraband

For Faughie's Sake

Laura Marney

Saraband

Published by
Saraband
Suite 202, 98 Woodlands Road
Glasgow, G3 6HB, Scotland
www.saraband.net

ISBN: 9781908643629
ebook: 9781908643636

Cover illustration and design: Scott Smyth
Text layout: Laura Jones

Printed in the EU on paper sourced from sustainably managed forests.

1 2 3 4 5 6 17 16 15 14

This book is for Holly, Max, Benjamin and David.
And for Faughie.
Another Faughie is possible.

So come all ye at hame wi' Freedom
Never heed whit the hoodies croak for doom
In your hoose a' the bairns o' Adam
Can find breid, barley-bree and painted room

Hamish Henderson

Chapter 1

Hollywood had come to the Highlands. Not the widescreen, surround-sound, 3D Highlands. Or the misty moors of Scotchland: the wee deoch an doruis, granny's hielan kailyard, heuchter-stick-it-up-your-teuchter Highlands.

No, the actual Highlands.

Filming of the blockbuster *Freedom Come All of You* had already begun around the village. It wasn't glamorous like I'd thought it might be, just inconvenient. Traffic tailed back behind convoys of location vehicles: long trucks full of lighting and camera equipment and endless snaking coils of greasy black cables. The steep-sided trucks parked on the grass verge and hung there at such an alarming angle I worried they might keel over in a strong wind.

To recreate the Highlands of yesteryear, informative road signs were taken down, and not replaced, and roads were often closed without notice or explanation, incurring four-mile detours. I wondered when, or indeed if, they had permission to close roads like that, but it was Global Imperial, they had bought the town; they could do anything they wanted.

As I drove down to the village, Faughie FM was playing *Freedom Come Aw Ye*, the song by Hamish Henderson from which the film had taken its title. As DJ Andy Robertson played this song in heavy rotation, I was unable to stop tapping my toe and humming along. Despite this constant reminder of the film title, I'd overheard people in the village giving it the nickname *Brigadoom*.

Driving past, I noticed that the new helipad was nearly finished. The tarmac had set and two men were rolling a paint cart to form a huge white H inside the circle. That had not taken long. It was strangely exciting to think that anything urgent enough to warrant a helicopter could happen in Inverfaughie. In the three months I'd lived here the most urgent thing I'd ever seen was a tourist jump out of a moving coach and sprint to the public toilets.

The village was bustling with activity now, and everyone was making money, lots of residential homes had suddenly become B&Bs and people were out tidying their gardens or polishing their windows. Taxis were dropping off and finding new fares within minutes. The influx wasn't just the usual Berghaus-clad climbers: intelligent dafties who spent their days humfing expensive kit up the north face and their evenings boasting about it in the Caley Hotel. No, these visitors were snappy dressers with sports cars. Audis, Subarus and Mazdas were everywhere. It actually took me a few minutes to find a parking space.

Global Imperial's production office was a Portakabin, but inside it was remarkably plush: thick carpets and thick curtains, behind which thick wads of cash were being exchanged for accommodation contracts. Jenny had already told me to insist on a block booking, and advised me on the going rates.

'I can't ask for that kind of money, they'll chase me,' I'd told her.

'You'd be a fool not to. That's what everybody's charging. You don't want to undercut everyone else, Trixie. Giving Global Imperial a reason to drive the price down won't make you popular.'

She was right; I didn't want to be even less popular than I already was.

'Highlanders don't get many opportunities,' she'd lectured me, 'we have to grab them when they come along.'

Pleased to meet me, the Accommodation Manager ushered me straight in. Her assistant had apparently been delighted with my B&B facility. She didn't quibble about the price, didn't bat an eye. She wanted to reserve all six double rooms for the duration.

'If you let me have your bank details, Mrs McNicholl,' she said in a lovely American accent, 'I'll ping the deposit over to you now. Oh, and may I take a copy of your Accommodation Licence?'

*

This was the first time I'd actually met a Member of the Scottish Parliament. I'd expected a sharp-suited, thrusting, handsome charmer, but Malcolm was more of a baggy-arsed, corduroy pantywaist. As I'd come to appreciate since moving here, life in the Highlands was replete with disappointments. I smiled politely and folded my arms. This was going to be a long night. Jenny Robertson, the local postmistress and shop owner, had invited me round to her house for what she'd billed a 'soiree'. We weren't exactly contemporaries: Jenny had at least twenty years on me. I would have put her in her early sixties but she had all the energy of a spider monkey and the nous of a city fox. She was skinny and a bit wrinkly, though you could see she'd been a good-looking woman in her day. And nosey? Jenny's nosiness knew no bounds, but I, a recent incomer, had no other friends. Never having been invited to a soiree before, I'd accepted immediately, but if I'd known that 'soiree' was Jenny's word for a night of envelope stuffing and political chat, I'd have politely declined. I had more important things to think about.

'It doesn't matter how small you are,' Walter tried to inculcate us, 'if you have faith and a plan of action.'

Worried that I'd giggle, I tried not to look directly at him. Walter had his passionate face on: his head tilted heroically, his eyes bright with visionary gleam. This would have been moving if it wasn't for the cake crumbs that were trapped in the creases round his mouth.

Malcolm snorted, looking to Jenny and me for support.

'Not *my* words: but Fidel Castro's,' Walter continued, holding his hands up to demonstrate his lack of influence with the Cuban revolutionary. 'Fidel Castro's, who – just to remind you – took on the United States of America.'

3

Walter pushed the pile of *Vote for Malcolm Robertson* leaflets to one side, leaned right into Malcolm's face and whispered, 'And won.'

'We couldn't do it even if we wanted to,' scoffed Malcolm. 'We don't have the resources.'

'That's the problem with you LibDems,' Walter retorted, his nostrils flaring, 'no ambition, no imagination. You're a shower of lily-livered Jessies.'

Jenny hooted and so, taking her lead, I laughed too.

When I'd helped her get the tea things earlier she'd assured me that this was just good-natured banter between the lads. From their spirited debate, Walter appeared to despise everything the other guy stood for, and yet here he was, Malcolm Robertson's official campaign manager. And here I was, stuffing envelopes to help Malcolm retain his seat. This wasn't what I'd come for. I needed to ask Jenny's advice on something but now that we were bogged down in this tedious debate there was no opportunity.

'We're easily self-sufficient,' Walter argued relentlessly, 'we'll not be eating many mangos but we have all the crops and livestock and dairy we need.'

'So we won't starve, but what about creating wealth?' countered Malcolm.

'What do you want, Malky? *Opum furiata cupido.*'

Right, that's it, I thought, Walter's started with the Latin, I'm out of here.

'What is this frenzied lust for wealth? I'm talking about transformational politics,' Walter boffed on, 'egalité, fraternité, liberté: education, health care, housing. We create the wealth the same way we always have, from our exports: salmon, fish, whisky, green energy, fresh clean water. The only difference is that we get to keep the revenue. Open your eyes, man, we're rich beyond the dreams of avarice!'

We looked to Malcolm for a comeback.

'Maybe,' he said meekly, 'but apart from the, eh, wealth, and equality, fraternity and um, oh yeah, the liberty, what else have we got?'

Walter sighed heavily and slammed his head down on the table. After all his rhetoric, he was finally defeated by Malcolm's complete lack of an argument. But I had bigger problems.

I didn't want to be here any more. Not here, in Jenny's living room. Not here living in this small suffocating Highland town. I needed to get back to civilisation. How could two old geezers having an abstract argument about independence fix that for me? It was patently such airy-fairy nonsense. That's what annoyed me about politics: it never went anywhere, never solved anything. I'd been offered no alcoholic refreshment whatsoever, not so much as a small sweet sherry. Having had no advice from Jenny, I still had the same problems I came in with, only now I was bored, frustrated and still sober.

I didn't have the head space for politics, I had my own troubles: my only neighbours had vanished and an ugly fence had gone up around their property. The Accommodation Inspectorate was due any day and the fence might mean I'd never get my Bed and Breakfast licence. No licence, no accommodation contract; no money, no exit route. I'd never get out of Inverfaughie. I'd die alone here in the damp mist, encased in cobwebs and wispy white mould.

Action was what was required, not pointless political sparring. As I made my apologies and got my coat, I decided that in future I should steer well clear of politician types, so much balloon juice only wound me up. I'd concentrate on solving my own problems and leave the politics to those with nothing better to do.

Chapter 2

'*Hooch Aye the Noo!*' the sign said, '*The Management would like to extend a warm Highland welcome to Harrosie: Bed and Breakfast, all mod cons, groovy atmos.*'

I'd found the wooden sign at the back of the garden shed, dusted it off, painted it and, in a fit of optimism, hung it back on the rusting bracket outside the front door. But that was before the house next door was fenced off like a condemned building, a place of plague.

The place that I'd lived in for the last three months, and that I'd grudgingly had to accept was my home – for the moment at least – was one of two houses that sat on a hill overlooking the dreich village of Inverfaughie.

If you enjoyed dreichicity, Harrosie was an ideal B&B: there were eight bedrooms, three with their own bathrooms, another bathroom and toilet, a big kitchen, dining room, a wee back room and a long lounge facing the front. The view to the right was of purple and grey mountains that skulked around Loch Faughie. To the left it looked out to sea at the islands, swathed in mist, like tropical islands, except with a sub-tropical, sub-zero climate. All the bedrooms even had brass plaques on the doors and were all named after whiskies.

When I repainted the sign I picked out the letters in heather colours, purple and yellow. The bit about groovy atmos I'd added myself, anything for a laugh. Underneath I'd reinstated the three thistles. Until I'd lived in the Highlands, using thistles as a mark of excellence had struck me as weird; thistles were jaggy and inhospitable, but now I totally got it. For an accommodation rating system, they could just as well have used midgies.

Elton John was dead right: life was a circle. My old mum Elsie, god rest her soul, had come here to Harrosie all those years ago to work as a housemaid. After my fortieth birthday, forty years after mum had left Inverfaughie, I'd returned. Just because I was a bit fed up with my job and wasn't getting on with my ex, just because some distant relative had left me something in his will, just because I was bored and lonely and horny and, seeking excitement, I'd thrown the dummy out of the pram. It might have been my mid-life crisis, or something to do with my ex-husband being shacked up with an au pair half his age, but I'd given up my home, my teenage son, my pals, my well-paid job and all my worldly pleasures. What a donkey.

And now I was about to carry on the work that Elsie had begun – changing sweaty sheets and cleaning stain-streaked toilets for paying guests. Not because I was going to enjoy performing intimate ablutions for strangers, but because it was the only way I'd ever earn enough money to go home. The mid-life crisis had been a huge mistake, I knew that now. I could hear how Elsie would have laughed: Miss High and Mighty Medical Sales Rep of the Month (April Thru Oct), scrubbing kitchen pots and toilet pans. But I'd have the last laugh. My mother had been a mere housemaid; I might not own the building but I was the proprietress of the B&B business, the Mistress of Harrosie.

I'd been reluctant to move out of 'Glenmorangie', the best-appointed room in the house. The wee room at the back, 'Tullibardine', would have to do as my bedroom – that was, if I ever managed to get rid of the smell of boiled sheep. In the olden days when Harrosie had been a farm building, this wee back room must have been where they did those quaint agrarian things like sheep boiling, although why they would haul sheep up two flights and a landing was a mystery to me. With persistent rumours of sheepshaggery

7

it was better not to think about it. No, the wee room would do me fine. The slightly bigger room, 'Old Pulteney', next door to mine, would do for Steven. That would leave me six bedrooms; six lucrative revenue streams. And this was set to be Inverfaughie's best ever summer. Not because of the mintcake-munching climbers, but because of the movie.

When I'd first arrived in this wee village I'd tried to integrate: I volunteered with the guitar group, worked at the annual gala day. Ok, I'd got a bit drunk at the ceilidh, aye, fair enough, I'd said some things, been a bit inappropriate, but it was hardly a hanging offence. Highland villages were hard unforgiving places, loyal to their own. I'd never be accepted here, I was a white settler, and a gobby Glaswegian into the bargain. I was as welcome as an outbreak of Legionnaires' Disease in high season.

Inverfaughie was no place for incomers; my English neighbours had worked that out before me. They'd left suddenly, packed up their kids and their suitcases. They didn't even stop to take their furniture. The first I knew of it was early last Sunday morning when I saw them standing in the rain like bedraggled refugees. The kids were wailing, their thin shoulders heaving in the Highland drizzle. Rebecca, their eight year old, and my only friend in this friendless place, clung to Bouncer and wiped her tears on his fur. She sobbed so hard she induced a bout of hiccups.

'I'll miss you Trixie,' she gulped, 'and you too Bouncer.'

When she hugged me it wasn't easy to let her go.

Once the taxi had pulled away and the noise of the distressed young family faded, their house was like a bricked-up tomb.

'Bring out your dead!' I cried into the wilderness.

They had left me their keys, mumbling something about letting the estate agent in, but it was builders who came.

The builders didn't want the keys, they didn't need access to the house, they said. They rolled up with two huge trucks and within three days had built an eight-foot-high perimeter fence. No matter how much I plied them with tea and my home baking, the foreman couldn't, or wouldn't, tell me who had instructed the work and, more importantly, why.

Harrosie now stood, isolated on top of the hill next to a sealed fortress within an ugly fence of untreated wood. It was like living next door to Guantanamo.

'Bring out your dead,' I shouted as the builders drove away.

I phoned Steven but he was more curious than outraged.

'But what's the purpose of this mysterious erection?' he said.

'That'll do, Steven.'

'Is the fence keeping something out?' He took a loud theatrical in-breath. 'Or keeping something sinister in?'

Chapter 3

'You're looking well, Trixie!' Jenny gushed as I entered her shop. 'Your wee detox programme is working wonders.'

Although it sounded like a compliment, you had to watch with Jenny. Though often entertaining, she could be hard work. I'd been toying with the idea of treating myself to a wee half-bottle, well earned I thought after all my frantic cleaning, but Jenny's mention of my 'wee detox' instantly scuppered that plan. A girl has her pride. And her vanity. Perhaps Jenny was right, maybe I did look better. My pink mottled skin and red alky nose were definitely heading towards a beige tone. It was true, these last few days I'd been feeling a bit healthier.

'What can I get you?'

'Just a Twix please, a packet of cheese and onion, a Bounty and a big bottle of Diet Coke. Oh, and I'll take one of those family bags of Minstrels.'

That lot should get me through an evening's TV viewing. Since I'd given up my best friend, whisky, I'd built a comfortable nest of loneliness and disappointment, nestling down every night under my rustling sweetie wrappers.

While Jenny was assembling my order, Walter walked in. I had wandered away from the counter, into a dark corner where I was examining a multipack of toilet seat seals, so Walter probably didn't realise there was anyone else in the shop. I did nothing to warn him I was there. I wanted to see what happened next.

Holding out his arms, Walter waltzed slowly, in his graceful old geezer way, towards Jenny. He was going to kiss her: he was headed behind the counter where he was going to grab her into a passionate clinch and winch her, right in front of me.

'Toilet seat seals!' Jenny squawked, 'I have them on special, Trixie, they're a popular seller.'

Alerted, Walter smoothly altered course for the customer side of the counter. There would be no clinch and no winch, not while I was there to witness it.

'Hello Trixie,' said Walter, in his dignified Highland whisper, 'Malcolm has asked me to pass on his appreciation of your help and to enquire after your health. I'll be pleased to report that you're looking well.'

'I'm grand, Walter, and you? You're looking great too,' I said, 'they'll be wanting you to star in the film. All the girls will be after you, Jenny'll be jealous.'

Walter smiled tightly, politely, but otherwise they both body-swerved it. This was the annoying thing about Inverfaughie, the bare-faced hypocrisy of the town. I knew Jenny was his girlfriend, everybody must have known, it was obvious, but for some reason she and Walter always insisted on pretending, even to me, that they were just good friends. Jenny now glared at Walter.

'I've only come to bring you more leaflets,' he said defensively.

Walter went into his rucksack and produced a clipboard and a bundle of leaflets. I assumed it was more 'Vote for Malcolm' leaflets but these were different. As I peered at them he explained.

'We're trying to keep the tweed mill open. Would you like to sign the petition?'

'Eh, ok,' I agreed.

'Leave it on the counter and I'll ask everybody to sign,' said Jenny as she buzzed about filling my order. 'God knows, most of Inverfaughie depends on that mill one way or another. What the firk were they thinking? Excuse the language, but I knew this would happen.'

I braced myself for one of Jenny's well-worn rants. I'd been hearing this for weeks since the mill, which had previously made more than eight thousand individual tweeds, had reduced production to just a handful of popular patterns.

'Here's a perfect case in point,' she said, tugging at the sleeve of Walter's tweed jacket to demonstrate, 'look at the colours through that. Is that not a thing of beauty? That's a work of art,' she declared, answering her own question.

'That's why I'm wearing it: in solidarity with the mill workers.'

As I dutifully stared at his jacket I saw that Jenny was right; what seemed at a distance to be boring grey twill, when looked at closely, with its bright yellow, green and pink threads woven together, was really quite beautiful.

'*Now* they've realised what sells tweed isn't a few restricted patterns on trendy trainers,' Jenny fumed, '*Now* they've realised, when twenty-three people are being made redundant and this village is losing the only industry it has left. *Now* they get it. When it's too late.'

'It's not too late yet,' said Walter, 'Malcolm's working with the government to find a buyer.'

'Are you kidding me on? The Scottish government? Jeezo, if they were any more apathetic they'd be sleeping.'

'Now don't get yourself all worked up, Moo, it's not fair to the customers,' he said, winking at me. 'Many thanks for taking the petition, if you give me my parcel I'll be off home.'

'Och,' said Jenny, impatiently, 'can you not wait for Jan to deliver it? I've never met such an impatient man.'

Jenny spoke with such familiar contempt and Walter, long used to it, hardly seemed to notice. Like a kid at Christmas, he ripped the parcel open right there and then. It was a book, a heavy tome, dirty with yellowed dog-eared pages.

'Don't be getting your fusty book dust all over my clean shop,' Jenny warned, as she shooed him out of the shop, his book under his arm and his feet hardly touching the floor.

'Cheerio Trixie!' he called cheerfully.

'Bye, Walter, happy reading!' I called back.

I was ready for her.

'Moo?' I smirked, as Jenny came back into the shop.

Chapter 4

Jenny returned behind her counter shaking her head and smiling.

'Walter and his history books.'

'Yeah,' I agreed, 'I don't understand why people get so excited about history.'

'You might not understand this, Trixie, but that man is a superbly political animal and esteemed scholar,' said Jenny, pointing in the direction she had just hustled him out. 'Don't write him off just because he had to retire.'

'I wasn't going to.'

'He's successfully run Malcolm's campaign every election as far back as I can remember and he's not even a LibDem. He does it to get people to engage with politics.'

'That's very –' I struggled for a positive about something that was so clearly a waste of time '– admirable.'

'And politics isn't the only string to his bow; he's actually better known for his Highland history, a recognised authority.'

'I wasn't saying anything against Walter, I just meant that history in general was a bit boring, I hated it at school.'

'Well you know nothing. Walter's right: history explains to us who we are, and why we are the way we are.'

I was offended and was torn between taking the huff and letting it pass; we'd just got over her tweed mill tirade, I'd been looking forward to a bit more light-hearted chat.

'They're always phoning him; asking him to come on the radio: Radio Scotland, Radio Four, they're all after him. Walter's been on the radio more times than ...'

'Terry Wogan?' I ventured.

'Than you've had ...'

'Terry Wogan?'

'Help ma Boab! You've *had* Terry Wogan?' she asked, mock wide-eyed.

'Tee hee,' I said, in acknowledgement of her old-fashioned 'Oor Wullie'-type banter.

'Onyhow,' she continued, 'Walter's been on the radio plenty, that's all you need to know. Now, what was it you wanted again? Aye, that was it: Twix, cheese and onion, Bounty, Minstrels and diet coke. Anything else I can get you?'

'Eh, no, I think that's it. Got to watch the old figure, you know.'

'You're not wrong there,' she said, looking me up and down over her specs as she scanned and bleeped and bagged my items, 'And will you be wanting any toothpaste today?'

What was this? A barb at my tooth-rotting confectionery consumption?

'I've plenty toothpaste at home, thanks.'

'Are you sure? Computer says you haven't ordered any for two months, you must be running out by now. And didn't you say your Steven is visiting next weekend?'

'See, this is where your superfast, all-whistling, all-farting computer system falls down, Jenny. What Computer doesn't know is that the last time Steven came he brought a large tube of Colgate and left without it. I'm up to my stumps in toothpaste.'

'But you'll be needing to stock up for your B&B guests. Actors take dental hygiene very seriously, you know, especially Americans. They must drink bleach to get their teeth that white. It wouldn't be me.'

'Well,' I said, bewildered by her determination, 'I'd kind of assumed that guests would bring their own toiletries.'

'Ah, but the odd time someone will have forgotten to pack their toilet bag and there you'll be: ready to supply them with a nice fresh tube of toothpaste, deodorant or what have you, and make a nice mark-up on it too. Upselling, that's how to maximise profits. God love you, Trixie, but you've a lot to learn about running a business.'

Did she really think I hadn't noticed she was trying to upsell to me?

'Yes, but as I keep trying to tell you: I won't have any guests unless I get my B&B licence and I might not get it because of that godawful fence.'

'Don't you be worrying your head about that fence,' Jenny said, 'you just make sure Harrosie is spick and span for the Licensing Inspectorate.'

'It is,' I said. 'It couldn't be spicker or any more span.'

My cleaning of Harrosie was so thorough I'd even hosed down Bouncer's manky basket. He'd sulked for a day and half. Whenever I came into the room he made a great show of getting up slowly, in that passive aggressive way, and skulking out with his head low and his tail wedged tight in his undercarriage. If I tried to speak to him he only gave me those lingering reproachful looks that were supposed to make me feel guilty.

'The Inspectorate will be the judge of that,' said Jenny. 'And by the bye,' she added, as if butter wouldn't melt, 'your boyfriend will be here in a minute.'

'Which one?'

Her eyes narrowed. 'How many boyfriends have you got?'

'You tell me, you seem to know everything that goes on in this village.'

'Oh now, I wasn't meaning Jackie,' she said softly. 'You know fine I meant Jan. He'll be in to pick up the postbag; I thought you'd be pleased to see him. You two have been spending a lot of time together.'

'Jan teaches the guitar club, I help out with the guitar club kids, that's it. Sorry to disappoint you, Jenny.'

And I was. The bored, lonely, horny thing hadn't gone away.

'Aye, but Jan told me this morning he took you up to the hippies' place for your dinner.'

Thanks Jan.

'They're not hippies.'

'Och, those New-Agers he's moving in with, you know who I mean. They're all living together, whatever you want to call it,' she continued.

The shop was empty, I was her only customer, but Jenny was not one to stand around shooting the breeze. She preferred to get on with stocktaking or wiping down tins while she was breeze-shooting, gossip-mongering, or just generally character-assassinating.

'What did they feed you? Something oaty? Oats are the only thing they buy from me. I don't know what they live on, it must be air, and porridge, and free love. I hear they have a couple of goats now. God save us. And the young fella, a nice enough boy, but he's not right in the head. You know, those hippies are as close to family as Jan's got here in Scotland. Things must be getting serious between you two.'

She was fishing, throwing chum out the back of the boat.

'Actually, you're right,' I murmured, 'he doesn't want me to say anything but you've guessed it ...'

Jenny had been dusting a tin of sweetcorn but her cloth stopped mid-wipe. She gave me a quick suspicious glance and then leaned in, she couldn't help herself.

'Steven *is* coming up next weekend, I think I will take some toothpaste, thanks.'

Chapter 5

Jenny had guessed right: Jan's friends had fed me oats. That sounds like they hooked a nose bag round my ears and called me Dobbin, but actually they served up a lip-smacking dish of smoked mackerel and 'skirlie', which turns out to be fried oatmeal and onion. They had grown the onions themselves and caught the mackerel in the loch. They apologised that the oats were shop-bought but they'd had a minor crop failure. The soil was all wrong apparently, but they were planning another crop with their own organic oats later in the year. I'd never eaten skirlie before, it was delicious.

'Like a furry worm in your belly,' said Brenda, which sounded weird in such a posh English accent.

I recognised Brenda and some of the others from 'Fat of the Land', the TV show that had been on telly about two years previously. I'd never met anyone off the telly before and I had to resist the impulse to ask for their autographs. They were so nice, so down to earth. They were much less skinny than they had been on TV. On telly they'd been positively emaciated and TV was supposed to make you look ten pounds heavier. Maybe since then, having successfully lived off the fat of the land, they'd each gained at least ten pounds. Of fat. Of the land.

A TV company had taken a group of city folk, businesspeople and the like, out to an uninhabited island north of Faughie. Like most of them, Brenda and her son had never set foot in the countryside, never mind north of the border. Once on the island they were housed in portakabins and experts were brought in to teach them self-sufficiency. After the most basic of training they gave them some livestock and a bag of seeds and left them to it. That's not to say they left them alone – they filmed every throbbing minute of it – but they did nothing to help them. Their cameras simply observed them maiming themselves on farm machinery or slowly starving to death. It was riveting. Me and Mum had been avid viewers. Of course, the participants eventually turned it around. Some of the people who had started out totally useless, the flashy car salesman, crusty university lecturer, ditzy fashion model, these were the very ones who began to thrive in this environment. By the time the series ended they were competent farmers with roses in their cheeks swearing that they'd never return to the city. And some of them didn't.

They came here, to Inverfaughie. They clubbed together, leased some land and a row of broken-down cottages and called themselves Ethecom, short for Ethical, Ecological Community. They were restoring the cottages, slowly building the place up, and doing it all sustainably. Like Old MacDonald's Farm, they had every kind of farmyard animal, a few of each running round. They had planted crops, they even had horses and carts instead of cars. It was really cute. And Jenny was wrong: it wasn't true that they all lived together, that was just village gossip. And, disappointingly, there wasn't any free love either.

Jan was about to become their first local member. They had allocated him one of the knackered old cottages, which he had agreed to restore. He was moving in next week and the dinner was to welcome him. The only reason he invited me was because, as a Dutchman and therefore a rank outsider, he had no friends in the village. The only reason I agreed was because I hoped that after a good dinner and a few glasses of wine, Jan might feel the urge to jump on my bones.

Brenda and her son Mag, who were our hosts, were a respectable family, as were the rest of them, and hospitable; they made me very welcome. They had become friends with Jan the same way I had, through his guitar lessons. Mag was about Steven's age and was exactly like Steven in that he was difficult and deliberately weird. He barely acknowledged Jan and me when we arrived. In their living room was a wall of books stacked from floor to ceiling, no doubt providing excellent and sustainable heat insulation, not to mention a fire hazard. Always stuck for reading material I cocked my head sideways and looked for titles I might enjoy but there was no fiction, they were all manuals: every kind of 'how to' book imaginable. Before dinner, Mag sat with his head buried in a book called *Electromagnetics for Dummies*. It didn't look like much of a page turner but he was totally absorbed in it. When his mother called him to the table he leaned over and whispered to me in a conspiratorial way, 'If you're not part of the solution ...'

I rocked on the back foot. Was there a problem? Was I part of it? I was about to ask when Mag continued:

'You're part of the precipitate!' he cackled and rushed past me to the dinner table.

Weird kid.

While we were eating, Jan asked him how he was getting on with a new guitar piece. I expected Mag to sulk and give the standard teenage 'dunno' but he surprised me by jumping up and hurrying out. This teenager didn't slouch in a bored, reluctant-to-shift way – instead he tore around crashing into things like an excited toddler. He returned swiftly with his guitar and stood over us while we ate, practising scales over and over again until his mother loudly cleared her throat.

'Can you play the new grade eight piece for us, Mag, please?' Jan asked diplomatically.

He did, faultlessly. It should have been romantic to eat a candlelit dinner while being serenaded by beautiful guitar music, but it wasn't. Mag's excruciating expression of concentration, which made him look constipated, put paid to that.

Chapter 6

As we left, Brenda discreetly pressed a small wrapped parcel into Jan's hand.

Jan wasn't moving to the Ethecom community for another week so I offered him a lift back to the village. I'd made the mistake of telling him about my 'wee detox', and to encourage me, Jan and his friends put a cork in their home-made elderberry wine. It was a more abstemious affair than I was used to, but despite not drinking and being, probably for the first time in my life, the designated driver, I felt relaxed. Of course it couldn't last.

Within a few minutes a dreadful guff began to soak up the air and poison the available oxygen in the car. It smelled like pond slime, or putrefied rodent. Or putrefied rodent lightly drizzled in pond slime.

Maybe Jan was a little too relaxed. He wasn't even embarrassed and made no move to open a window. It might have been the scent of muck spreading from the fields but it didn't smell like the light sweet manure odour I had gradually come to enjoy. This was a heavyweight stench and getting stronger by the minute. Why was Jan not reacting to it? Surely he didn't think it was me? I tried to take shallow breaths but my gag reflex kicked in.

'It's pretty strong, *ja*?' said Jan, at last rolling down the window.

I was by this time parked outside Jan's house. I'd cut the engine, I'd even unclipped my seat belt, all he had to do was invite me in.

He removed the parcel off the dashboard and held it at arm's length out the open window.

'I think it was getting too hot on the dashboard.'

'Oh, is that what's stinking? What the hell is it?'

'It's a goat cheese,' said Jan. 'Ethecom encourages everyone to pay where possible with goods or services, like a barter system. Brenda gives me cheese for Mag's guitar lesson. Although it smells pretty strong, it's really delicious. Would you like to try some? I can give you half to take home.'

Jan began hauling his arm, and the howfing cheese, back in the window.

'No, no, you're alright.'

To grab a breath, I rolled down my own window, turned my head sideways and sooked up two lungfuls. I wanted Jan to put the moves on me but I was also trying not to yack. Ok, he wasn't the handsomest, he was actually quite ugly: big jaw, big nose, scowly face; but outsized features looked better on a man, I always thought, and anyway, what made Jan irresistibly attractive to me was his rarity. But despite being the only available man in downtown Inverfaughie, if he was going to invite me in and jump my bones, he'd better be ready to wash his hands. It would take the full four-minute surgical scrub to get that honk off him.

When I turned back, Jan was suddenly much closer to me, right up against me. By the hurt on his face I realised that, at the moment he'd sidled over, I'd turned away. He'd made his move and I'd missed it, inadvertently dodging his kiss.

Jan slid defeated back to his own side. The atmosphere, which might earlier have been described as sexually charged, was now ripe with mortification and the stench of nanny goat.

Our timing was all wrong.

Crestfallen, Jan made his excuses and left. Which, I later reflected, was just as well.

If there had been any bone jumping, it would have been for one night only. Jan was a decent man. He was looking for a long-term relationship, a nice girlfriend who was going to stick around. I was only looking to get out of this dreich waiting-room of a town.

I had to get B&B certification. I'd spent a week, and a small fortune, preparing for the licensing board inspection; there was a lot riding on it. All the rooms had fresh new bedding and towels, the bathrooms stocked with upmarket soap, shampoo and shower caps. I'd even bought a 500 pack of Jenny's seals that read, 'hygienically cleaned and sealed for your protection', and stretched them across the toilet lids. The toilets weren't sealed, obviously; a thin strip of plastic had limited powers when it came to preventing germs, but it looked professional. Business was all about the customer's perception. In my previous life as a medical sales rep that was always a key point at sales training. With the customer's, and more importantly the Inspectorate's, perception in mind, I folded the toilet roll ends into a wee point. I drew the line at leaving chocolate on the pillows. That reminded me too much of my previous life. So many times after falling into my hotel bed drunk at a conference I'd woken up with an After Eight stuck to my face.

On the morning of the inspection the house squeaked with cleanliness. If the Inspectorate wiped a white glove across any of my surfaces he would find not a speck. The doorbell rang at 10:57, three minutes early, but I was ready for him.

Chapter 7

I had envisioned a council employee, an official in a suit with a measuring tape and a clipboard, but I opened the door and there stood Betty Robertson, the blowsy bitch who'd stolen my rose bowl. Two weeks earlier I'd won that trophy fair and square, but fair and square wasn't a concept that was familiar to the judges of the Inverfaughie Gala Day Flower Show. Nepotism; out and out Robertsonism was much more their line. My roses had been the obvious standout winners, admired by everyone who came into the marquee; a blind man with a head cold knew that.

'She only won because her name's Robertson like the rest of them,' said Steven when he'd phoned, trying to cheer me up, 'that way they don't have to get it engraved, and anyway, they probably can't spell any other names.'

Betty Robertson was held up to be a pillar of the community, though you wouldn't know it after the way she'd comported herself at the ceilidh: throwing her head back and showing everyone her fillings; throwing her legs wide and showing everyone what she'd had for breakfast. She was a fine one to be inspectorating anything. And there was someone else with her.

'Well, if it isn't my old friend Jenny,' I said, smiling sweetly. I was using the word 'old' to mean geriatric, not long-standing. 'Please do come in.'

I indicated towards the front lounge where I had put in a trendy new rug and curtains, but they swept past me and headed straight for the kitchen. By the time I caught up with them Betty Robertson had her head in my freezer. What was she so frantically searching for? Body parts? She would find nothing more damning than a multipack of Magnums and half a Black Forest gateau. A girl had to have some pleasures. Betty Robertson emerged looking disappointed and slightly snow-tinged.

'Now, as the appointed representatives of the licensing board,' she began.

'In a voluntary capacity, you understand,' interjected Jenny.

'Thank you, Jenny,' said Betty, 'Miss Robertson and myself have been instructed to undertake an inspection of your premises to ensure that they meet the minimum criteria for the issuing of an accommodation licence and to ascertain the appropriate number of thistles you may be awarded.'

I assented and Miss Robertson and Mrs Robertson then worked their way through every room in the house, inspecting. Or, to be more accurate: having a right good nosey. They were very thorough. They were inside pillowcases, under mattresses, I half expected them to strip search me. And then the dog.

'I've laid out the tea things in the lounge, ladies.' I said, once they'd exhausted their rummaging. 'If you'd like to follow me through.'

'No thank you,' said Betty. 'We can't accept refreshments of any kind.'

She made it sound like an inducement when I had only been trying to be hospitable.

'It could be interpreted as undue influence,' she explained. 'The committee takes a very dim view.'

I found this suggestion of bribery offensive. I was annoyed after all the trouble I'd gone to, making such extravagant cup cakes. I'd done a double batch and had planned to give them a box each to take home. Still, they wouldn't go to waste.

Their resolve weakened when they actually saw my cakes. Jenny was salivating. After the sell-out success at the gala day, my home baking had already gained a reputation in the village. I'd pushed the boat out and finished these with butter cream, fresh strawberries and chocolate shavings.

'Och, I think we can make a wee exception,' said Jenny. 'Trixie's cakes are mouthgasmic, Betty, you should try one. Box those up for me would you, dear?'

As they left, with their cake boxes under their arms, I enquired as to whether Harrosie had passed muster.

'Oh, we have to present our findings to the committee,' said Betty loftily. 'I'm afraid I can't predict the outcome, but it is by no means certain.'

*

Four days later and not a dickie bird from the licensing committee. New B&Bs, restaurants and cafes were opening on a daily basis. Everyone was soaking up the rich gravy that was sloshing around the village, everyone except me. I wasn't going to ask Jenny, I wouldn't beg, I had my dignity.

Day five and another van rocks up next door, this time it's a removals van. There are three guys squashed together in the front. The driver, a fat guy, gets out, unlocks the gate in the fence and drives the van inside. That fence; not only had it destroyed my view over the loch, it also meant I couldn't see a damn thing that was going on next door.

An hour later the van emerged and drove off, this time with only two guys in it. One of them must be in the house. Next thing my front door was being chapped.

'Hello, I'm Tony, pleased to meet you. I'm going to be staying next door, thought I'd introduce myself.'

'Oh hello, I'm Trixie. Come away in, I'll get the kettle on.'

He was a young guy, a Glaswegian, thank you Jesus. He said he'd rented next door for the summer. I didn't want to ask too many questions too soon, didn't want to scare him off, I'd have all summer to interrogate him. And anyway, Bouncer, who was as starved for company as I was, got a bit excited. He started what

I sometimes called his mad half-hour: dashing from one end of the house to the other. He'd rush up to Tony, jump up to lick him, and then bound off again. It was difficult to sustain a conversation when a furry bullet blasted through the kitchen every few seconds.

'Calm down, Bouncer, get a grip! Sorry about this, he likes you.'

'He's a great wee guy. He's got plenty of energy, hasn't he?'

'Oooft,' I agreed, 'he could run from here to Byres Road and back again if he'd forgotten his keys.'

Even just sharing a wee joke and the memory of Byres Road with a fellow Weegie was cheering me up. Tony laughed and said, 'Are you from Byres Road? I thought I knew your face.'

'Funnily enough, you look familiar to me too.'

That was one of the things I missed about Glasgow and particularly the West End: the ability to see people on the street on a regular basis without them having to know all your business. Byres Road had the feel of a village but the anonymity of the city.

Tony stared hard at me and then suddenly snapped his fingers and pointed.

'Double vodka and diet coke, no ice. Right?'

'Absolutely spot on. How did you know that?'

'I used to work in Tennent's, years ago. I can't remember customers' names but I never forget an order.'

'Double vodka diet coke no ice', that had been my tipple of choice back in the good old days. In the good old days, I used to drop by Tennent's for a sly drink after a hard day's medical repping. From this distance they still seemed like the good old days. How I longed for a double vodka now.

'You don't remember me, do you?' he said, smiling.

'Not specifically, but you look familiar.'

Tony shrugged. He was a good-looking guy but he was only about twenty-five, a bit young for me. Put that tiddler back in the water, I thought, probably wouldn't see much of him anyway. He'd probably be working round the clock in one of the hotel bars. There was plenty of money to be made now that the film company were coming to town. Americans were famously good tippers.

'Have you come up because of the filming?'

'Yeah.'

'You'll be working your arse off, the whole town will. Probably not see much of you then.'

'Probably not, but it's got to be done.'

'Oh, I've got something for you.' I fumbled in the kitchen drawer for the keys Polly had left with me. 'There you go.'

'Oh,' said Tony, surprised, shoving them deep into his pocket, 'cheers. Wouldn't want the paps getting their hands on these.'

'Yeah,' I said. I didn't know what he was talking about, but I smiled and passed him his tea.

Chapter 8

Shockaroonie on the front page of *The Inverfaughie Chanter*. Malcolm Robertson M.S.P. for Inverfaughie and district had keeled over and died. Heart Attack, no warning; sitting eating *Chicken Tonight* and boom. I phoned Jenny but she seemed disinclined to gossip and could only manage funereal platitudes.

'A sad loss to this community,' she mumbled through her hanky.

'How's Walter feeling?' I asked.

'He's sad, Trixie,' she said, somewhat coldly. 'Obvs.'

Even I was a little sad, Malcolm had seemed a nice man, a bit boring but still; if he hadn't prematurely gone with the angels he might, in the fullness of time, have become my friend. He was an M.S.P. after all; he probably got invited to loads of parties. It wasn't as if I had pals to spare. But, as sometimes happens, one friendship portal closes and another opens up. That very day I met someone new.

In the grassland that ran down to the beach, the place the locals always referred to as the machair, Bouncer spotted something and bounded away from me. Usually the machair was heaving with sheep and cows roaming freely, making it out of bounds to dogs, but that day there were none so I'd thought it was safe enough to let Bouncer off the lead.

Hah.

I eventually caught up with him down near the water's edge sniffing at another wee dog. More than sniffing, actually. He had wrapped his back legs around the wee dog's head and was thrusting back and forth in a familiar rhythmic motion.

'Bouncer, stop that right now!' I shouted.

'She might be more receptive at the other end, old chap,' said a calm voice.

A woman lay sprawled in the long grass, her face tilted to the sun, blowing cigarette smoke in an upward stream like a steam engine. I was thinking how strong her lungs must be when she suddenly exploded into a strenuous coughing fit. With the effort she was putting in she'd be lucky if her underwear didn't get at least a wee bit damp.

I didn't recognise her from Inverfaughie. She must be a tourist. By her clothes and hair and thread-thin figure she seemed young, but up close she had what used to be known as a 'lived in' face. She should have been pretty, she had nice regular features, but whoever had lived in her face had obviously trashed the place. Instead of the usual crinkles and laughter lines there were deep trenches round her eyes and mouth giving her the look of a hunted animal, probably from all that extravagant coughing. When it finally subsided she seemed relaxed, or maybe exhausted. She sat up on her elbows, stubbed out her ciggie and squinted at the dogs.

'I think she rather likes it, actually,' she said in an aristocratic accent. 'Mimi, you're such a little tart.'

Mimi, a beautiful little King Charles spaniel, seemed to resent this remark. She wriggled free of Bouncer and ran off along the sand. Taking this as a come-on, Bouncer gave chase.

'Bouncer, come back here this minute!' I yelled in my how-dare-you voice, and then turned to the woman, 'I'm so sorry about this.'

This posh lady might not be so relaxed when my grubby mongrel impregnated her pedigree pooch.

'Oh, leave them to it. Don't worry on Mimi's behalf. She's a flirtatious little bitch, she enjoys letting dirty dogs run after her. But then, we girls are all the same, aren't we?'

She smiled at me, a leering all-girls-together smile, which, out of politeness, I returned, rolling my eyes for good measure. I hear you sister, my rolling eyes said. The woman rose to her feet and stuck out her hand.

'Dinah. Pleased to meet you.'

She reached into the back pocket of her jeans and pulled out a hip flask.

'Snifter?'

I was so surprised I didn't say anything. It really was a beautiful hip flask, silver or maybe pewter, and all engraved with a fancy coat of arms on the front. Dinah took my hesitation for acceptance and thrust it towards me.

'It's Auchensadie,' she said, nodding her head towards the village and the distillery beyond, 'good stuff.'

'I really shouldn't,' I mumbled.

The flask had a wee silver cup attached as a lid. I poured a teaspoonful, just to be sociable, and necked it. It burned all the way down. The breeze on my face suddenly felt exhilarating. As I handed the flask back I was about to tell her my name when Mimi leapt between us and up into Dinah's arms. Bouncer wasn't far behind and, in his enthusiasm to get at Mimi, he nearly pushed the anorexic woman over. Almost as quickly as they'd come, the dogs were off again, this time with Mimi chasing Bouncer. Dinah might be right about her wee spaniel, but it was clear both dogs were enjoying themselves.

'It's lovely to see them having such fun, isn't it?' she said, as she poured herself a large one and sipped at it.

We stood and watched the dogs romp around on the sand before they came tearing towards us again. Luckily Dinah had put the flask back in her pocket. This time she was ready for Bouncer and grabbed him by the collar.

'Good boy,' she said enthusiastically, as she fondled his ears.

I took my cue from Dinah and patted her little dog. Mimi was adorable, with a cute wee squashed face and dangly ears.

'Oh, her fur is so soft!' I cried in surprise. Not like Bouncer's shag-pile coat.

'Yes, and she makes an excellent foot warmer,' said Dinah. 'Oh crumbs, what have we here? I'm afraid your little chap has a tick.'

I didn't know what she was talking about.

'Just here, behind his ear. See? They get them all the time in this long grass.'

I peered down while she held Bouncer's collar and separated his fur.

'Oh my god, it's moving!'

Something was embedded in his skin, something alive with flailing limbs and tentacles.

'Sheep tick. Don't worry, it's easily removed,' said Dinah evenly, reaching into her other back pocket and producing a green plastic thing that looked like a miniature crochet hook. 'This is what I use when Mimi has one, I swear by 'em. Now, it's important to get the whole of the little beggar, head and all, so slide it in like this, twirl it round, pull upwards and, there!'

Dinah held up for my inspection the blood-bloated beastie, head and all.

Not sure how to respond, I nodded. Dinah scraped the tick off the hook with her boot and ground it into the sand where it left a faint pink stain. She held out the small green hook for me to take.

'Now that you know how to use it,' she said, 'keep it for next time he picks one up.'

'Oh,' I blustered, baffled by this casual kindness, 'that's kind of you but ...'

'Oh, don't be silly, I have another one at home and it'll save you a fortune in vet bills.'

'I'm hopeless with that kind of thing. I've never had a dog before. Sorry, I meant to say, my name's ...'

Somewhere deep in her clothes Dinah's phone began to ring. She smiled an apology and stuck her hand down the neck of her jumper.

'Trixie, pleased to – meet you ... ' I tailed off.

Dinah fumbled and jiggled until she located the phone and immediately opened it.

'Sorry, I have to take this. Here,' she whispered, thrusting the tick-winkling tool into my hand.

I stood for a few minutes while she shouted into the phone.

'Oh Georgie, please, you know I can't do that. There must be another option,' she wailed.

Dinah turned away out of the wind and remained with her back to me, intermittently shouting and pleading with her caller. I wasn't sure what to do. Which was more rude: listening in to her private business or leaving without saying goodbye? Slowly I began to realise that she didn't expect, or indeed, want me to wait, but by then I had foolishly lingered too long.

'Oh for goodness's sake,' she yelled, 'I'm back in London tomorrow. I'll do it then.'

So she was just a tourist, then, a high plains drifter, just passing through. That was a shame, we could have walked our dogs together, maybe got together socially. The main reason I'd given up drinking was because I'd had no one to drink with, and I'd never been comfortable with what they say about people who drink alone. She was kind. It was frustrating.

Now I began to understand a little of what the locals felt about the tourists. What was the point of getting to know them? Why even bother learning their names? They were only here for the weekend, they were free to leave any time they liked, they had a life to return to.

I dragged the toe of my walking boots through the wet sand and scraped out 'thank you'. She was still shouting down the phone and didn't even notice. It was an intense conversation and it looked like it might be a long one. Her mind was probably on the glamorous life she lived in London. By tomorrow Inverfaughie would be a memory, nothing more, but I hoped she'd at least see my pathetic little sand message before the tide came in and washed it away.

Chapter 9

Bouncer and I came home to discover a canvas shopping bag that had been stuffed through the front door. It was from Ethecom, a free gift for everyone in town apparently. The bag was of untreated calico, not exactly a fashion item, but it looked like it could hold a few kilos of potatoes and it had a certain rustic charm. The hippies were always coming up with ideas to make Inverfaughie more green. Last week they had set up a stall in the village and offered home-made sweets for the kids and a free compost bin for every household. They even gave demonstrations on how to compost. Their philosophy seemed to be that there was no such thing as rubbish, everything was recyclable.

Brenda, bless her heart, had popped a small goat's cheese into my canvas bag, thereby rendering the bag useless, at least until it had been through a boil wash. This time the cheese wasn't wrapped in hygienic plastic, but in recycled paper with a note scrawled on it. 'Lovely to meet you, Trixie, hope we'll see you at the meeting tonight?'

One of Ethecom's latest projects was the setting up of a credit union. A meeting was planned in the village hall to introduce the idea to Inverfaughie. They had talked about it at dinner that night but I hadn't paid much attention. Before 'Fat of the Land' had changed their lives forever, they'd all been IT programmers and bankers. Brenda had been some kind of corporate lawyer. Between them they had now devised an online local bank. It was a wee night out. God help me, I was so stuck for a social life I was actually looking forward to spending my evening at a talk on personal finance.

*

The village hall smelled of damp tweed and Scotch broth, a reminder of the pensioner lunches that were held there. I had expected to see Jan there too but there was no sign of him and I was relieved. The turnout wasn't great, but those who had come seemed prepared to give it a fair hearing. Three different speakers outlined what the credit union offered: current and savings accounts, cheap loans, insurance, mortgage advice and help with budgeting. It was going well until someone raised the question of cash. I had assumed that we'd be able to get money the usual way – from the mobile bank that trundled round the village three times a week but no, the Inverfaughie Credit Union was to be a virtual bank. There would be no bank building, not even an office. Everything was supposed to happen online. Cash could be deposited and withdrawn only once a week here in the village hall between the hours of 5 and 7 pm on a Friday. The atmosphere changed after that. People started whispering amongst themselves and rumfling in their pockets, digging out car keys, impatient to go. When the presentations were over the crowd quickly thinned out.

Jenny caught my eye and made her way towards me against the traffic of people exiting.

'Take-up is low. Disappointing,' she said, shaking her head.

There was only a handful of people filling in the application forms. I was surprised that Jenny would be supportive of this initiative; I had only ever heard her disparage the hippies as incomers, them and their free love.

'I think people prefer the convenience of getting cash from the mobile bank,' I said.

'They prefer the convenience of buying pirate DVDs from Hamish, more like.'

'No way! Hamish sells pirate videos out of the mobile bank?'

'Hah! And the firkin rest,' said Jenny, still shaking her head, 'excuse language.'

I used the mobile bank all the time. Hamish had never even hinted at the offer of dodgy DVDs. Another sign, if I ever needed one, that I'd always be an outsider in this distant town.

'He's killing my rental business. I've a good mind to report him to his superiors.'

'Why don't you then?'

'I know, but – then we'd have no bank at all.'

For a bit of banter I said, 'I see you're sporting Inverfaughie's latest fashion accessory. You're really working that eco look.'

Jenny laughed and struck a modelling pose. I thought she would scoff at the plain canvas bags, but she had one casually slung over her shoulder.

'D'you know how much I've paid that cash and carry for poly bags over the years?'

'No, how much?'

I was impressed that she had such a handle on costs.

'I've no idea,' she said, disappointing me, 'but it's a lot. I've kept this town in free bin liners for years. It's time we were all doing our bit for the environment. From now on if anyone wants a poly bag in my shop I'll be charging them 5p.'

'That seems a bit steep.'

'If it's good enough for Marks it's good enough for me. The free poly bag gravy train stops here.'

After exchanging pleasantries with Brenda, Mag and some of the others from Ethecom, I joined the small queue to sign up for the credit union, more out of solidarity with my fellow outsiders than anything else, but I was pleased when Jenny fell in behind me. Her motives were probably more of a protest against Hamish's contraband but at least we were making up the numbers. It was only as we were leaving the hall that Old Thistle Knickers herself, Betty Robertson, wafted past us. I wasn't about to ask her about my application to the licensing committee, I wouldn't give her the satisfaction. Jenny at least had been tactful enough not to mention it, but Betty volunteered the information, or rather, the lack of it.

'Hello Mrs McNicholl. The Inverfaughie Council sub-committee are yet to deliberate on your case,' she said, making me sound like a criminal. 'You'll be informed of our decision.'

She was so obviously enjoying her game of bait-the-incomer. I would rather appear on 'Embarrassing Illnesses' than let Betty Robertson humiliate me like this, but what could I do?

Chapter 10

I couldn't believe it, there she was, exactly where I'd left her yesterday on the machair, still shouting down the phone, giving someone a right ear bashing. Did she still have the same clothes on? I couldn't remember.

After my last faux pas, hanging about waiting for her to get off the phone, I was all set to give her a friendly wave and walk past but the posh woman held out her arm to stop me.

'Got to go,' she shouted into the phone. 'No, seriously, Julian; I've just run into an old friend, I'll call you later.'

And with that she hung up.

'Hello!' she cried, with an enthusiasm bordering on hysteria. This was more than was appropriate to the occasion and required me to stop.

'Hello Dinah,' I replied, 'nice to see you again. It's Trixie by the way, Trixie McNicholl.'

'Oh crumbs yes, Trixie,' she said, and promptly dried up, leaving me standing there like a numpty.

Clearly she couldn't think of the next pleasantry. I smiled. The wind blew a fine layer of sand along the beach. The moments ticked past. Bouncer and Mimi were by now barking and jumping all over each other, joyfully reunited, making our human discomfort all the more conspicuous.

'Sorry about last time,' she said, taking an awkward half-step towards me, slapping her leg and then retreating. She was much more jolly hockey sticks than I remembered her. She made an exaggerated phone gesture, her thumb and pinky at her ear, shrugged and pulled a face. 'Business.'

She went quiet again, forcing me to state the obvious.

'So, did you decide to stay on?' I asked.

Dinah looked puzzled. I almost blurted out that because the last I'd heard, she was off to London in the morning. I managed to stop myself. I didn't want her to think I'd been listening to her conversation. I wasn't listening, I was involuntarily hearing. Two different things.

'Have you extended your holiday?' I said by way of trying to rescue a dead-in-the-water conversation.

Dinah laughed. 'Golly, no!' she said, 'I'm not on holiday. I only wish I were.'

'Oh,' I said. Now it was my turn to look stupid.

'I live here. Over there.'

She bobbed her head towards the other side of the loch. Did she really mean the castle on that huge big rambling estate across the loch?

'You don't mean Faughie Castle?'

'Yup,' she said, fists shoved in pockets, rocking forward on to the ball of her foot and then down again, her head bobbing. She seemed almost embarrassed. 'Although I think the term "castle" is a bit of a stretch these days for the old ancestral pile.'

'Have you just bought it?'

Only that day I'd read in the *Inverfaughie Chanter* that the place was up for sale. Wow, I thought, she must be mega loaded. Even an old broken-down place like that, the land alone must be worth millions.

'Bought it? God no. I was born here.'

So, I reasoned, if she wasn't buying she must be selling. There was some famous American billionaire interested in turning it into a polo resort, so the paper had said. The local council was backing his bid; they were right behind the jobs and the dollars it would bring into the area.

The dogs ran along the lochside and, now that the rust had been scraped off the wheels of our conversation, Dinah and I walked together towards them.

'We moved away when I was eight,' she continued, 'but we always open the house every summer for a few weeks. Or at least we always did. We used to have such good times here. I don't know if it was the cold clean Highland air or just being with my family but I remember summers in Faughie when I'd feel almost hysterical with happiness, high on life, you know?'

She looked at me, perhaps expecting me to recognise this hysteria of happiness. If I'd ever had such a feeling I'd long since forgotten it, but it was only polite to nod earnestly.

She slowed down her walk and I was obliged to do the same, which seemed to bring a greater intensity to the conversation.

'I never get that any more.' She smiled. 'I'm usually too hungover.'

How did she know? Was this just dog-walking chat, a passing observation, or did she instinctively recognise in me a fellow alky?

'Me too,' I blurted, 'although I'm trying to stay off it.'

'Me too,' she echoed.

Neither of us mentioned yesterday's hip flask and we carried on, following behind the jubilant dogs, in silence.

*

The next morning I scurried down to Jenny's shop for baking soda. Truth be told, I had a sufficiency of baking soda, as Computer would no doubt be able to tell me, but I was dying to quiz Jenny about my new friend.

'I know the woman who's selling Faughie Castle.'

'Dinah?'

'Yes,' I reluctantly admitted, my thunder stolen, 'd'you know her?'

'Of course I know her. Lady Murdina Anglicus, to give her her full title, has been coming into this shop since she learned to say "dolly mixtures", but she's too posh to mix with the peasantry.'

I wasn't about to tell Jenny why Dinah was mixing with me: the reasons being we both happened to have dogs and an alcohol problem.

'Ah, well,' I bantered, 'that's obviously why she wants to be pals with me. Amongst the unwashed peasants of Inverfaughie she's finally found a fellow Patrician.'

Jenny snorted. 'So,' she began the interrogation, 'was it buttered scones for tea at her place then? They haven't had any staff in there for years. I imagine the castle must be in a right state these days.'

'I haven't seen the castle,' I answered honestly. 'We mostly just walk the dogs together,' I continued slightly dishonestly. 'Dinah loves Bouncer, she gave me a present for him.'

Having implied regular meetings with Dinah, I didn't want Jenny cross-examining me any further, exposing my pathetic imaginary friendship as lonesome wishful thinking.

'Is she really a lady?' I asked, throwing the gossip ball back to Jenny.

She gave me a stare that begged me to stop being so naive.

'Murdina Anglicus ain't no lady. But she has a title. Lady of the Heather. Her family have been lording it over us for centuries. They own all the land in these pairts. Her father Murdo, the old laird, was never here. Absentee landlord; he was always off down in London chasing skirt. And her half-brother, the new laird, Robin – god love the wee soul – he died last November. She must be devastated. When they were kids they were always close those two. And as for that son of hers ...'

'She's got a son?' I blurted.

Dinah hadn't mentioned a son to me, but then, why would she? 'And no husband.'

Something else Dinah and I had in common.

'Never has had,' Jenny continued in her whispery gossipy voice. 'People say she used a turkey baster, you know ...'

For one horrible moment I thought Jenny was going to give me a demonstration of how Dinah had used the turkey baster. Time to change the subject.

'How old is her son?' I asked. I was still hoping Steven would come and spend the summer with me. Maybe he and Steven could be friends. 'Och, he'll be grown up now,' said Jenny. 'Haven't seen him up here for years.'

Poor Dinah. Her family was dead, no husband, no son; we had so much in common we really should be friends.

Chapter 11

'So, you might as well know, I'm going to run for M.S.P.,' said Jenny.

I inhaled.

'No way.'

'Yes way. Well, you know that Malcolm died.'

I exhaled. Yes, I knew that. Other than the movie coming to town, old people dying was the only thing that ever happened in Inverfaughie.

'So H.M.B., I'm running for M.S.P. I know. It's madness, I'm too old and I've no experience, and Walter would make a far better M.S.P., but he can't be running up and down to Edinburgh every week. He's not fit for it, not in that parliament of ...'

By the look on her face she seemed to be fumbling for a derogatory term.

'Badgers?'

'What?'

'That's the collective term: a parliament of badgers,' I explained.

'Huh! I wish they were badgers, I'd cull the lot of them.'

'Jenny, don't do it.'

'Somebody has to go down there and, let's face it, it's the only way I'll ever get out of this fusty wee shop.'

'You're not giving up the shop?'

'Keep your knickers on, Trixie. I'm not closing it. I couldn't, the villagers would lynch me. No, there's a salary for being an

M.S.P.; I'll get in a manager for the shop, become an employment provider, whatever it takes.'

What an opportunist, I thought. Jenny obviously saw the death of Malcolm as a chance to get the hell out from behind that counter. She was clearly dressing up her personal ambition as altruism, she'd just said so. After so many years behind the counter of that wee shop, the bright lights of the big city were calling her again.

A few weeks ago, Jenny had told me that she'd lived in London through the swinging sixties.

'There were tons of Highlanders in London if you knew where to find them, and Irish and Australian, American, you name it. Musicians, actors, painters, London was full of it. I met them all, you know,' she'd claimed. 'Mick Jagger, Mary Quant, I even knew Jimi Hendrix. Aye, all you see is a wee Highland spinster, but let me tell you, Trixie, I won't die wondering.'

She'd been assistant manageress of a Woolworths on Oxford Street for twelve years before they offered her her own shop out in Kent.

'I know that doesn't sound very grand, but that was in the days before women were managers.'

But after twelve years in the metropolis, she had ended up permanently back in Inverfaughie.

'Ach,' she'd shrugged, 'I never liked Kent anyway, too many English.'

It was just selfishness. She was going to bail out and leave me here to rot. Jenny was the only friend I had in this godforsaken dump. Standing gossiping in this shop was the only entertainment I ever got.

'But if you don't have any experience? It's a wonderful gesture, but seriously, Jenny, politics these days is no place for the well-intentioned amateur. I'd be worried for you.'

'Thanks for your concern,' she said dryly.

'I'm only thinking of you, Jenny. Are you sure you're fit enough? You're not getting any younger.'

'There's no one else to do it. All the young people go off to university and don't come back. What have they got to come back to? To work in the tourist trade or the mill, and if we don't fight they won't even have that. The town is dying, even the incomers have retired before they get here. Seriously, we need everyone on board with this. Everyone thinks it's great now, while the filum's here, and it's big bucks all round.'

'I'm not seeing *any* bucks from the filum,'I said.

Most people in the village called it a 'filum'– something to do with there always being a vowel between consonants in Gaelic.

'You will, we all will, but what we need to remember is: it's temporary. In a few weeks the circus will have moved on and the mill workers will still be under threat of redundancy. This village will go down the toilet if we lose our mill.'

'Well, you don't need to worry. It said in the paper that this is a safe seat for the LibDems.'

'Och, give me credit for some intelligence, Trixie. I'm not standing as a LibDem.'

My mouth fell open. 'But – wasn't Malcolm … ?'

'Look, Malcolm could have stood as the Monster Raving Loony Party candidate, dressed as a giraffe, and he'd have been elected. People liked Malcolm, we all trusted him. He was always a constituency M.S.P., an honest man, it hardly made a difference what party he was in.'

'So if you're not going with the LibDems, what are you standing as then?'

'Well, there aren't a lot of choices, are there? Tory?' she snorted. 'SNP? I spent years in London, remember, and if I ever did hold with any of that petty-minded nationalism rubbish, I've outgrown it.'

'Which only leaves Labour. No, I couldn't go Labour, I'd have to support that Westminster crowd; they're more Tory than the Tories.'

'Well that only leaves the Monster Raving Loony Party,' I said. 'All you need now is a giraffe costume.'

'Hah! That might inject a bit of fun into the proceedings, get people engaged with politics, but,' Jenny sighed, 'knowing Betty, she'd veto it.'

'That Betty Robertson would veto her own mother, oooh I'd love to ...'

'Hey,' said Jenny clapping her hands together, 'd'you know what would really sicken Betty Robertson?'

'What?'

'If you joined Faughie Council.'

'Aye right.'

'I mean it, I can propose you, Walter will second you, not a thing Betty can do about it. We're meeting tonight.'

'Nah, I don't ...'

'You know, Trixie, as a local businessperson you might want to think about joining.'

'Well, thanks to Betty Robertson's licensing inspectorate, I'm not a businessperson.'

'Not yet, but maybe if you joined the council ...' Jenny dipped her head to the side. 'I can think of lots of reasons why a person might want to volunteer on the council, get involved in local decisions.'

'I've told you before, Jenny, I'm not political.'

'Course you are, everybody is, well everybody who wants gas and electric and roads and street lights is. You want your licence, don't you? Aye, so you are political.'

'Are you saying that if I want an accommodation licence, I need to join the council?'

Jenny dipped her head again, a longer slower dip. 'It couldn't hurt.'

Chapter 12

The Faughie Council and Business Club second quarterly meeting lasted not quite two hours but it felt like a week in the jail.

The great and the good were here. There being no show without Punch, Jenny was in attendance, of course, and of course her clandestine consort, Walter. To preserve the secret of their love, they sat at opposite ends of the big table, but they weren't fooling me. Caley Ali from the Caledonian Hotel nodded hello and I recognised the Faughie FM radio DJ Andy Robertson from when he'd hosted the gala day. A group of men stood around together who, from their turned-down wellies and the faint whiff of manure, I took to be farmers. I was surprised to see them engaged in conversation with Brenda and her son Mag. Brenda was much more of a weirdo outsider than I was but she seemed able to chat to people. Since influential opinion leader Jenny had endorsed Ethecom's canvas bags, they had become de rigueur around the village.

I smiled at Brenda and she gracefully brought me in to their conversation, which seemed to be about bore holes and heat pumps. They might as well have been speaking Gaelic. After a few tedious minutes I excused myself and made for the tea urn where I encountered Mrs Moira Henderson, the guide from the Auchensadie Distillery, unmistakeable in her big tartan cape. I could only hope she wouldn't remember me.

A few weeks ago when Steven had visited he'd insisted we take a tour of the local distillery. I'd had a heinous hangover and was begging god to just let me slip away quietly, so I wasn't really up for it but, so that Steven could get a free whisky, we had to endure a guided tour led by Mrs Henderson in her kilt, tartan tammy and big daft tartan cape. Long story short: Steven shoved my head in a huge circular vat and the smell made me boak into the whisky mash. That batch was going to have an interesting tang. Maybe that's what was called 'whisky sour'.

There were a few notable absences. I knew Jackie was on the council because Jenny had told me. She'd also told me Jackie had sent his apologies, probably because he'd heard I was coming. No sign of Jan either, no doubt for the same reason. Betty Robertson looked at me as if I'd come in with something unpleasant on my shoe, but as chairwoman she called the meeting to order and everyone sat down around the big table.

'I'd like to open this meeting by paying tribute to a man we all knew and loved,' she began, 'our M.S.P., Malcolm Robertson, who shall be sadly missed.'

Everyone nodded gravely and made approving comments. I chimed in with my own muted 'hearhear'.

'Mr Walter Robertson will now deliver a eulogy that will form part of our formal minutes.'

Walter spoke for a few minutes in a husky grief-worn voice and everyone kept their heads down. He talked of Malcolm's many years' unstinting service: the meetings, the personal guarantees he'd often made to his constituents, the petitions, the early train to Edinburgh in all weathers, the late nights on committees, speech writing into the wee small hours, the fundraising, the marches, the protests, his work on the Cross-Party Transgender Adoption Group. I had no idea there even were transgender kiddies, but good on him, I thought.

'As you all know, I was Malcolm's election agent,' Walter said, 'and I'm proud to announce tonight that his legacy of sterling work will not be forgotten but will be continued and built upon by the new candidate, Miss Jenny Robertson, to whom I have offered my services.'

Everyone looked at Jenny, who nodded in confirmation of this news.

'Jenny will stand as an independent M.S.P. supporting our tweed mill among other local concerns,' he continued, 'and we hope we can count on your votes.'

Betty swiftly shut him down. 'Yes thank you, Walter,' she simpered, 'I'm sure we all wish Jenny our best, now if we can move on, we have rather a lot of business to get through tonight.'

Once they had circulated the sederunt and apologies were noted, Betty moved straight to the business of new members. This was just as well because, just like on my distillery visit, the fear in my stomach was threatening to make a dramatic entrance on to the committee table. I was the only new member being proposed. Jenny stood up and read, with frequent smiles in my direction, a paragraph from a prepared statement on my suitability as a member of the Faughie Council, mentioning my supposed friendship with the local landed gentry. So that's why she wanted me to join! The wily old vixen. She cited my exemplary voluntary work with the kids' guitar group. With no shortage of superlatives and blandishments she was bumming me up to be Philanthropist of the Year.

'In short, I believe Trixie McNicholl would be an asset to Faughie Council and wish to propose her,' said Jenny.

'Seconded,' said Walter.

Within minutes it was ratified and I was confirmed as a member of Faughie Council; as quick and painless as that. A shoogly tooth extracted by a string tied to a slammed door.

Chapter 13

The meeting moved on. Andy Robertson reported to the meeting on Faughie FM's appeal, *Visit a Veteran*, to find volunteer 'friends' to visit old people who lived in outlying districts. I'd heard him talk it up on the radio. The idea was to phone them, visit them, maybe even invite them to lunch occasionally. I could see this would be good PR for a community radio station but obviously doomed to failure: who in their right mind would voluntarily spend time with cantankerous oldsters? God knows I'd done my time with my own mum. But Andy dumbfounded me. He was pleased to report that Faughie FM had identified twenty-three volunteer visitors for the elderly and he was now requesting the disbursement of funds to pay travel expenses. A ripple of approval went round before it went to a vote. Betty was staring at me with one eyebrow almost meeting her hairline.

'Do you intend to vote, Trixie, or would you prefer to abstain?'

'Eh, sorry,' I bleated, as I raised my hand.

Bringing joy to the lonely lives of local coffin dodgers, this was important work we were doing here. I sneaked a glance at my watch and wondered what time I'd get home; there was a good film starting soon.

'Support for this and our other outreach projects has only been made possible due to a very generous endowment from our funding partners, Global Imperial. And today I'm delighted to welcome their representative, Miss Jacqueline Yip,' Betty said, a full curtsey in her voice.

I followed Betty's fawning expression up the table where it rested on a young woman. Miss Jacqueline Yip was a tiny wee thing, no more than a child really. In her exquisitely cut suit, top-knot hair-do and designer specs, she had all the accessories of an expensive corporate lawyer. She reminded me of a toddler in her mum's high heels but when she slowly bowed her head in receipt of Betty's tribute, Miss Yip displayed the delicate mannerisms of an Oriental princess. She was delightful.

'We have another application to the welfare fund,' said Betty, 'and I believe we are to have a presentation from Ethecom. Brenda?'

All eyes on Brenda, whose lips were closed.

'Eureka!' shouted a voice from the back of the hall.

People recoiled in fright.

'Who famously said that?'

'Archimedes,' piped up Walter, like the class swot, 'Greek scholar and mathematician.'

'Correct,' said Mag, Brenda's weird kid, as he wheeled the tea trolley to the table.

People tutted, perhaps because of the loud theatricality of the presentation or perhaps because, like me, they had no idea what the hell Mag was on about.

'What has this to do with your funding application?' asked Betty, glaring at Brenda while her glance alternatively flicked towards Miss Yip.

Brenda, probably mortified by Mag's shenanigans, made an apologetic face.

'He famously ran through the streets naked but he also invented the Archimedes screw,' said Mag, scrunching two fingers into inverted commas, 'a machine for transporting low-lying water to irrigation ditches. I've made a model.'

On the tea trolley he had rigged up two basins of water, one six inches higher than the other on top of a cardboard box. Bridged between the basins was a plastic spiral glued round a wooden stick.

He turned the stick and, sure enough, water was transferred from the lower basin to the higher one.

Some people stood up to get a closer look.

'This principle has been established for hundreds of years, but only very recently did we experiment with reversing it.'

Mag stopped turning the stick and tilted the top basin slightly. Water now began pouring through the screw in the opposite direction into the lower basin.

'But what alchemy is this? As the water falls, the weight of it pushes on the flights and rotates the screw. With a generator connected to the main shaft, the rotational energy can be turned, not into gold, ladies and gentlemen, but electricity.'

Mag went on to explain, in his hammy stage-magician style, how he had designed a hydrodynamic turbine to put on the weir on the River Faughie. This would provide electricity for Ethecom's domestic and farm use. He'd obviously done his homework because he easily batted away every objection: a middle-aged man wearing a canvas hat decorated with colourful fly-fishing hooks who introduced himself as Calum McLean was worried that a hydro-turbine would kill the fish.

'Not this kind, Mr McLean,' said Mag, dropping the theatricality and becoming pragmatic, 'Archimedes screws are fish friendly. Think of it as the luge in the Winter Olympics,' he said curving his hand to demonstrate. 'It lets the fish, even the big ones, safely pass down the screw. As the water passes through the turbine it gets churned and oxygenated, improving the water quality and, subsequently, the quantity of fish. Until, of course,' he said in a quieter voice, 'they get hooked and yanked out.'

I was impressed with his nerve; Mag was probably Steven's age, sixteen. He was weird but there was no doubt he was smart.

'We work hard at Auchensadie to create the right atmosphere for our visitors to enjoy a little piece of Highland magic,' said Mrs Henderson, 'a Scottish idyll, if you will.'

It was true: Auchensadie distillery was immaculate, the gardens so scrupulously tended there wasn't a leaf out of place; oak barrels, sherry casks and antique equipment artfully placed around the courtyard, buildings so white they hurt your eyes. It was perfect, a whisky paradise. It occurred to me then that if drug dens were this appealing, lots of people might switch from alcohol to heroin. Drug dealers simply hadn't worked hard enough at getting the marketing right.

'I'm a little bit concerned that the turbine will be, well, I'm sorry, there's no nice way of saying this – an eyesore,' continued Mrs Henderson, 'and for that reason,' she said, apparently mistaking herself for a dragon out of *Dragons' Den*, 'I'm out.'

'Hang on,' piped up one of the farmers, 'I've got sheep up that way. What happens if one of my animals falls into your screw? It'll get all chewed up; that's not exactly going to enhance the tourists' experience!'

The farmers all laughed at that one, clearly tickled by the image of live minced lamb.

Brenda now found her voice and chipped in.

'We can put a guard over the turbine so that nothing can fall into it.'

'I don't see a costing for a guard,' said Betty, reading from the application form. 'What do you think, Miss Yip?'

Miss Yip leaned forward to see and be seen by everyone around the table. She was obviously dying to get her oar in and had just been politely waiting to be asked.

Although she looked lighter than a soap bubble, Miss Yip's opinion was heavyweight.

'Members will be wise enough to make their own decisions,' she began respectfully in a gentle but firm American accent, 'but if I understand your objectives correctly, Faughie Council desires not only to be performing good works but also to be seen to be performing those good works.'

'You understand our objectives perfectly,' Betty simpered.

'Perhaps this project,' Miss Yip continued, 'as it is located outside the main village, is not quite visible enough.'

'Not visible enough to whom?' asked Mag.

No one answered him.

Again he made a good point. Miss Yip was hinting that Global

Imperial had given the council funds to spend however they pleased – so long as they did what Global Imperial wanted. So long as it made them look good.

'Now,' said Betty with an exhausted exhalation, 'are we finally ready to vote?'

'Point of order, please, Mrs Chairperson,' said Miss Yip. 'With great respect: as it's owned by Faughie estate, the River Faughie is not within the purview of the council. It is Global Imperial's assertion that to place anything on the river would require permission, along the lines of a fishing permit, from the laird.'

'Ah, thank you, Miss Yip, so we can't vote on it anyway?' said Betty, giving Mag a withering glance. 'I'm sure Lady Anglicus will give this project all the attention it deserves, now please, can we move on?'

What a waste of my precious time. That film had probably started by now. I should never have got involved in these petty small-town politics; when were they going to get around to granting me my licence?

Chapter 14

Next up was extended licensing hours for hotels and from there it got progressively more esoteric: fishery reports, approval for a proposed wind farm, wholesale milk prices, slurry pits, manure management. Manure management indeed. My shoulders drooped and my lips were struggling to maintain an upward curl. The Faughie Council meeting appeared to have entered the fifth dimension; time had slowed to a trickle while the forces of gravity were getting much heavier. Dear God let it end soon.

'Well that brings us to the end of our agenda items,' said Betty. Thank you Jesus.

'So this might be the time to give you all some very exciting news,' she continued. 'Global Imperial has kindly offered us – free of charge - the services of one of their fitness coaches and, right here in this hall, we are going to have our very own ...'

At this point Betty beat her forefingers on the table to create a drum roll. 'First. Ever. Weekly. Genuine ...'

She stopped drumming.

'Zumba class.'

Inaudible crash of cymbals. Gasps of delight from the women. Quizzical expressions from the men.

'The ladies know what I'm talking about and don't worry gentlemen, there's something for everyone. I've negotiated a nice little windfall that I think you're going to love,' Betty added smugly.

'What time is the Zumba, Betty?' asked Mrs Henderson.

'Don't worry, Moira, you can make it. Thursday 7 till 8. That's when most of the ladies in the village can make it.'

Moira gave a big theatrical sigh of relief.

'May I be the first to congratulate you, Betty, on your procurement of such valuable services,' said Walter quietly.

'Thank you, Walter,' said Betty dismissing him with a gracious nod.

But he wasn't finished.

'And may I raise another point of information: the hall is already booked on a Thursday evening with my Scottish history class. This term, as we have a film being made on that very subject, the curriculum will include the Highland Clearances. I will of course give way to the ladies and move it to another night, should that be the wish of the committee.'

'I'm afraid there isn't another night, Walter. We're booked solid with rehearsal space for Global Imperial, I've had to suspend the mother and toddler group and even cancel a few pensioner lunches. A Thursday evening's no use to those groups so I thought we might as well have the benefit of ...'

'In that case, I must insist that my booking stand.'

'But Walter, you don't have a booking, there's nothing in the diary.'

'Betty, you know fine that Walter runs this class every year,' said Jenny, trying, and failing, to keep the anger out of her voice.

'Of course I do, but no booking was formally made and now the slot's been taken, there's nothing I can do about it. I'm sorry, Walter, really I am, many of us are making short-term sacrifices for the good of the community.'

'Which community?' said Walter, pulling himself unsteadily to his feet. He may have been softly spoken but there was no doubting his indignation. 'Our community that fundraised for years to build this hall, or the Global Imperial corporate community?'

It wasn't clear to me if the guttural rumble that had gone around the room was disapproval for Walter's outburst or Betty's ruthless scheduling, but the mood of the meeting had turned darker.

Betty shook her head sadly. Andy Robertson, superstar DJ and Inverfaughie's most gallant man, stepped into the fray and threw Betty a lifeline.

'Betty, you mentioned something about a windfall?'

She grasped it with both hands.

'Yes! The machair, the cash bonus! Thank you, Andy, I nearly forgot. As you all know, we were all delighted – and jealous,' she quipped, '– when Murdo's low field was chosen as the spot for one of the large-scale battle sequences in the film. But the film crew have hit a problem getting all their trucks and equipment down there. The field is lying fallow at the moment and apparently it's far too soft. The trucks will churn it into mud before shooting even starts, so, Miss Yip has put together a very interesting proposal. Now, some of you are shaking your heads, but please, just hear me out. Our machair has the unique advantage of having a better turning circle for heavy vehicles and its views of the mountains across the loch are unsurpassable.

'The machair belongs equally to each and every one of us. Obviously there are grazing rights, but we all have a stake and therefore we all have a say in the decision. Global Imperial are offering every household in Inverfaughie a very generous fee of 240 pounds, as well as a separate agreement for everyone with grazing rights. Although technically we'll be temporarily waiving our access rights, apart from while they're actually filming, our use of the machair will not be affected. So long as we fulfil the conditions, everything will carry on as normal.'

'Will our visitors be allowed to walk on the machair?' asked an anxious Moira.

'Absolutely, except obviously when filming is taking place, and when they're filming that fight scene, my goodness, won't that be the biggest tourist attraction of all? I wouldn't be surprised if we got the television cameras up here from Edinburgh. It'll put our wee village on the map.'

Most people seemed to agree and were excited about the filming on the machair. Like me, most of them were probably already plotting how they were going to spend their 240 quid.

'And what about those of us with grazing rights?' asked one of the farmers, 'how much are we getting?'

'No, hold on a wee minute,' said another one, 'I'm short on grazing as it is this year. I don't want compensation. I want my grazing.'

'But it isn't compensation,' said Betty, the soothing balm of her voice like calamine lotion. 'You won't lose any grazing and you'll still be paid the honorarium.'

'How much?'

'That very much depends on the size of your flock and the shooting schedule. Miss Yip has kindly drawn up some figures. I'm afraid there wasn't time to have them copied but if you'd care to look.'

'I'll need to see them as well before I agree to anything,' said yet another farmer.

'Yes, of course, you'll all have your chance.'

Jenny raised her hand and was given the floor.

'We can hardly expect anyone to make a decision if they haven't seen the figures. I propose a break. That'll let the lads see how much they're getting before we vote on these two important matters.'

'Two matters?' said Betty.

'Aye. The machair agreement and the Thursday night history class,' said Jenny, 'that's yet to be sorted to the committee's satisfaction. Nobody leaves this hall until it is.'

Chapter 15

As soon as I got home I phoned Steven to tell him the good news.

'Well, my bum was numb by the end of it, but they finally gave me the licence.'

'Quality!' Steven yelled.

'So, you'll be arriving into your luxurious three-star B&B this weekend, or three thistles, I should say.'

'I've never stayed in a hotel before, I don't think Gerry has either.'

'Gerry's coming?'

It was out before I managed to rein in the sharpness in my voice.

'I told you he was. You said.'

I'd lost so many battles over the years when, in an unguarded moment, and just for some peace, I'd *said*.

'Yeah, ok, but this is the last. Once I'm properly up and running as a hotel Gerry will have to pay like everybody else. And I don't want you two doing your usual: out all night drinking.'

'Oh no,' he quipped, 'That would be treating the place like a hotel.'

*

He'd been in a strange mood since they'd arrived. When I'd picked him and Gerry up at the station Steven wasn't full of his usual cheeky banter. He wasn't even interested in my new Glaswegian barman neighbour. A peck on the cheek and an 'alright Trixie?' was as much as I got.

He sat in the back of the car with his head bowed low, his knees wide and his two thumbs a blur working across the screen. I could imagine how much fun this was going to be for me: silently watching Steven stab at his phone all weekend. I didn't want to get on at him in front of Gerry so I asked cheerfully, 'Are you still playing Grand Theft Auto?'

He screwed his face up. 'What? I'm not playing a game. Leave me alone. Mind your own.'

Unjustly chastised, I left him alone. I minded my own. I didn't speak again the whole way to Harrosie, nobody did. The only sound in the car was the imaginary noise of hot steam being forced out of my ears. How dare he speak to me like that. If he wasn't playing a game he must be texting, which showed how little interest he had in spending time with me.

I didn't normally wait up for them but I felt something wasn't right. When 3 am came and went, I knew it. Even the Caledonian Hotel's lock-ins didn't go on this late. They were probably at a party somewhere in the village, 'an Empty Hoose', that was to say a hoose empty of parents but paradoxically full of drunk sex-crazed teenagers. I really hoped that's where they were.

I heard a diesel engine climb the hill out of Inverfaughie and stop outside, the van's engine ticking as I rushed to the front door. It was Jackie, he had him, he had Steven in a fireman's lift, slung over his shoulder, slack as a sack of turnips. I rushed forward and threw my arms around Steven as he lay slumped on Jackie's chest and immediately felt the wetness. I jumped back to stare at my hands.

'What is that? Oh God! What is it?'

'Stop panicking woman, it's only water,' said Jackie, the first words he had spoken to me in weeks.

He strode past me into the lounge and laid down my precious son. The care he took with him, placing his head gently on the cushion, made me realise how precious he must be to Jackie too. Steven was pale but he was breathing, his eyes were closed but he wasn't unconscious. When I stroked his face he moaned and curled into a ball.

'There's nothing wrong with him,' Jackie said gently. 'He fell asleep in the van.'

It might have been relief that Steven was safe but I felt a gush of warmth towards Jackie. The memory of him lying on that very same couch a few weeks ago, half asleep like Steven was now, reminded me of how I'd felt about him then. When I remembered how I'd tried to kiss Jackie, and how he'd reacted, I felt another gush, this time of black mortifying shame.

Steven stirred.

'See?' said Jackie, 'he's fine. He'll have a hangover in the morning but nothing a sick bucket and a couple of paracetamol won't fix.'

I turned and looked at Gerry.

'Would you like to tell me what the hell happened tonight?'

Gerry remained mute, standing behind Jackie, trying to look invisible. His clothes were soaked too, and he was dripping on my new rug.

'I'm sworn to secrecy but you might as well tell her,' Jackie said to Gerry.

'Yes, please do, Gerry.'

'She'll only keep going till she twists it out of you.'

With both of us badgering him, Gerry looked as if he might cry.

I hadn't seen Jackie for ages; he always scurried away if he saw me in the distance. We hadn't been on speaking terms since before the ceilidh, but now here we were working together; playing good cop/bad cop with Gerry.

'But I have to warn you,' Jackie continued, 'Trixie's not much good at keeping secrets. She has the terrible affliction of blabbing other people's business to the whole town.'

No, my mistake, we weren't working together. Jackie was using the occasion to have a go at me.

My rage was swift and overwhelming. I turned and pushed my snarling face into his.

'Oh for god's sake get over yourself!' I roared.

Jackie backed out of the room and as I followed I realised I could still hear the diesel engine running. He had obviously intended to dump Steven quickly and be off. His snipe at me was an unexpected extra, for both of us.

'Get out!' I shouted redundantly.

I was gratified to see he was taking my advice, scrabbling to get into the cab of his van.

'Yeah, go on: flee, that'll solve everything. Fleeing's all you're good for, you pathetic flee-er!'

But he had fled.

Enraged by Jackie's talent for escapology and outstanding cowardice, I marched back into the house. This wasn't over.

Gerry was halfway up the stairs.

'Not so fast young man. Get down here; you've a bit of explaining to do.'

It could have waited till morning, but with that amount of adrenaline buzzing through my system, I hadn't vented enough yet, not nearly enough. I pointed to a chair. Gerry meekly trotted over and sat down, perching on the end of the chair trying not to soak it with his wet jeans.

'We just went for a few drinks in the Caley then we went to Shona's.'

'Shona's?'

'Yeah, one of the girls from the village, she had an empty.'

'And?'

'And, that was it.'

'Where was this house, at the bottom of the sea? I don't know if you've noticed, Gerry, but you're both soaking my suite.'

He shifted awkwardly as if he'd netted a crab in his pants.

'Me and Stevo went out to the island.'

'At this time of night? Did Jackie take you out there fishing? I'm going to report him to – somebody. I'll ...'

'He didn't take us there. He brought us back. He helped us, we were stuck.'

'Well, how did you get out there then?'

'We took a boat.'

'You stole a boat?'

'We were going to put it back but when we landed on the island Stevo forgot to stow the oars. They must have floated away. We nearly lost the boat as well. It was funny at first, but it got really cold.'

'Why didn't Steven phone me?'

Gerry shrugged, 'Jackie's got a boat.'

I had no boat. No argument. I had nothing.

'Why go to the island in the middle of the night? Who d'you think you are, Tom Sawyer?'

'It was Stevo's idea. He nipped a wee burd early doors but she bolted.'

'Steven nipped a burd?'

As far as I knew he'd never had a girlfriend; Steven had always been shy around girls. This probably explained his earlier huffiness, but I was concerned about the bolting. I didn't want my son's first encounter with the opposite sex to be humiliating. God knows he'd have ample opportunity for humiliation during the rest of his life.

'And you say she bolted?'

'Aye, she didn't want to go home, she was well into Stevo, but she had to get up early to milk cows. It was still early and we just wanted to ... I don't know, do something mad.'

'Well, you certainly achieved that. Didn't you, Steven?'

At the mention of his name Steven stirred. This was the burd-nipping Lothario who had stolen a milkmaid's heart and then gone on a drunken boat-stealing rampage. Sweet sixteen, he was still so cute, so vulnerable.

'Help me get him upstairs,' I said.

'You're not going to phone my mum,' pleaded Gerry, 'are you Mrs McNicholl?'

Chapter 16

Of course I didn't phone Gerry's mum – Steven would never have spoken to me again – but I grounded them for the rest of the weekend. I think it suited them, it gave them a chance to eat off their hangovers, scoffing every cake on the premises, but house arrest hardly made for the fun family weekend I'd planned.

I took Steven up a cup of tea to his room. He lay on the bed in his T-shirt and boxers, spread-eagled and face down, ignoring the tea.

'How are you feeling?' I asked.

'Quality,' he mumbled through a mouthful of mattress.

'Steven, why are you being so snarky with me? Have I done something to upset you?'

He sighed, 'No.'

I stood awaiting further revelation but there was none. I looked at him lying there. Steven was blessed with a strong healthy young body, his hair shone and his skin was flawless. How did I ever manage to produce such a magnificent creature? And at the same moment I was burning with fury that he would so casually jeopardise this magnificence; throw away his beautiful young life, in a moronic boating misadventure.

'Oh not again,' he said, wrinkling his nose, 'I know what you're checking for.'

I had no idea what he was talking about.

'Do you indeed, and what's that then?'

'Tired and irritable, check. Decrease in appetite, check. Poor personal hygiene, check. Dark shadows under the eyes, check.'

I knew now what he meant, and dreaded what was coming.

'Puncture marks or bruising on the body.'

At this point he rolled over and held his arms open wide, a Christ figure, showing me his mercifully unbruised, unpunctured arms.

'Not check.'

I honestly hadn't been looking for tracks on his arms but he must have seen the relief on my face.

'Ah, but I've fooled you. I actually am a hopeless addict.'

'No you're not.'

'It's just that I've decided to go down the slightly more alternative route of spit meth addiction.'

'Just stop it, Steven.'

When I'd been a medical rep part of my job was to visit pharmacists. While chatting in the back shop I'd seen plenty of heroin addicts being given their dose, knocking back the little cup of bright green methadone under supervision, but I was shocked to discover what some of them did with it next. Instead of swallowing there and then, some of them walked out the shop, spat it out into another cup, and sold it on for a fiver to someone even more desperate than themselves. It was me who had told Steven about this disgusting spit methadone practice, not for laughs, but to warn him of the indignities of addiction; to frighten him. And now he was trying to frighten me.

'They usually throw in some food particles for free and, if I'm lucky, sometimes a nice chewy bit of phlegm.'

'Right, that's enough, Steven. I know you're not an addict, I never said that. So if we've established that you're not hooked on spit meth, why would your irresponsible behaviour be acceptable?'

'Oh just leave it alone, Trixie, will you?'

'Look, I have to live in this town. What are you going to do about the boat you stole? What you think is just a prank is also known as common theft; the owner could press charges. At the very least you'll have to apologise and make good the damage.'

'The boat is taken care of,' he sighed. 'Jackie towed it back from the island with us. I phoned him this morning to apologise and he said he'd returned it to Murdo with a set of oars he has spare. He said Murdo was alright about it, he just laughed.'

'Oh yeah, what a hoot! You could easily have drowned in that drunken state. I could have coped with *you* drowning, Steven –'

'Cheers.'

'– but what would I say to Gerry's mother?'

'We were fine.'

'So fine that you had to phone Jackie to come and rescue you.'

My throat closed a little as I said his name. In a life-threatening crisis Steven had thought to phone Jackie instead of me. Jackie rescued him, Jackie supplied replacement oars, smoothed everything over with Murdo. I didn't even know Jackie's phone number. Steven had him on speed dial.

'It was getting cold.'

'Exactly; you could have died of hypothermia.'

'Me phoning Jackie, that's what's really bugging you, isn't it?'

I had to walk out of his room.

Steven stayed in bed most of the day. The next morning he and Gerry took the early train back to Glasgow. He wasn't speaking to me. No gossip whatsoever on the burd he'd nipped; no sexual health or relationship advice sought or given, no vicarious thrills for mother. I didn't even get the burd's name, but at least Steven and Gerry had made it out alive – not drowned or dead from hypothermia. As a means of enticing Steven to spend his summer with me, the weekend had been an unqualified disaster. He was never going to come back.

Chapter 17

When Global Imperial's Accommodation Manager asked me this time for my bank details I gave her my new Inverfaughie Credit Union account. This might be the ideal way to sneak it past the tax man.

'Right,' she said, sweeping her index finger across her iPad, 'I've pinged a 30 per cent deposit across for you now. We settle in full on completion of the contract.'

I laughed at how surreal this seemed. She had just contracted to pay me enough money for a deposit on a flat in Glasgow. All I had to do now was cook full Scottish breakfasts for a few weeks. That and start looking online at properties for sale in Glasgow. I could be back in the West End by October. I'd better get stocked up on full Scottish breakfast gubbins: tottie scones and the like.

*

They were beautiful, in the way that all young girls are beautiful, their faces blameless and rosy with expectation. Hardly a moment ago they had played with skipping ropes and dollies. Disenchantment hadn't had time to weary them, yet, and so, in period costume, jeans or mini-skirts, they waited. Tall thin ones, small fat ones, and every other female body shape checked their appearance in compact mirrors, applied more make-up, fixed each other's hair. The longer they waited the more their chatter and laughter increased. From the kitchen the sound made me think of a flock of seagulls that had lost its bearings and swooped down the chimney into the village hall. The girls were here to audition for a part in *Freedom Come All of You*. Jenny was a key holder for the village hall. She'd asked me to help her serve coffee and cake and wash up afterwards. It wouldn't normally have been a very enticing proposition but when she told me it was for the movie I'll admit I was nosey. When she showed me the net curtain she had draped over the serving hatch, I was in.

'Obviously we won't be in the hall when the auditions are actually taking place but – and here is where the net curtain reigns supreme –' she said, 'it's as good as a two-way mirror. If we keep the hatch open and stay quiet we'll see the whole show. Ringside seats.'

'I always had you down as a Curtain Twitcher.'

'This audition is what's known in the biz as an open casting call – anybody can try; like the "X-Factor". Global Imperial say they want to fully engage with the community, so they're seeing local girls. It's only four lines but it's an important part: the wife of the hero, Tony Ramos. There's to be a long lingering kiss between them. If he was ten years older I'd break him in for them myself,' Jenny tittered, 'although there's no sign of Tony yet,' she said, peering through the curtain.

I took a turn at the old ladyish white lace net curtain. I had to admit, it was a pretty effective camouflage. The film director, Hollywood wunderkind Raymondo Land, sat with four Global Imperial staff at a long table at one end of the hall with the hopefuls at the other, corralled behind a plastic tape barrier. After we served the movie people their coffee – the girls were to be offered no such hospitality – Jenny and I returned to the kitchen. There we organised our own coffee and cake, made ourselves comfortable behind the net curtain and watched the drama unfold.

The girls were called forward one at a time and asked to read just one line. It was dialogue between the hero and his wife, Raymondo Land explained. The wife was to beg the hero not to go into battle as he would surely die. The American man standing in for the Tony Ramos part, a tall thin bald man, mumbled his way through the lines, never looking at the nervous, faltering girls.

'I must go not for self but for country for Scotland,' he mumbled.

'Please don't go, they'll kill you,' the girls replied, with varying degrees of credibility.

I wasn't impressed with the script so far. If this was going to be the standard, *Freedom Come All of You* would probably go straight to DVD, Tony Ramos or not.

Mr Land asked the young women to read in different moods. Sometimes he wanted them to say it sadly, or angrily, or as if they didn't care. Then he got them to do it again, this time with their own interpretation. I would have thought the words indicated that this was a serious matter but some of the girls tried a jocular approach.

'Please don't go!' one tall buck-toothed girl laughed maniacally, 'They'll kill you!'

'That's Maureen Templeton,' Jenny whispered, circling her finger at her ear, 'from Bengustie.'

Isla McPhail was next: a gorgeous statuesque redhead wearing high heels, a tight-fitting black silky skirt with a split up the side and a red top that showed her heaving bosom to great effect.

'Please,' she wheedled huskily, running her open palm up the hero's thigh, 'don't go.'

Then she threw her leg, with great agility it must be said, up onto the shoulder of the confused, frightened man and smiled seductively, 'They'll kill you.'

With this sexy display I nearly choked on my fruit scone. Due to the disapproving looks coming from Jenny I tried to do it silently but this only led me to an uncontrollable fit of the giggles. At this she tried to stuff a tea towel in my mouth. The afternoon was very entertaining. Some girls shrieked the line, some purred, some said it with conviction, and eventually the director whittled the crowd down to six.

During a lull while Mr Land consulted his assistants, Jenny and I started tidying up the kitchen. As I was emptying the coffee dregs, we suddenly heard a commotion in the hall. To the sound of excited squeals from the remaining girls, Jenny rushed back to her look-out post by the serving hatch.

'H.M.B., I knew it!' she whispered. 'He's come at last. Tony Ramos is here in our wee village!'

Chapter 18

'I hate to tell you this Jenny, but that guy's not Tony Ramos.'

Jenny and I had just had a silent but vigorous elbow war at the kitchen hatch. I felt bad wrestling with a woman who had twenty years on me and possibly osteoporosis, but she was stronger than she looked.

'I know that guy, he told me he's here to work the season.'

'Rubbish!' Jenny puffed, squashing in beside me, 'He's come to personally cast the right girl. That's how much of a pro Tony Ramos is.'

'He's a pro alright, a professional barman. A couple of years ago he regularly served me in my local pub.'

'Yes, and now he's a filum star,' Jenny insisted.

'But he looks nothing like Tony Ramos in *The International Brigade*.'

'FFS, Trixie, he was playing a real-life character, it was a prosthetic nose, surely you knew that?'

I did not know that, and now I was starting to doubt my own argument. When my new neighbour had told me he'd come because of the filming I'd assumed he was, like the rest of us, cashing in on the gold rush, supping up the movie gravy.

Jenny tutted but never took her eyes from the serving hatch. 'Hopeless: you're living next door to one of the world's highest grossing filum stars and you don't even know it.'

Jenny moved aside to let me stick my face against the curtain.

'Read any of the gossip mags; it's well documented that Tony was a barman before he made it,' she insisted.

My neighbour, the wee barman from Glasgow, was graciously receiving deferential greetings from Raymondo Land and his assistants. The girls were almost wetting themselves. Taking the mickey, I opened up Jenny's couthy wee acronym and dramatised with long pauses like a hysterical boy band fan, 'Help. Ma. Boab!' I said, 'Tony Ramos is my next-door neighbour!'

They began the audition process all over again, exactly the same as before. The director asked each of the girls to speak again, but this time it was Tony Ramos feeding them their line. Tony smiled and gave them a wee peck on the cheek as they came forward. He was very encouraging, thanked them when they were done and gallantly walked them back to their chair.

'He's every inch the gentleman,' said Jenny, drooling. 'I'm putting my money on number 3 getting the part.'

'How much money?'

'Fiver?'

'You're that confident?'

'Och, alright then, a tenner, but I'm telling you, she's a cert.'

After we shook on it, Jenny explained why she thought this girl was a shoe-in for the role of Tony's young wife.

'Morag Fenton, Bobby's daughter. What you don't know – amongst other things – is that although Morag's only fifteen she's the most experienced of the lot of them. She's had training: Scottish Youth Theatre summer school, she goes every year. Costs her dad a fortune, and she's the best looking.'

I couldn't disagree. Morag, with her creamy skin, softly curling auburn hair and flashing green eyes, was certainly a beautiful girl, but I'd been more taken with number 5. I told Jenny this.

'Och, away you go! She's not even local. That one works in the Bayview round the coast. A nice enough wee girl but she's not a Highlander.'

On the second run-through I had to admit Morag Fenton was a standout. As she came forward she didn't appear to be starstruck and silly like some of the others; she behaved professionally, standing calmly beside Tony as she prepared for her cue.

'I must go,' said Tony. 'Not for self, but for country.'

I had pitied the actor, having to work with such poor material, but he soon made it clear why he was one of the world's highest grossing stars. Tony's delivery was so nuanced it didn't matter how cheesy the dialogue was. He said it like he understood that these were high-minded words and he felt unworthy of saying them but still and all, they must be said.

'For Scotland,' he said humbly.

Jenny went a bit glassy-eyed.

Morag took Tony's right arm with both of hers and pulled him gently towards her, as if she was preparing to physically prevent him.

'Please. Don't,' she said.

There was pleading in her voice but no whining. She shook her head slightly, as if she was trying to deny the reality of her man leaving her. She turned her face from his to shield him from her tears. She was really crying. Real tears were flowing from her eyes. After a few seconds her grip on him slackened, as if she knew the futility of trying to persuade him. She turned back to him and smiled.

'Go,' she said, respecting his wishes, giving him her blessing, accepting what must be; loving him so much that she was prepared to let him go.

'They'll kill you,' she whispered. She was smiling, nodding, as if she knew it for a certainty, but yet rebellious: as though the notion that death could separate them was ridiculous.

There was silence in the hall. No movement, no breathing: absolute silence. We were in the presence of pure transcendent love.

Applause broke out in the hall and Jenny and I joined in. No contest. Fair doos, she was amazing. When everyone had had their turn Morag was called forward to the desk. As the director spoke to her the others were discreetly let go.

'That's a tenner you owe me,' Jenny gloated. 'Oh, and by the way, the other thing you don't know: Morag Fenton is currently your Steven's main squeeze.'

Chapter 19

Claymores, scabbards, shields, dirks, axes, bows, arrows, flags, bagpipes, spears, pikes, powder horns, muskets, kilts, belts, helmets. And six hairy Scotsmen.

They arrived in a minibus with a trailer for all the gear.

I went out to meet them at the gate, where I introduced myself and then delivered my wee speech. It was the professional thing to do.

'Welcome to Harrosie, where we offer the very best in Highland hospitality. We hope your Bed and Breakfast experience will be a memorable and pleasant one. If there is anything that would make your stay with us more comfortable, please do not hesitate to ask.'

A look passed from one to the other that made me nervous about what it meant. No one spoke. A burly bearded man with a big red nose took the lead. Oh dear, I thought, with that swollen conk he was obviously the type to take a right good drink. I didn't want any trouble.

'Stan McCauslan, Claymores Battle Director,' he said, shoving a surprisingly small hairy hand in my direction. 'We've been billeted with you. Have you somewhere we can store our equipment, love?'

'Eh, I have a shed out the back,' I said, stretching my lips, smile-like.

The Accommodation Manager told me I was being allocated combat performers but I never dreamed I'd end up with a shedload of medieval weaponry.

'Lockable?'

'Well, I've never needed to lock it before. It's pretty safe around here.'

He looked at me through blood-shot boozy eyes.

'But I could put a padlock on it. I think I have one somewhere.'

I didn't want to lose my guests before they were even in the door.

'Aye,' he said, signalling to his men. 'A lot of expensive kit here, hen.'

It took ages for them to put the stuff in the shed. With Red Nose barking orders at them, they unloaded everything from the trailer, carried it round the side of the house to the shed and then entered into a lengthy discussion about how to stack it all.

I had bundled Bouncer upstairs into my bedroom, I didn't want him bouncing around while I was trying to get my guests settled in and I was looking forward to the welcome tea I had laid on. I'd dug out the best bone china: a full tea service, hand painted with tiny bluebell flowers, even inside the cups, so light and fragile they were translucent. Everything matched: cake stand, milk jug, sugar bowl, side plates; there was even a gorgeous set of silver sugar tongs with the bluebell emblem on the handle. I'd ordered sugar cubes from Jenny especially. Napkins, doilies, tiny silver teaspoons, one for each plate. I'd baked a Victoria sponge for the cake stand and, if I said so myself, the sponge was so light it was in danger of floating away. To fit on the side of the neat little saucers I'd baked dinky wee macaroons and cute button-sized meringues, all in pastel shades. Who knew running a B&B was going to be this much fun? It was so unbearably charming I was getting high off the cute rush.

The men still hadn't agreed how to stack their stuff. It seemed their weapons were more precious than their personal belongings, which they had dumped in a heap at the front door. From the open kitchen window I could hear a lot of swearing coming from the shed as they cursed and joked with each other. The Battle Director looked up and caught me earwigging at the window. I grabbed the teapot and waved it at him.

'Ewan, Colin, Dave, Will and Danny,' he said by way of intro-
duction when they all finally trooped into the lounge.

The six men were a homogeneous blur of the Highland warrior
cliché: big, burly, beardy or bald. Stan and Ewan – beardy; Colin
– baldy; Dave and Will – beardy and burly; Danny neither burly
nor baldy but slightly beardy. They were of a similar mid-thirties
to mid-forties age range, and could have been brothers.

'Pleased to meet you, please do take a seat, don't stand on ceremony,' I said as I handed round cups and poured tea.

The rest of them took their cue from the boss, who didn't
seem to want to sit down, so they just stood around in a semi-
circle. No one spoke. As I handed them their teacups a few of
them flapped; with the exception of Stan, their big sausage fingers
were too unwieldy to curl inside the finely wrought handles. I
served Stan first.

'Milk?'

'Please.'

'Sugar?'

'Three please.'

With something approaching euphoria I lifted the exquisite
sugar tongs and plopped three perfect cubes into his teacup.

'Sorry about the swearing, hen,' said Stan pointing backwards,
obviously referring to the cursing in the shed.

'Please, don't worry, Stan,' I said. 'While you're in Inverfaughie
my home is your home. I'd like you to feel at home.' I turned to
one of the others. 'Milk?'

'That's kind of you, hen, and by the way, you don't need to
call me Stan. You might as well call me Rudi.' He leaned his head
towards his men. 'That's what these yins call me.'

I nodded. It seemed rude to ask why; I already had a good idea.

'The nose,' he said, pointing to it, and then, more to the men
than to me, he said, 'not used to being around ladies. I'll need to
mind my Ps and Qs. I nearly said the *fucking* nose but then I ...'

'You just did,' said Danny, halting Rudi's nervous chatter.

Rudi stopped and reviewed his last few sentences then, mortified, he whispered, 'Sorry.'

The men shuffled, staring at the floor and pinching the handles of their teacups awkwardly. No one spoke.

Now I realised how badly I'd misjudged how to play this. I'd thought running a B&B was all about impressing the guests with my best china and my pastel-coloured meringues. Now I saw that these guys would have been more comfortable with bacon butties and builder's tea in a chipped mug. They must be dreading having to spend the next six weeks in this stuffy atmosphere. I tried to think of some way to put them at their ease.

'I've heard worse swearing than that, Rudi, believe me,' I said. 'Yeah?'

'Of course,' I said, passing round the macaroons, 'haven't we all?'

The men nodded and smiled, apparently relieved. The genteel crockery must have given them the idea that I was some kind of sad, old-fashioned Highland spinster. Now they'd see I was as broad-minded as the next person. At last the tension was lessening; the atmosphere was beginning to thaw. Maybe we would all get along after all.

'So,' Rudi asked, 'are you alright with the cunt word, love?'

Pinkie in the air and my cup poised at my lip, it was all I could do not to spray the parlour with tea. I didn't know where to put myself. The rest of them fell about laughing.

There was no redeeming it; my posh tea party was a farce.

'It's the C word,' Danny corrected him, giggling, 'you're supposed to say, *are you alright with the C word?*'

But by this time we were all laughing.

Chapter 20

No sooner had they come than they were gone again. Rudi ordered them to get their weapons and follow him up the hill for battle practice. It was raining slightly, a light smirr, but they didn't even seem to notice. They didn't come back for hours, by which time Bouncer and I were relaxing in the lounge in front of the telly. When they returned I went to leave, to give them the lounge to themselves, but they insisted we stay, all of them making a big fuss of Bouncer.

'Leave him be, hen, he's comfortable where he is. He's a great wee dog,' said Rudi.

The rest of them agreed, clapping him and tickling his belly.

'Yeah, he's charming,' I conceded.

If they were going to share the lounge with me and Bouncer they'd better know what they were letting themselves in for.

'Except when he's eating his own sick or licking his willy,' I added.

That got a laugh and no one demanded Bouncer leave the room. Now that we'd got the measure of each other I was going to get on fine with these men.

'That's a helluva fence next door,' said Will.

I told them that Tony Ramos was staying there and how I hadn't recognised him as a filum star but as the wee barman from

Tennent's. They all laughed. It turned out they knew him too. They had worked with him on *The International Brigade* and he had actually got them the gig on this movie. They were all great pals by the sounds of it.

'Wee Tony's stayin' next door, eh?' said Will, 'I thought that was him when I saw the fence.'

I asked what he meant.

'Press intrusion. Tony cannae be doing wi' them peeking in his windae, rakin' his bins,' he said. 'Och, well, he'll no' have far to go if he wants a game of poker.'

Poker? I wasn't sure if I liked the sound of that, not with Rudi and his boozy red nose, they might be up all night drinking and carousing.

'Where did you go for dinner?' I asked.

'We haven't had our dinner yet,' moaned Dave, 'Rudolfo wouldn't let us. I'm starving.'

'I could maybe rustle something up for you, if you'll take pot luck.'

I still had the chicken curry I'd made for Steven and Gerry. When they went home early I'd put the rest of it in the freezer; it would stretch at a pinch.

They loved it. They nearly licked the pattern off the plates. A few days later, after they had exhausted the restaurants in the village, Rudi came to me.

'Trixie, we'll have to square up with you for the lovely curry you cooked us the other night.'

My cunning plan had worked.

'Your curry's the best dinner we've had since we got here. Global Imperial gives us a subsistence allowance, you know, it's quite generous. It would suit me to have all my lads eating dinner here together; gives us more time to rehearse. What do you say we come to an arrangement?'

We came to an arrangement. They would give me wads of cash, and I would give them dinner. All the more money for my flat deposit fund. The money would be great – the slightly ticklish bit would be the drinking.

Rudi's men would want a drink with their dinner, a pint or maybe a glass of wine. It wasn't unreasonable for them to want to relax after a hard day's claymore wielding, but I was nervous. I didn't know if I had the willpower to resist temptation. I was keen for us all to feel relaxed with each other; I just didn't want them to see me lying slumped, paralytic in a chair, trying to sing 'Flower of Scotland'.

Chapter 21

When I went into the shop, Jenny was busy serving a young girl, or what looked, from the back, like a young girl. Up close it was clear she was a rather more mature lady with an overperky boob job and lashings of botox. To complete the look she also had a fluffy wee puppy in her huge Dolce and Gabbana handbag. They were obviously discussing the pup, or at least the woman was. Jenny seemed, by her body language, not to give a toss.

'And there are quite a few interesting crosses,' the woman lectured Jenny, 'a poodle and Labrador, that's a labradoodle. A Bichon Frisé and Jack Russell, which I have to tell you is absolutely adorable, they're called Jacky Frost. Isn't it cute? I nearly got one of those but then I found my little Vivienne; she's the best, aren't you, darling?' she said, pulling the dog out of the handbag. 'She's half-cocker spaniel and half-poodle. She's my beautiful little Cockapoo.'

'Eh?' said Jenny, barely managing to keep a sneer at bay, 'cock a what?'

'Cockapoo. She's a designer breed. I'm not sure if you'd have designer dogs this far north.'

'We have a different name for them in the Highlands.'

'Really?' said the woman, dangling the Cockapoo above her face. 'D'you hear that Vivienne? You have a Highland name. So what would you call her then?'

'Ach,' said Jenny, 'we just call it a mongrel.'

She slapped an expensive brand of cigarettes on the counter and smiled sweetly. 'Nine pounds thirty please.' With a designer yelp Vivienne was shoved back in the bag, the cash was handed over and the woman flounced out of the shop.

I waited a moment and said, 'Thank God I stopped smoking. Nine pounds thirty! Is that how much it costs for a packet of fags now?'

Jenny burst out her malicious tee hee laugh, 'It is if you buy them here.'

I gave her a disapproving stare and then joined in with the tee heeing.

'She won't be back, you know.'

'Pffff,' said Jenny, 'I'm the only place that stocks her fancy fags.'

'You're the one who told me we have to be nice to the visitors.'

'She's not a visitor, she's filum company, can you not guess? And anyway, how else am I supposed to have any fun around here? Yes, can I help you, sir?'

A crowd of customers had come in. Jenny's shop was going like a fair. I hung about in one of the aisles, pretending to be interested in her latest marketing wheeze, a 'Brussel sprout event', while she serviced the lunchtime rush.

'And what exactly is a Brussel sprout event?' I asked her, between customers.

'Och, it's just a bit of nonsense. For the tourists and filum people, it's more what they're used to. Posh shops don't have a sale, they have an "event".'

'You mean like a blue cross event?'

'Exactly. Except mine is sprout themed. D'you want a kilo? They're 20 per cent off.'

'Eh, no thanks.'

'Nah,' she said, making a face, 'I can't stand them either.'

While I lingered, customers came and went and in almost every case Jenny was able to extract information from them.

'Are you still working on the old village up by the lochan?' she asked some of the Global Imperial workmen. 'Nice to be out in the sunshine. Och well, I hope this lovely weather keeps up for you,' she chirped, 'cheerio for now. Laters!'

When the men left and the shop was empty again Jenny began restocking her cold drinks fridge, a sure sign that she was ready to recommence gossiping.

'Well, don't torment me,' she said, 'who did you get for your B&B? Anybody famous?'

'Six combat performers, but they seem nice enough.'

'Handsome?'

'Nah.'

'Still, six fellas all to yourself. Your Jan will be getting jealous.'

I smiled, but I still wasn't taking the bait. Time to change the subject.

'I've walked Bouncer up to the wee lochan a few times and I've never seen an old village. Where is it?'

'Well, it's not a village any more, there's only ruins now.'

'D'you mean those oblong walls?' I asked.

'Aye, that's it.'

'I thought they were old-fashioned cattle pens.'

'Nope.'

'But, Jenny, I've seen those oblong pens other places in the Highlands,' I argued, 'they're everywhere.'

'Maybe they became sheepfolds after they burned the villagers out, but before that, they were family homes.'

'So what are Global Imperial doing?'

Jenny rolled her eyes.

'The magic of Hollywood,' she sighed. 'They're recreating the village. They're making a terrible mess up there. I hope they're going to restore it but I suppose those lads will do what Global Imperial tells them. Like the rest of us.'

I wasn't comfortable with Jenny's bitter tone, not when Global Imperial were paying me enough to buy an exit visa and a flat in Glasgow. Another swift change of subject was required.

'Why did you say "laters" to that workman?' I asked.

'Och, just a bit of banter. They're good lads those workmen, and he's from my old manor, Pimlico.'

'Tell me more.' Since she'd given up louche London years ago and returned to be buried alive in Inverfaughie, Jenny had lived her life through other people in the village, other younger, more exciting people. People like me. But London was always an excellent topic of conversation. She'd hinted darkly about her life there, in the fleshpots of Pimlico, and had claimed she *wouldn't die wondering*. I shuddered at what kind of weird experimental sex that might mean. It was hard to imagine Inverfaughie's postmistress in love beads and a mini, ash from a fat spliff dropping onto her naked breasts. Breasts that were now, and had been for years, safely encased within a dark blue polyester overall.

'Och aye, in Pimlico I was a free spirit.'

'Really? I thought you were the manageress of Woolworths.'

'That was just my day job. By night I turned on, tuned in and, eh, what was it again?'

Still fixated on Jenny's bosoms I sniped, 'Drooped down?'

Chapter 22

During the day I hardly had time to be lonely. Every morning I walked Bouncer, cooked breakfast, washed up, changed sheets and towels, washed and cleaned, walked Bouncer again and popped down to Jenny's before it was time to cook dinner, but something was missing.

'Hi son,' I said, trying to communicate a smile down the phone.

'Who's calling?' said Steven, apparently for real.

'How many mothers have you got?' I joked.

He didn't laugh.

Since our tiff over his boating incident I'd phoned Steven every day and always got a lukewarm reception. I wanted chummy conversation, a bit of light relief, but it became interrogation: me asking him question after question and getting nothing back. He was hiding in his dunno cave and nothing, not even that fact that I had a film star living right next door, would winkle him out. I was forced to continue as if my monologue was a dialogue.

'The Claymores have worked with him loads; they all play poker together. They're talking about having their poker nights here in Harrosie. That's going to be a laugh, a house full of big rufty-tufty men and Hollywood stars. He's a nice guy, dead down to earth. You know who Tony Ramos is, don't you?'

'Dunno.'

Steven had to have been impressed, it wasn't everyone who had a film star next door, but he forced himself not to be.

'Is everything alright, Steven?'

'Quality.'

'Is Gary still giving you all that overtime at the warehouse?'

'Dunno.'

It's simply a yes or no answer! I wanted to scream.

'Because if you want to earn money, there's plenty of work up here.'

Silence.

This was getting me nowhere; if I asked him any more questions he'd do his usual: start huffing and puffing and then say he had to go. The only avenue I had left to me was to give him my news and hope to sell him the wonderful benefits of living in Inverfaughie.

'Talking of earning money, I've turned into quite the business-woman. I've even joined Faughie Council, well I had to really. D'you remember I told you about Betty Robertson?'

Nothing.

'She was the one who came round for the inspection, you know, the one who got the rose bowl at the gala day?'

'Please, I'm begging you, not the rose bowl story again,' he said, 'let it go.' I ignored the impertinence; at least he was responding.

'Well, she's on the council. Betty says that with the movie in town we're all going to be millionaires. There's full employment in the village, lots of opportunity. Oh, and the big news is that a local girl got a part in the film.' I tried to keep my voice light. 'Morag Fenton, she's playing Tony Ramos's wife. I don't know if you've met her yet?'

I hoped a reminder of the creamy-skinned, auburn-haired beauty might provoke a response, but he left this hanging in the air unanswered. At least he wasn't denying it – that was a good sign.

'Global Imperial want to give villagers work, put something back, that sort of thing, so if you were here for the summer you'd have your pick of jobs. Even acting, they're looking for extras for the film. D'you not fancy trying your hand at acting? You could end up a big star like Tony Ramos. '

'Nah ... bsolutely.'

At last, I thought, an affirmative response!

'Seriously, d'you fancy acting? I could speak to Jenny about getting you a part in the ...'

'Y ... unlikely,' he scoffed.

Steven sang this in such a tormenting taunt as to convey to me that I'd been duped by his earlier reply.

'Even though I have a house full of cool Highland warriors and a film star next door; even though I'm up here all on my lonesome and missing you more every day, you still won't come. Will you, Steven?'

Silence.

'Steven?'

'What?'

A ratty impatient 'what'.

'Nothing,' I sighed.

After that there was a very long silence where we listened to each other's angry breath.

Eventually Steven spoke. 'That's Gerry at the door for me, I have to go. Nice talking to you.'

'Quality,' I said sarcastically. 'Let's do this again soon.'

*

Jan contacted me, not for a dinner date, thank Jehovah, but to help out with the guitar group again.

I gladly agreed. It was another fundraiser, but this time the kids wouldn't be playing their guitars. The parents had signed the contracts – Global Imperial were paying the guitar group big money for the kids as 'supporting artistes' in a big scene they were shooting and Jan had asked me to chaperone the girls.

The film company had already tried to recruit from the school but the headmistress had had to refuse on health and safety grounds. It seemed that although Global Imperial had plenty of supporting artistes, they were short on oldies and children. They were now specifically seeking vulnerable types and had sent scouts round the village picking off anyone who was limbless, toothless or glaikit-looking. Jenny teased Walter remorselessly about being targeted until the scout came for her. She saw him off with her broom and literally swept the guy out the shop. I was surprised that Walter was up for it; he was becoming increasingly anti-G.I., but he said he wanted to see at first hand 'what the sneaky bodachs were up to now'.

I expected we would be taken up to the lochan and ruined village but the bus stopped at the bottom of the hill. Parked on both sides, creating a dark narrow canyon, were the mammoth production vehicles we had become so used to seeing around the village. Beyond, the road was single track, so the film company had set up base camp here, ferrying crew and equipment up and down in one vehicle. Although it was now nearly midnight and as dark as it was likely to get, the crew moved around at an industrious mid-morning pace, working like profit-share bees. Even the air was busy with the smell of hot electrical cables, fried food and hairspray.

Jan took the boys and I took the girls as we were quickly hustled into 'wardrobe'.

Inside there were heavy rails of elaborate period ball gowns, lush silks and velvets in every flavour of pink and green. Sadly, on this shoot everyone was to be dressed in nightclothes, so we were issued with uniformly drab, long collarless shirts.

Jan bounded off the gents' costume bus to meet us with a big smile on his face. He wasn't in a grubby nightshirt like the rest of us; he was in an old-fashioned top coat, knee-length boots and breeches. The breeches didn't have a fly fastening, they buttoned down either side. Which kept drawing my eye to between the buttoned area. It could have been worse; it could have been a codpiece.

'He's playing one of the factor's henchmen,' explained Walter, 'the dirty traitor.'

The kids laughed at Walter's get-up too: a long goonie and a night cap. They taunted him by singing 'Wee Willie Winkie', which he took in good part, turning quickly towards them to scare them and make them giggle. Walter, with his skinny blue-veined legs, looked like something out of Dickens. We all did.

'What factor?' I asked.

'Patrick Sellar,' said Walter, 'the Duke of Sutherland's factor for the most brutal of the Highland Clearances. Wait and see what happens here tonight,' he said portentously, 'just you wait.'

Chapter 23

The Claymores were next to emerge. Most of them were in dark-shirted uniforms, like soldiers, but Danny and Will were in the same grubby nightshirts as me and the kids.

We were sorted into groups, our nighshirt group being led up to the lochan by a guy with a clipboard. It had been raining on and off for days and the bracken was soaked. I had to keep a close eye on the kids. One of them, Rachel, wandered off the path and nearly lost a welly in the bog. As we breasted the hill and caught sight of the village there was a collective gasp.

The village was completely restored, the houses rebuilt. Black-houses, with thick stone walls and thatched roofs, now covered the ruins. Highland cattle were tethered outside. G.I. had even planted vegetable gardens in front of the houses, but when we got closer we saw the reality.

The dry stane walls of the houses were fibreglass facades. Held up with wooden frames, there was nothing behind; they were two-dimensional. Some of the grassed areas were actually artificial turf – even the cabbages they had planted were plastic. Amidst the lighting and camera hardware set out in front of the village, the crew, in fleeces and Gore-Tex jackets, stood staring back at us.

Clipboard Guy stationed groups of extras behind each of the fibreglass facades, sorting us into what seemed to be families. Me and the kids along with Walter, Danny and an old lady, became one such unit. Rachel was perhaps not the first person to notice our demographic but she was the only person to comment. Developing her theory out loud she explained that Walter and Jean (the old lady) were grandad and granny, she and the rest of the kids were the kids, obviously, and, lastly, to my huge embarrassment, Danny and I were daddy and mummy.

'Ok folks,' Clipboard Guy – whose name turned out to be Tristan – said placidly, 'take it easy for now; it'll be a while before the scene's ready to shoot.'

I wondered why they had brought us up if they weren't ready. We could easily have waited on the buses. It was sheltered down there. Up here a sharp breeze blew across the hill.

'Now,' said Tristan, 'can everyone see that man over there?' He spoke to someone through his earpiece and a figure behind the cameras began to wave at us. 'Ok, keep your eye on him and when he gives you the signal, take your shoes off and leave them here.'

The kids looked to me for clearance on this. I looked to Danny – he was, after all, a seasoned film actor – but he shrugged lightly. It must be ok. I nodded.

'Keep watching him, and when everything's ready, he'll give you another signal. This time you'll run out through that doorway and down towards the cameras. Don't stop; keep running until you're told to stop and whatever you do, don't look at the camera, ok?'

I mulled this over, but everyone else agreed it was ok.

'Remember, you've just woken up, you're tired.'

The kids, used to playacting, began yawning and stretching.

'That's it,' he said, 'but your house is on fire so you have to get out quick. You're screaming, you're crying. You're running for your lives.'

At this the kids began to squeal and rush around.

'You'll be great,' said Tristan, moving off to the next house, 'just don't look into the camera.'

'Danny,' I whispered so that little ears wouldn't hear, 'what did he mean by "your house is on fire"?'

Danny laughed and shook his head. 'No. There won't be any actual fire. It's shot digitally.'

'Aww, not fair!' Rachel and Michael grumped simultaneously.

'CGI?' Walter asked, showing off.

'Yeah,' said Danny, 'they'll add the flames post production.'

Taking their cue from the bigger ones, all the kids sighed and slumped in disappointment. I sighed too, with relief. With Jan off elsewhere, swanning around in his fancy breeches, I was on my own. Solely responsible for the safety of these eight small children. Up a hill in a soggy field. With no shoes on. Running around electrical equipment. In the dark.

But at least we weren't required to pass through a flaming building. I had a horrible image of one of the kids catching fire, their skin bubbling as their long flowing nightshirt turned them into a human candle. Thank God for CGI. There wasn't going to be any actual fire, everything would be fine...

Chapter 24

Take after monotonous take we did it, over and over again; running out on an adrenaline high and then hanging around behind the facades, bored and tired, for what seemed like hours. The first time the problem wasn't technical, it was one of the extras. No one in our family, one of the other houses. An old man, stage-struck and a bit too stoked, got his signals mixed up. While everyone else was removing their shoes, he ran screaming through the doorway, still wearing his bright blue Adidas Sambas. Raymondo Land, the director, shouted 'cut!' and turned away in disgust. A moment later we heard the squeal of the loudhailer being turned on again and everyone held their breath.

'I don't think three stripes were fashionable in the nineteenth century,' joked Mr Land, and everyone laughed.

But the laughter drained every time the phrase, 'positions, please!' was yelled at us through the loudhailer. Several takes later another extra – again not us, we behaved impeccably – bumped the fibreglass and the whole facade nearly fell on top of him. This would no doubt become comedy gold on an out-takes show and it would have been funny if it wasn't so dangerous.

Once we'd made it through the doorway we ran on to an obstacle course. Apart from the uncharted boulders in the bracken, tufts of heather and foul-smelling bog water, we had to dodge the equipment. A huge camera mounted on a platform, which could glide up and down and from side to side like a fairground ride on its own wee train tracks, followed us as we ran. We were not to look at it. We were not to engage with the other actors who stood around, calmly overseeing our village being sacked. Jan was one of them. I had to constantly remind the kids not to smile at him. Jan stared us homeless peasants down as if we were shit on his shoe. Either he was a really good actor or the power of being one of the factor's men had gone to his head. Perversely, he had never seemed more attractive.

As we were four adults and eight kids, the arithmetic was easy: two kids apiece. Walter and Jean were happy to hold hands with two kids. I had allocated the oldest kids to granny and grandad; this would provide stability for the oldsters and slow the kids down a bit. As Danny was likely to be the most sure-footed I asked him to take the two smallest, Lucy and Benjamin.

'Sorry, Trixie, I'll take them through the doorway but once the horsemen come I have to work.'

'What horsemen?' I asked.

Out of the mayhem, Rudi and Dave came galloping towards us on horseback. They rode fast and certain, standing up in the saddle and holding the reins in one hand like Cossacks. In their other hands they held what looked like flaming rocks tied on strings. They swung these round their heads and let them fly through the windows and doors of the house. There was a strong smell of smoke and singed hair. Had anyone still been standing on that side of the facade, they would surely have been killed or, at the very least, slightly maimed.

We ran, and as the hot rocks whistled past our ears, I worried about Walter. His poor wee blue legs were getting tired, he wasn't up to this. He must have been as nervous as the rest of us but, perhaps for the sake of the kids, he didn't show it.

'Goodness gracious,' Walter muttered as he dodged a flaming missile, 'great balls of fire.'

'Why didn't they tell us about this?' I asked Danny between takes.

More to the point, I thought, why hadn't Danny warned us?

'They want to make the experience as authentic as possible, get the best performances,' he explained, 'the old-fashioned element of surprise.'

'Huh, element of terror, more like,' I said.

At last things moved on. We didn't have to come out from behind the facades any more. Rudi and Dave had stopped throwing fire bombs at us, but we had to stay on set. I now saw why Danny couldn't take the kids. As we emerged from the house and Dave rode past, Danny jumped onto Dave's horse and pulled him to the ground. It was highly choreographed but impressive none the less. The next few scenes were of Danny fighting Dave. Every few blows they had to stop and either do it again or move on to the next part of the fight sequence. We simply stood around behind them, decorating the set, no more than human wallpaper.

It had been a warm night but it was colder up here on the hill. They let us put our shoes back on between shots; we were only barefoot for a few minutes in total but by now our feet were wet and muddy and cold and we weren't getting the chance to dry out.

Danny did the whole fight sequence in his bare feet but he didn't even seem to notice. It wasn't method acting – I actually felt proud of him trying to defend our village from these marauders. It wasn't a fair fight – Dave had a pair of boots and a knife – but, like every other inept movie bad guy I'd ever seen, he wasted too much time posturing. He seemed more interested in showing off his flashy knife, throwing it hand to hand and smiling a leery smile. Bootless and unarmed, Danny was focused, his bare feet kicking Dave's knife away before overwhelming him.

'I don't think kung fu was fashionable in the nineteenth century,' commented Walter dryly.

Now that we were required to stand still – for continuity purposes, not to move an inch – the kids were fed up.

'Auntie Trixie,' said Rachel, 'Lucy needs to go to the bathroom.'

Wee Lucy nodded shyly.

'I do too,' piped up Ailsa.

'Ok, I'll ask them,' I said.

As soon as they cut I waved Tristan Clipboard over.

'Sorry. The girls need the toilet, is there one up here?'

'Hmmm,' he said, 'I'm not sure. We're nearly finished with this sequence and then I can take you back down to the portaloos. In about five minutes?'

'Oh ... ok,' I said, there being no other option, but he had already ducked back behind the equipment.

Danny and Dave fighting: Dave punching Danny, Danny kicking Dave. Danny beating Dave and Rudi entering the fray. Rudi jumping Danny from behind and Danny going down for the last time.

'No fair!' said Michael.

'And thus the powerful tame us,' sighed Walter.

But the fight wasn't quite over yet. Everything stopped for a few minutes while Tony Ramos, dressed in the same grubby nightshirt the rest of us peasants wore, was escorted on to the set by six or seven people.

'Ho, Rudi!' Tony yelled, pointing at Rudi, 'you're gettin' it, Big Man!'

Everyone laughed. It was funny, an international film star behaving like a Ned.

'Hiya Trixie,' he yelled next to me.

'Auntie Trixie?'

'Don't ask, Rachel, it's a private joke. Just for the grown-ups.'

'Ailsa really needs to go to the bathroom.'

'Ok,' I said turning my attention to Ailsa. 'Ailsa, are you ok?' She didn't look ok.

'Excuse me,' I discreetly asked Tristan as the Tony entourage passed, 'can I take the kids to the toilet now?'

'Sorry, we're bringing Mr Ramos on set just now.'

'Yes I can see that but ...'

'I'll be with you in a few minutes,' he smiled obsequiously.

'Everything cool, Trixie?' Tony asked me.

I obviously wasn't as discreet as I'd thought.

'Toilet?' he whispered.

I nodded.

'Use my trailer. Hey Tristan, take them down to my trailer, will you?'

'Certainly, Mr Ramos.'

'Eh, now please, Tris?'

'Of course.'

I turned to Walter, 'Can you keep your eye on the rest of them please? Ok girls,' I said, shoving my frozen feet back into my shoes, 'let's get you to the loo. Ailsa, why are you crying pet, what's wrong?'

Chapter 25

I almost wished we were back on set. Up there at least it was well lit. Here, halfway down the hill, it was so dark I couldn't see my hand in front of my face.

We hadn't made it to Tony's trailer, but on the plus side, due to Ailsa's little accident, Walter, the children and I had been 'released'.

'Stay together,' I ordered the kids, but I hardly needed to. They huddled round me, hanging on to my jacket as we blindly shuffled forward over the uneven ground. Once we'd got our own clothes back on, there was no one available to escort us back to the bus but Tristan said we could leave. We could have come round the lochan – there was a straightforward path down the hill from there – but Walter would have none of it.

'Och, it's best to stay well away from that horrible wee lochan,' he said dismissively. 'There's all sorts of horrible beasties round there, big ugly pikes that jump out and eat you; I've even heard there's a kelpie and we're not wanting drowned now, are we? No, no, we don't need to go all the way round, we're much quicker just going straight down the hill.'

Jan had been asked to stay on and film another scene where he and other henchmen dragged a pregnant young woman from a house and set fire to it. He was donating his fee to the guitar group, so although it was distasteful, it was for charity. I kept thinking about those breeches they made him wear. They were ridiculous, and yet …

The kids were moaning about the walk.

'Cheer up you lot,' I said into the pitch black, 'we'll be sitting on the nice warm coach soon.'

But, cold and exhausted, none of us had enough energy left to cheer up.

'I know,' Walter said gleefully, 'we can use my iPhone.'

'Brilliant! Do you have a flashlight app?'

'Nope,' he replied chirpily.

Walter had finally lost the plot. Shock and trauma can do that to old people, turn them demented, I was starting to feel a bit Alzheimersy myself.

Walter set his phone to camera and took a photo of the darkness. A flash illuminated the path before us for a millisecond, only enough to give us a brief light-blinded impression. When I opened my eyes again it was even darker than before.

'Cheers for that, Walter.'

'No,' he said, 'look.'

He passed me his phone and sure enough, there was a clear photo of what lay ahead for at least the next thirty yards or so. In the photo, about five feet in front of us, there was a deep trench to the right-hand side. If it wasn't for Walter's techno nous we would have toppled like lemmings into it.

'I thought as much,' Walter muttered, 'so much water comes off this hill, see where the irrigation ditches criss-cross? Come on everybody, get in behind Trixie and me on the left-hand side.'

Walter took up the position but the kids were reluctant.

'C,mon now. It'll be just like in *The Lord of the Rings*,' said Walter, 'where Frodo and his companions are blindfolded and led through the forest.'

'So, are you and Trixie elves?' asked Michael.

'Aye, that's it,' Walter agreed with a wink to me, 'not many people know this but Trixie is actually Galadriel, the elf Queen.'

Taking photos every twenty yards, Sherpa Walter saw us safely off the hill, but when we made it to the coaches they were deserted and locked.

'Gone fishin',' said Walter clicking his tongue, 'the fishing waistcoat over the driver's chair is gone. He could be gone for hours. We might as well keep moving, it'll be warmer than waiting, and at least the road is easier to walk.'

The kids instantly commenced whining and slumping to the ground, too exhausted to walk any further.

'Och weesht!' said Walter, his patience threadbare, 'are you really complaining because there isn't a luxury coach to take you home?'

Here we go, I thought, we're going to get the standard Grumpy Old Man's you-kids-don't-know-you're-born-it-wasn't-like-this-in-my-day speech.

'Hey, c'mon Walter,' I joked, trying to coax him, 'we were all getting on like a house on fire.'

Walter shook his head sadly.

'You have no respect. Laugh Trixie, laugh away, it's just a filum, silly playacting. But years ago the people from that village actually saw their houses on fire, their homes burned down. They were forced to walk away in bare feet. This is the exact route they took and plenty of them froze to death or later starved.'

'I'm sorry, Walter, I wasn't thinking.'

'They didn't have nice warm beds to go home to. They had to build the houses that you all live in today. You can be grateful your ancestors did that for you.'

'We don't have an Aunt Cestor,' said Rachel, 'we've only got an Aunt Pauline.'

'No,' explained Michael, 'ancestors; like grannies.'

'Not our granny,' shrugged Rachel, 'she lives in Tenerife.'

Walter sighed. I thought he had given up, finally defeated by their indefatigable carelessness but still he carried on.

'Not your immediate granny but her granny and her granny before her, and many more beyond ...'

'So how many grannies ago?' said Rachel.

'Well ...' said Walter.

Energised by the question, he was now striding ahead. Curious to know the answer, we trotted along behind.

'Let's say twenty years per generation, five grannies per century, that would roughly mean that the villagers are your granny's granny's granny's granny's granny's granny's granny's granny's ...'

The kids fastened to the hypnotic sing-song of the two-syllable chant and we marched back into Inverfaughie beating out the rhythm of '... granny's granny's granny's granny's granny's granny's granny's ...'

Chapter 26

The place was hoaching with strangers. Even the machair, usually a desolate place, was busy. As I drove past there was a crowd standing at the gate. The same builder's truck that had fenced off the property next door to Harrosie was waiting to go through, loaded with long wooden poles. Not another fence. Another beautiful view spoilt. Less Highland idyll, more Russian gulag. People were talking to the driver. I recognised some of the farmers, and in the midst of them, Jackie. I pulled over and parked.

This was too good an opportunity to miss. Jackie always did his utmost to avoid me in the village, even changing direction when he saw me coming, so I rarely had the chance to observe him up close these days.

For those brief golden months while he'd been my gardener I'd had good reason to look at him: I was entitled to supervise his work, and I took full advantage, sneaking peeks at the muscles on his shirtless back as he leaned into the digging.

I thought back to what my first impression of Jackie had been: he was breathtakingly beautiful. I think I'd actually gasped at how handsome he was. He certainly didn't look like a gardener, more like a hunky fireman or a guy from a diet coke ad. Not far off six feet and broad as a house. Not fat, muscley: down and dirty. Manly.

I shivered. It gave me the creeps to remember how I'd lusted after him.

Now, at this distance, it was fascinating to see how he behaved when he didn't know I was watching. He was talking passionately to the people standing next to him, his face fizzing: eyes burning, teeth flashing – but not with his lady-killer smile; he didn't look happy at all.

For the first time I noticed how old Jackie was beginning to look. Because of his good looks it was easy to forget that he was sixteen years older than me, and I was no spring chicken. What was he doing here at the machair? Surely he wasn't working as an extra? Operating his boat tours and all the gardening and odd-job work he took, he was already working too hard for a man in his fifties. I felt a slight panic at the idea of Jackie ageing, becoming a pathetic old man, but that's what would inevitably happen. The cords in his neck stood out and his coat drooped forwards off his shoulders. He looked tired, beat; like a boxer losing his last ever humiliating bout. Maybe it was only when he knew someone was watching that he sucked in his gut and set his face to handsome. I put the car in gear and drove away hoping he hadn't spotted me.

*

'It's all kicking off now,' said Jenny.

This as I entered the shop.

'What is?'

'Everything. It's a scandal.'

Before I had the chance for further questions her mobile began to ring. To halt me she showed me the underside of her index finger, holding it in front of my face in the annoying schoolteacherish way she had.

By the terse 'uh huh's and 'right's she was barking into her phone I could tell this call was scandal related. Everything was kicking off. I felt a delicious ripple of anticipation. Pure uncut scandal would very soon be flooding my system, my whole body tingling, the pleasure centres in my brain going off like roman candles. Jenny was my dealer in this town, my gossip orgasmatron. I only had to wait until she got off the phone. I cast around the shop looking for something to distract me. A filum.

In the last few weeks the stock in Jenny's shop had changed radically. Until recently she'd stocked such exotic fare as pickled onions and mayonnaise on her 'world foods' shelf. Now she had all manner of organically certified wholefoods. The packaging was a uniform dreich brown paper, but despite this the products were three times the price. I wasn't complaining – overall it was an improvement. In the past the chill cabinet had been full of brick-sized bargain-brand cheese wrapped in cling film. Reading the label I discovered it wasn't even technically cheese. It was legally required to be called 'cheese food' and looked and tasted more like plastic explosives than actual cheese. Now at least she had some quality local cheese and, to go with the new food, she'd introduced a line of kitchen gadgets. You could now purchase a fish kettle or a pasta maker if you were so inclined.

Jenny had also revamped her DVD rental section. Until a few weeks ago the rack had only Hollywood blockbusters. Now it was full of films where nothing happened, usually in Russian or Japanese, in black and white, and where characters often unaccountably took their clothes off. That must be why they were called movie buffs. Why anyone would want to watch naked foreign people not doing anything was beyond me. Jenny said it was kinky and I readily agreed.

'Not kinky!' Jenny had laughed, 'although some of those filums are a bit raunchy, I grant you. No, I mean KINKIE: Keep It Niche, Keep It Expensive. It's a good business model when your customer base shifts to the chattering classes. Och, shut your gub, Trixie, you'll catch a fly.'

Kinkie, indeed. Jenny could make even a business acronym sound daring. This was going to be great. Finally she got off the phone. My scalp tingled as I felt the anticipation rise.

'Do you not read your emails?' she snipped.

'Aye.' I hesitated. 'Well, not today, not yet.'

'They've locked us out of the machair.'

I was still on the backfoot about the email so I didn't react with the level of shock to this news that Jenny was obviously expecting.

'G.I. have locked everyone out,' she reiterated.

'I didn't know they were filming there just now.'

'They're not,' she said, 'they're putting in a perimeter fence to stop us getting access. The farmers can't graze their cattle.'

'But why?'

Jenny lifted her shoulders and opened her hands in a gesture of bewilderment. I finally caught up with her indignation and managed to muster some of my own.

'That's not on,' I asserted. 'The deal was that everyone could use the machair except when they're actually filming. I remember Betty Robertson saying that.'

Jenny nodded. That was obviously the way she remembered it too.

'We've called a public meeting; this concerns us all. Seven o'clock tonight. We've requested that G.I. send a representative to explain this outrageous behaviour. That wee Miss Yip would be the one I'd expect. We need a full turn-out tonight,' she continued, 'a show of strength, show them they can't mess with us. I emailed you asking you to put the word out but I think between Walter and Jackie they've covered everybody.'

As a rule, Jenny never mentioned Jackie's name to me, she seemed to sense how raw it was, and she was always careful not to stir up any resentment. But as she was the one who'd mentioned him, I took my opportunity to find out more.

'I just passed Jackie there.' I omitted to mention that I'd parked and watched him. 'He's standing at the machair gates with a crowd of other people.'

'Pickets. They're trying to persuade the G.I. staff not to cross the picket line, but they've had no luck so far.'

I wanted to talk a bit more about Jackie. Why was it so difficult? I'd love to be able to casually mention him in conversation, ask after his health, the way normal people did. But Jenny had already moved on.

'There are other things we can do. If G.I. want to play dirty we can do the same. For example, we could stop offering them accommodation. How would they make their filum if they had nowhere to sleep?'

I bristled involuntarily at this but quickly covered it by pretending to feel cold. If I lost my B&B income now I'd never be able to buy my flat in Glasgow. I'd never get out of Inverfaughie.

'Och, it'll probably blow over,' I said. 'You know what they're like, always having equipment breakdowns; they've no doubt shut the machair because of some technical problem. It'll only be for a couple of hours.'

'I don't care why they've shut it, or for how long,' said Jenny, leaning over the counter. 'They don't have the authority. Our farmers are being denied their grazing rights. G.I. have used their money and power to take whatever they want without our permission, but we run this village, not G.I. We need to show them that.'

'I don't think we need to throw them out on the street just yet, Jenny. We don't want to do anything rash.'

'For the good of the village we have to pull together or they'll win. They'll try to play us off against each other, divide and conquer by buying some of us off with their pathetic windfall. We have to be strategic and political; this isn't the time for self-interest.'

I took a step back at the sheer brass neck of the woman. Self-interest? She was a fine one to talk. She was in this to enhance her career prospects as M.S.P. and increase her votes. She had bent over backwards to accommodate G.I., not out of kindness or good old-fashioned Highland hospitality, but for her own kinkie profit. She was making a fortune out of this hand-knitted wholefood malarkey. This shop was full of Jenny's organically certified self-interest.

'But if some lost their B&B income while others continued to profit that might divide the village even more.'

'You mean me, don't you? Well, I'll have to think about that but I'm only suggesting a possible strategy. That's what the meeting's for, but meanwhile I'm not going to show the enemy my hand, am I?'

'Oh, are G.I. the enemy now? Last week they were the best thing that ever happened to Inverfaughie.'

'God love you, Trixie,' said Jenny, as she expertly slashed open a crisp box with a Stanley knife, 'you've got a lot to learn about politics.'

Chapter 27

It was all about percentages. G.I. had paid me 30 per cent of the contract up front – 100 per cent of the contract, plus 100 per cent of what I earned feeding the Claymores, might, if I was very lucky, amount to a 10 per cent deposit on a flat in Glasgow, but if I didn't get paid I'd be stuck forever in Inverfaughie, 100 per cent miserable. If Jenny was going to make this radical proposal I'd have to vote against it. Thank god I was a council member with full voting rights.

As I drove past the helipad there was a row of six black Land Rovers parked nose to tail. The smoked glass windows made it impossible to see anything, but whoever was inside must be important. Maybe the American president had come to Inverfaughie. That's what it looked like: one of those convoys of armoured vehicles I'd seen on telly, where the American Secret Service jog alongside wearing suits and sunglasses and talking into their sleeve.

When I got back to Harrosie there was a visitor waiting for me.

I walked in to find Steven wrestling with Bouncer. When they saw me they both exploded in enthusiastic greeting. Steven pulled me into a bone-crushing hug – he even kissed me, mushing his lips on my cheek till it was painful.

'Steven! Nice to see you too,' I said, struggling to break free. It was lovely that he was being so affectionate, lovely but weird.

'How did you get here?'

'Train to The Sneck and then hitched.'

'The Sneck?'

'The Sneck, Inversnechty, that's what us locals call Inverness, surely you knew that Mum. How long have you lived here?'

Mum.

Hugs and kisses and Inversnechty and actually being called Mum. It was all a bit overwhelming. I hadn't even seen Steven for such a long time without his conjoined pal Gerry.

'No Gerry?'

'Gerry's working.'

'I didn't know he had a job.'

'He does now. I got Gary to give him mine. Everybody's happy.'

'You gave up your job at the warehouse? Nettie won't be best pleased at that. You did tell her, didn't you? Your Auntie Nettie knows you've chucked your job?'

Steven gave an exasperated, 'Yes.'

'And your dad?'

'You don't seem very pleased to see me, Mum. I thought you wanted me to come up here for the summer, spend some "family time".'

'I did. I do. Honestly, this is brilliant,' I said, as I collapsed yawning into the sofa, 'I'm overjoyed.'

We both laughed.

'Sorry, I was up all night. Not what you think. Don't worry, I'm still on the wagon.'

The relief on his face told me that was exactly what he'd been thinking.

'I worked last night on the film.'

'Really? You're in the movie? Quality!'

'Och, believe you me, it's not as glamorous as it sounds, I'm knackered.'

'D'you think I can be in it?'

'I don't see why not, they're always looking for extras.'

I hoped this machair spat wouldn't stop Steven getting work.

'Are those weapons in the shed from the movie?'

'Don't you touch those weapons. They're not toys. They don't belong to you and they're dangerous.'

'They're not dangerous,' he scoffed, 'they're for dummy fighting, all the blades are blunt.'

'It doesn't matter. If you drop one of those things you'll lose a toe. Please Steven, promise me you'll stay away from those weapons, they're scary.'

'Keep your wig on, Trixie, I was only looking at them.'

And with that he stormed off to his room.

So I was back to being Trixie. Mum didn't last long.

It was probably my fault, these things usually were. I might have been a bit short with him but I was worried about being paid and the meeting and getting dinner ready for the Claymores. I didn't really have time to run up to Steven's room with a conciliatory cup of tea and a flapjack. I'd done enough of that the last time. He'd have to understand that he couldn't just pitch up here any time he wanted stealing other people's boats and historical weaponry. As his mother it was my job to make him understand that. But of course Steven had me over a barrel. He knew I'd have to introduce him to the Claymores and that I'd want to play happy families. It would be too embarrassing not to.

I had missed my son so much I'd forgotten what living with him was actually like: the constant boundary testing, brinkmanship, power plays, the hard-fought negotiations – bickering, reasoning, begging. With a heavy heart I took a tray up.

He was, as I'd guessed he would be, open to arbitration but exploitative. Steven graciously accepted the tea and flapjacks and, after he outlined my heinous crime: doing my usual of treating him like a baby, he heard my confession and my tight-jawed apology. As the balance of power currently stood, if he'd wanted me to apologise for global warming I would have had to. What else could I do? In exchange he agreed not to touch the Claymores' equipment without their knowledge and approval. This meant I'd have to do a bit of double dealing with Rudi – get him to promise not to let Steven near the weapons – but in the end a deal was done. When I asked him to come down to dinner and meet everyone he nodded beneficently. I knew he was gagging to meet them but we both kept up the charade that he was doing me a big favour.

When I took him into the dining room the Claymores gave Steven a warm welcome. Following Rudi's lead they all shook his hand and introduced themselves before sitting down to dinner. As they sat round the table talking about football and discussing the new signings for Celtic they included Steven in their silly jokes and listened respectfully to his comments. Once dinner was on the table the football chat died away as everyone concentrated on eating. I scoured my mind for a topic that might be of interest. I wanted Steven to see how well I got on with the Claymores, and not just because I was their landlady. The lads treated me with respect and affection, like a big sister.

In my eagerness to stimulate conversation I very nearly blurted the gossip: the machair being closed and the public meeting Jenny had called to protest. Just in time, I remembered that the Claymores worked for 'the enemy', as Jenny had put it; best to keep my mouth shut, loose lips and all that.

'Did anyone see the big black cars at the helipad?' I asked.

'I saw them,' said Danny. 'I ran past them.'

'How fast were you running?' joked Dave. 'The limit's only 30 in a built-up area. You know his nickname's Insane Bolt, don't you, Trixie?'

'I made a speed camera go off but I was only jogging. You cannae touch me for it,' Danny quipped.

'Where did the cars go?' I persisted.

'They seemed to be heading round the loch to the big house.'

'I know the woman who owns that big house,' I told them. 'Dinah, she's a friend of mine.'

'Well, she won't own it much longer,' said Rudi. 'It's up for sale. There's talk of it being turned into a hotel; they're planning to build polo fields on the lochside. That's what the papers are saying anyway. And guess who's in town to make an offer? That guy, you know, the billionaire businessman Knox MacIntyre.'

So Dinah had found a buyer. Lucky dog. The sour taint of jealousy had stolen my appetite.

Chapter 28

I cleared the plates and stayed in the kitchen tidying up. I could hear sporadic bursts of laughter from the dining room. It was great that Steven was getting on so well with the lads. With a bit of luck they would set up the table for one of their regular poker nights and invite him to play. Then I could sneak out to the meeting.

But the Claymores had to work. Another night shoot, apparently. Just as Rudi was shuffling the cards he got a phone call, so Steven told me. The men jumped in their minibus and headed off. Within five minutes the house was quiet again.

Steven came and joined me in the kitchen.

'Alright?' he asked, while I stood over the sink impotently scrubbing a chilli stain on my stainless-steel pot.

'Yeah, fine. You?'

'Totes.'

I wasn't sure what 'totes' meant but it didn't seem entirely negative. So he wasn't in a huff.

'That was an arse-scorching chilli there, Trixie.'

The hot stink of adolescent insolence filled the air. I had to work to keep the disapproval off my face. It was beginning to dawn on me that if I wanted Steven to stay with me here I was going to have to put up with him swearing and showing off. He knew it too and, boy, was he exploiting it.

'A total anus roaster.'

His use of the word 'arse' I could just about tolerate but despite being more anatomically accurate, I found 'anus' distasteful. Button it, I reminded myself.

'So what film did you get?'

Oh dear. Steven had spotted the DVD box lying on the counter.

'Och, just some old black and white thing.'

'Quality. I've never seen a black and white movie, what're they like?'

'Eh, colourless. And Jenny only has arthouse films now, boring naked people.'

Steven's head came up like a meerkat.

'Naked?'

'Pffff,' I said, 'naked men, mostly.' And just in case that wasn't enough, 'Last one I saw was full of fat old geezers.'

'Rank.'

'Bits dangling right in your face. How is that artistic?'

That was inspired. Sometimes I surprised myself.

'Why don't you go on Facebook?' I suggested. 'Catch up with your pals.'

Steven pulled the DVD box open, '*Passport to Pimlico*. Says here this is a classic British comedy.'

'Really? Jenny must have mixed the boxes up.'

'Either that or you don't want to watch it with me.'

'Don't be silly, Steven.'

'Why did you even want me to come up here,' Steven's pitch had risen, 'if you don't even want to watch a poxy black and white film with me?'

He was close to losing it.

'I'm sorry, son, I think we got off to a bad start.'

'You think?'

The thing to do now was to sit down and talk to him; reassure him that I very much loved and respected him and wanted him with me here.

'Let's forget this arguing, put it behind us. We've not lived together for a while. It'll mean a bit of re-adjustment. From the both of us.'

At this last onerous point he tutted and drew me a sour look. This was going to take longer than I'd thought.

'Look, I know this is difficult, Steven. Everything has changed and it's a lot to take in at once.'

As I sought to make sincere eye contact with my son, I spotted the clock on the kitchen wall. It was three minutes to seven. It was at least a twelve-minute drive to the Village Hall, if I didn't get stuck behind a tractor.

'I think we both could do with a wee breather. I tell you what, why don't you watch the film and I'll get out of your face. I'm going to pop out for a wee while to grab some air, give you your own space.'

'Cheers, that's thoughtful of you.'

'And when I come back we'll start again: as if you've just arrived and we're pleased to see each other.'

'Just start again as if nothing happened,' he said, with the same optimistic tone I had used. I couldn't work out if he was being sarcastic or not, but I had to work with it.

'Yes. I'd like that,' I said, as I draped my dishcloth over the oven door and looked for the car keys. The clock was ticking towards seven.

'Aren't you going to take Bouncer?' Steven asked.

Hearing his name mentioned, Bouncer rushed over to me, big wet eyes all expectant.

'Maybe he could grab some air as well. Reflect on his behaviour. Take a long hard look at himself.'

Well, that was that mystery solved: he was definitely being sarcastic.

'Eh, no, it's fine, I'll walk him when I get back.'

Bouncer turned away, crushed, and slunk back to lie at Steven's feet.

'You know it's all crap, don't you?' said Steven, stroking the dog.

I had no idea what he was talking about but I couldn't be drawn in now. I found the car keys and pocketed them.

'They're all the same,' said Steven, 'all in it for what they can get; power, fame, money. Dodgy deals and sex scandals, they're all corrupt. Anyone who's involved in politics is not to be trusted.'

'Politics?'

'Aye. That's where you're going, isn't it? The meeting about the machair? Jackie told me.'

So he had already spoken to Jackie.

'Check you out: rushing down there, fighting for your community, trying to make a difference. I'm disappointed in you, Trixie, you used to be so cynical.'

Busted, I blushed, pride and shame reddening my face in equal measure. Pride that my son had assumed my motives were selfless, shame because they weren't. But, I rationalised, I was doing this for him, if he only knew it.

'I'm just being a good citizen, Steven,' I mumbled as I headed out the door. 'Just doing my bit.'

Chapter 29

I was nearly half an hour late but nobody noticed. The hall was heaving, standing room only. The whole village had turned out and I was lucky to squeeze in at the back.

I just hoped to God I hadn't missed the vote. If Jenny had somehow managed to convince anyone it was a good idea to give up their B&B income I'd have to come out fighting. I could barely hear the indistinct murmur of a voice speaking, but no matter how much I strained it was impossible to make out what was being said. The last thing I wanted to do was vote the wrong way.

'Speak up!' I said, a bit louder than I'd meant. 'We can't hear you at the back.'

The people in front turned and gawped in my direction. We were too tightly packed for me to duck so I joined them in looking around for the culprit, staring accusingly at an old woman slightly to the left of me. I knew no one was fooled but for my own dignity I had to keep up the pretence.

There was the sound of chairs scraping the floor and then a frisson rippled through the crowd, something was happening up the front. Through a gap between two red heads I saw Jenny suddenly grow four feet taller. She must be standing on the committee table. A flash flared and Jenny blinked. The flash pack screamed as it recharged and a man loaded down with cameras snapped a few more.

'As most of you will know, I'm standing as an independent in the forthcoming Scottish parliamentary elections, but I believe the future of our village is far more important than any party politics and I personally will work with anyone – of any political persuasion or none – to resolve the situation. At 17:42 this evening I received an email from the offices of Global Imperial,' she bawled, 'which I'd like to share with you now.'

She waved it around so everyone could see it, like Neville Chamberlain getting an email from Hitler. From her grim tone it wasn't going to be a good email, but we waited while Jenny put on her glasses.

'Dear Miss Robertson,' she yelled, 'thank you for your kind invitation, but regrettably Miss Yip has been detained on business in London today and is not expected back in Inverfaughie until the 12th. There is no legal representative of Global Imperial available to meet with you at this time.'

People started booing.

'However,' said Jenny, 'however ...'

She gave up trying to speak over the noise and waited, giving everyone who wanted it the opportunity for a good boo.

I'd expected that we'd be voting, like last time, but this was a rabble. G.I. must have packed Miss Yip off to London for her own safety, and no wonder. The way things were going, the mob would soon be outside G.I.'s portakabins with pitchforks and flaming torches.

Once everyone got it out of their system, the booing died away.

'However,' Jenny continued, 'with reference to your complaint I refer you to clause 5b of the agreement drawn up between the Faughie Council and Global Imperial as detailed below.'

She stopped and cleared her throat.

'Clause 5b states that during the period of rental of the machair pasture lands, neither party shall in any way damage or otherwise alter the appearance of said machair pasture lands and its environs. Any such damage shall result in breach of contract and preventative action being taken.'

'Aye, that's right!' shouted a nearby voice, Bobby Fenton the dairyman. I looked around for his lovely daughter Morag but there was no sign of her. Like Steven, she was probably contemptuous of politics, but Morag also had a role in the film – did that make her the enemy?

'But that was so only so they wouldn't build anything on our machair,' wailed Bobby, 'that was for *our* protection; for the fodder. What's clause 5b got to do with anything?'

Jenny nodded sympathetically.

'That's what we all thought, but it's how they're defining damage. They're trying to exploit a loophole, calling it a continuity issue.'

'A conti what?' shouted Bobby, but he wasn't the only one who was confused.

'Ok. Plenty of you have been extras so everybody knows how many times they shoot the same scene. And after they've dressed you up in a peasant costume they take a photo of you. Well, that's so that when they film it again you'll look exactly the same: same hair, same clothes and all that, as you did in earlier takes. So that when they put it together, the scene looks like it all happened with no breaks. That's what they call continuity.'

'But what the hell have peasant costumes got to do with my milkers?' yelled Bobby.

'I'm sorry,' said Jenny, 'Global Imperial is maintaining that live-stock presence on the machair is causing damage and they insist they're entitled to prevent it.'

'But my wee cows are only there to feed, how's that damaging anything?'

I thought Bobby made a good point. The cows weren't organising a rave or setting fire to anything. Hoofs were no use for striking matches.

'I know,' Jenny said, the exasperation beginning to show in her voice, 'but it's a contractual loophole. Cows or sheep grazing is obviously going to flatten the grass a wee bit. Standing on it, tearing it up, eating it and then, well, quite frankly, shitting on it, is bound to alter the appearance of it. Global Imperial has been very underhand and I'm sorry to say we've been conned.'

'I never agreed to that!' roared Bobby.

Lots of people joined in.

'Me neither!' seemed to be the consensus.

'Who signed us up to that?' a different male voice yelled, another angry farmer, I supposed.

A figure appeared on the table beside Jenny. The camera again flashed and whirred at Betty Robertson holding up both arms and looking embarrassed.

Well, well, well. The golden girl wasn't so golden now.

'I'm so sorry,' she began.

I didn't hear the words but I saw the shapes her lips made and the taste they seemed to leave in her mouth.

'I signed it. On behalf of the committee.'

A hiss of disapproval snaked from the back of the hall to the front.

'But I take full responsibility,' she quickly added.

The damage was done. Jeering broke out like loud burps directed into Betty's face.

'Who gave you the right to sign away our grazing?'

'My milkers are starving, you stupid cow!'

Things were starting to turn ugly. I began to feel something I would never have thought I could feel: sorry for Betty Robertson.

It was delicious.

Chapter 30

Poor Betty. Poor, poor Betty. She was getting pelters; dog's abuse as she was being mercilessly papped by the local newspaper. Bobby shouted into her face, spittle flying.

'And does it say in the contract,' yelled Bobby, 'the contract that *you* signed,' he jabbed an accusing finger at Betty, 'that they can put up a fence?'

'No!' was the horrified response of most people, including me. I already knew about the fence but I was caught up in the atmosphere. Being part of a mob was an exciting new experience for me.

'Aye,' Bobby confirmed with a grim nod, 'they put it up this afternoon; a big barbed-wire fence all the way round the machair. They've locked us out of our own property.'

'Nothing a good pair of wire cutters couldn't solve!' Walter shouted from somewhere behind Jenny.

Mob outrage, in broad agreement with the fence-cutting option.

'We are getting right royally shafted and you just stand there, Betty Robertson, with your head up your arse!'

Cue more booing. Betty Robertson didn't have her head up her arse but that might have been safer. People were sneering at her, pointing and yelling. The hysteria grew, reaching a crescendo, when someone hurled a shoe. A welly, in fact. Luckily, Betty was quick enough to duck and it bounced harmlessly across the table.

'Hey!' yelled Jenny, but no one was listening. 'Hey, hey! Don't blame her. Betty signed the agreement on your behalf. With your approval. We voted on it, remember? You were all quick enough to take the money, weren't you?'

And then, when no one answered, she bawled, her face turning purple, 'Weren't you!'

The noisy barracking faded to muted resentful muttering. We had voted in favour, accepted the cash, that was the inconvenient truth, and no one could argue.

'But my milkers,' pleaded Bobby, close to tears, 'they need fresh grazing, what am I going to do with them?'

Bobby went on to describe the horrible chain of events that would surely happen if the cows couldn't graze. No grazing, no milk, no income, no feed. His herd would slowly starve. The hall fell silent as Bobby painted a grizzly picture of his famished cattle with their ribs showing, their bellies hollow, their big lips mooing their distress before they keeled over and died with their legs in the air. He was quite the storyteller and he grossly embellished the yarn with a vivid description of carrion crows pecking at the eyeballs and innards on the bloated corpses, tugging on a particularly stringy sinew.

'Come on now, Bobby, it's not that bad,' said Jenny, 'we'll get it back in ten days' time. We're obliged to let them film their scenes, which we agreed was to take not more than ten days. That's in the contract.'

'Aye,' said a familiar voice near the front, 'I know for a fact, because I have a wee friend in the production office, and she told me they're only scheduled to be on the machair four days. Barring bad weather, that is.'

The voice was Jackie's, no mistaking it. The mention of the *wee friend*, no doubt some silly woman whose head was turned by a handsome Highlander swinging his kilt, was no surprise either.

'See, Bobby?' said Jenny. 'You're panicking for nothing. It's only going to be four days.'

With the news that Bobby's scenario of famine and pestilence wasn't imminent, the tension in the hall eased. I felt and heard sniggering, shuffling of feet and a collective letting go of breath. I wouldn't lose my B&B income after all. A flat somewhere in Glasgow still had my name on it. I would be kissing the Highlands goodbye at last. Thank you Jesus.

'Could I just ask,' said another familiar voice, this time a woman's, 'if the contractual ten days includes time taken to rectify damages or alterations?'

Jenny looked to Betty.

'Betty?'

Still shocked from the welly-hurling incident, Betty stood open mouthed and glaikit.

'We're not sure,' said Jenny, 'we'll get back to you on that, Brenda.'

So it was Brenda, from Ethecom. I hoped she wasn't about to complicate things. The meeting was going just fine.

'I'd like to volunteer my services,' said Brenda. 'This is an area where I might be of some help.'

'Thank you, Brenda,' said Jenny, her voice a bit clipped.

Jenny probably thought that Brenda's help would be in the art and crafts department. But Jenny, and most people in the hall, were completely wrong.

Now I remembered that before 'Fat of The Land' and Ethecom, Brenda had been a corporate lawyer, a specialist in property law.

'For God's sake, Brenda,' said Jenny when Brenda explained this, 'why didn't you tell us before? Please, everyone, let her through.'

The crowd squeezed and shifted and I caught sight of Brenda wriggling her way to the front. Jenny and Betty tried to haul her up on to the table but they hadn't the strength. My Jackie, gallant as ever, pushed through and came to the rescue. He tried lifting her into his arms, but there wasn't room for that. Then he pressed his shoulder under her bottom and pushed upwards. Brenda making it onto the table was by no means certain; she wobbled a lot and, like a strongman lifting a truck, Jackie's cheeks wobbled too. Everyone wanted to help. Many hands volunteered to support Brenda's bottom until eventually she arrived on the table, red-faced and adjusting her underwear.

Once she got her breath back, Brenda was impressive. If we could establish that we had been induced to enter the contract by misrepresentation, Brenda said, this would put us legally in a much stronger position. I noticed Betty nodding her head sadly at that. She suggested that Faughie Council call in the Environment Minister to assist in this dispute, after all, that was the government's job, although she was confident that an amicable solution could be found. However, she had concerns about clause 5b. The clause apparently allowing 'preventative action' might mean that G.I. could stay on the machair – and keep us off it – indefinitely. It was in our own interests that the filming be achieved as soon as possible with no avoidable delays.

'I know in a farming village what I'm about to say is blasphemy,' she said with a wee smile, 'but if we want the machair back soon we'd better pray it doesn't rain.'

Brenda counselled that, at all costs, we must act within the law. As she fixed a piercing look on Walter she reminded us all that tearing down the fence would allow G.I. to claim criminal damage, hold the machair for longer, and take the moral high ground.

The mob seemed suitable chastened by that.

'For the meantime,' she said with a gentler tone, 'we have two fallow fields that we can offer. You're welcome to bring your sheep or cattle for grazing if it helps. And of course when I say *we*, I mean the Ethecom community. Some of you might have the idea that we're a bunch of hippies.'

That got a great big guffaw.

'But community co-operation was Ethecom's founding principle.'

This was met by a barrage of warm approval. Smiles, nods and 'Hear, hear!'

'Good on you!'

Amidst all this optimism I suddenly felt miserable, and I wasn't sure why. I couldn't understand it, my B&B was safe, why did I want to cry? Maybe it was Brenda. She was more of an outsider than I was, she was English for god's sake, and yet she had done what I had spectacularly failed to do: made friends of these people and gained their respect.

Chapter 31

That week's *Inverfaughie Chanter* ran with the headline '*Local council intellectually defenceless*' above a photo of Betty Robertson trying not to look like a toddler baffled by simple arithmetic. The quote was from a meeting that took place between Global Imperial and the council's newly appointed legal representative, Brenda. Brenda was making the argument that as G.I. had used unnecessarily complicated jargon and stratagems beyond the council's limited understanding, the agreement should be null and void. The council had been hoodwinked, ambushed by its intellectual superiors, a pretty embarrassing defence I thought, especially for Betty, but it didn't do to gloat.

Brenda had asked that everyone leave their phone number and email address if they wanted to be kept up to date. Was she kidding? This stuff was mother's milk to Highlanders and there was no one who didn't want to guzzle on the teat of Inverfaughie gossip.

From that point onwards I was bombarded with information on an hour-by-hour basis. If it wasn't text alerts telling me that G.I. had now employed security guards, it was radio bulletins from Andy Robertson with the news that Knox MacIntyre was buying Faughie Castle. There was an email from Jenny warning that the security guards were not to be molested. The Scottish Minister was arriving for talks with G.I. Then, because of the dispute, Knox

MacIntyre was rumoured to be pulling out of the Faughie Castle deal. There was any amount of speculation that he was bluffing to get the price down.

The next crisis was that the grass had run out; despite Brenda's generous offer, the cattle had hoovered Ethecom's field in hours and now the farmers needed more pasture. Brenda appealed on Andy's show, offering a free 'eco-organic lawnmower' to callers. This was in fact a cow to come and eat the garden grass but Brenda was so charming and persuasive that even I found myself calling in. I hosted Donal and Mhairi, who chomped their way across my lawn in an afternoon and made a tidy job of it. I only hoped Global Imperial would find Brenda as persuasive as I had; their Accommodation Manager wasn't returning my calls.

Andy had a phone-in about Faughie Castle and people called to say how worried they were that the deal might not go through. There were going to be jobs created from this polo resort, all the more important once the movie eventually left town. Walter phoned in to say that Knox MacIntyre was only angling for tax breaks, sweeteners from the government to locate his business here. The airwaves were fairly crackling with the rumours and scandal. Inverfaughie was generating more political intrigue than the West Wing.

Despite Brenda asking everyone to pray that it didn't rain, it poured for the next four days. The following day it dried up in the afternoon and then started again after tea time. The whole village became avid weather watchers. All except its most recent resident: Steven. Waiting for the dispute to be over and the extra work to start again, he moped in his room.

Against Brenda's advice, Jackie continued to organise a picket line at the gates to the machair. It was almost pointless as, due to the persistent rain, nothing was happening there anyway. The security guards turned out to be Keek and The Bell Boy, two brothers from Annacryne, the next village. I had no notion why The Bell Boy had such a strange and unwieldy nickname but it wasn't hard to work out why Keek was so called. One eye on the fireplace and the other one up the lum – not a great asset for a security guard, Jenny sneered. I'd met them a few weeks ago at a drunken party with one of Jackie's pals, Spider. They were probably related to half the village; that's why G.I. had employed them, said Walter, in another round of angry emails. Divide and conquer, he said, it was a tactic that had been successfully employed in earlier Highland clearances.

The biggest shockaroonie of all was that lots of Global Imperial staff, or at least all the local staff, were laid off with immediate effect. Even the Claymores. G.I. were obviously trying to hit the village where it hurt, in the wage packet. Thank god the lads were paying me for their dinners, but as far as their accommodation went, who knew when or even if I'd see the balance? I phoned every day but only spoke to an answering machine. Did this mean my contract was cancelled? Could they do this without telling me? Everyone in the village was in the same position. A minister came up from Holyrood and held a pow-wow with Jenny and a few of the council worthies, but nothing as yet had been resolved. Brenda counselled villagers not to put their guests out; they expected the dispute to be settled imminently and everyone should sit tight. It was a waiting game. Worried that I might lose my escape route back to Glasgow, I was sitting so tight I could have yanked the cork out a bottle.

Chapter 32

The Claymores weren't the type to sit tight, certainly not Rudi, who seemed to have particularly industrious insects in his underwear. He made the rest of the Claymores go out and train all day in the rain, while he looked for alternative work for them. He asked all the local farms if they wanted help bringing the harvest in, which they did, but the rain was holding that up too. Word must have gone out on the jungle drums because on the fourth day Walter popped round and sat in my kitchen with Rudi.

'Would you know if any of the Global Imperial people are still up at the old village on the hill?' Walter asked him.

Walter was up to something. I sat down at the table and lingered over setting out the tea things.

'Nah,' said Rudi, 'they struck the set the following day. G.I. moved everything down to the machair. There's nothing up there now; the place is deserted. Why?'

'Och, it's just that when we were up there I noticed there were some good peat bogs.'

'Yeah?' said Rudi.

'And this is the interesting part,' said Walter, leaning forward and talking quietly out the side of his mouth. 'Since all this carry-on with the machair, I've had occasion to study the land register, checking our entitlement.'

Walter raised his eyebrows and sat back in his chair, 'And so forth.'

'Have you now?' said Rudi, aping Walter's mysterious manner.

'I've looked up the records on the hill village and there's no registered owner. I've always assumed it belonged to Trixie's friend, Lady Murdina, like everything else in this damn place, but no. There's no registered owner. Most irregular.'

'Yeah?' Rudi repeated. He was obviously as baffled as I was. 'I thought you were a local expert, Walter, I thought you would have known this area like the back of your hand.'

'Well, I do and I don't,' said Walter, scratching his chin. 'The lochan and environs, I don't like that place, I've never taken much of an interest, but during our guest star appearance in the filum the other night I got a good look at the village. I'm no geologist but it looks to me to be hoaching with peat. If I was a younger man I might have gone up there and cut it myself.'

Rudi shifted in his chair, making it screech on the kitchen floor.

'I might have dried it and brought it down. And, who knows, I might have made some money.'

The penny finally dropped. I caught Rudi's eye and nodded. He returned my nod. We looked at Walter and he joined us in a communal nod.

'Walter,' said Rudi, breaking the spell, 'thanks for thinking of us, it's a great idea, but we've never cut peat before. We wouldn't know where to start.'

'Och, there's nothing to it; I can show you how it's done. All you need is your tosg – the cutting tool – and I can lend you mine. Trixie, you've a few tosgs in your shed you can let them have. Och, if it comes to it you could use your old medieval weapons, it's not complicated. Now, I won't lie: it's dirty work, and back breaking, but a good cutter can cut a thousand peats a day. A few strong young lads might make a lot of money.'

'Yeah, that does sound interesting. And where might these strong young lads sell this peat?'

'Ah now, that's the shame of it. They couldn't sell it.'

Rudi looked at me again, but there was no more nodding.

'They would need a wholesaler. A fixer, if you will, who might have contacts with a third party.'

'A whisky distillery?' asked Rudi.

Walter smiled.

Who knew he was such a wheeler-dealer? With his unstinting voluntary work on behalf of the village I'd always thought Walter was a man of high principles, but it seemed that he, like everyone else in Inverfaughie, wasn't above a bit of jiggery-mac-pokery.

'So is it ok just to go up there and take it?' asked Rudi.

'Och, I wouldn't say it was illegal,' said Walter in his sneaky sing-song Highland lilt. 'There's no registered owner, so there's no one to complain, but I wouldn't say it was entirely legal either. It's maybe as well to keep it under your hat. Just our wee secret.'

Walter began a knowing nod, 'Between us three,' he added to include me.

'I must say I'm surprised, Walter,' I blurted.

'*Is treasa tuath na tighearna,*' he continued, ignoring me, 'the slogan of the Highland Land Law Reform Association. The first mass political party in Britain; they sent four MPs to Westminster.'

'Sorry, I don't speak Gaelic, Walter.'

Which Walter knew very well, and I really wasn't in the mood for yet another of his impromptu history lessons.

'The people are mightier than a lord,' he explained, puffing his chest out. 'Or in this case, a global corporation. We're only doing our duty.'

'I'm not sure I'm comfortable with …'

'Sorry, Trixie,' said Walter, getting to his feet, 'it was wrong of me to involve you in something …'

'No,' I said, cutting him short.

Walter had come to my house and proposed something potentially illegal, but he'd trusted me. 'No,' I said again more slowly, trying to recalibrate, '*I'm* sorry, Walter, please stay. Really, I'm sorry. I wasn't sure what you meant with all your Gaelic slogans. This is more excitement than I've had in ages.'

Walter sat back down and a smile passed between the two men.

'Not that kind of excitement,' I said, slapping them both on the shoulder, 'but seriously, I don't get it, what's the duty you're talking about?'

'Och, nothing really,' Walter smiled, 'just a wee bit of what the young people used to call "sticking it to the man".'

'Exactly,' said Rudi, 'let's have a dram.'

He stood up, bounded out of the room and a few moments later bounded back in again with a bottle of Auchensadie's finest and three glasses. I glanced at him, trying to transmit my anxiety. Had he forgotten he'd never seen me take a drink or had he just never noticed? Apart from that tiny snifter I'd taken from Dinah, I hadn't had a drink in what seemed like months. I'd really beaten myself up about that, promising myself I'd never touch it again, but, given the deal that was about to be sealed, how could I refuse?

This was a landmark moment: the first time I'd been involved in an Inverfaughie secret. There were rituals to be observed, honour amongst thieves. Here I was, aiding and abetting criminals, rebelling against authority, breaking off the shackles of the bourgeoisie and sticking it to the man. In this radical atmosphere, what was the harm in a wee nip of the old giggle water?

Rudi ceremoniously poured the Auchensadie into three glasses. I briefly wondered if this bottle was produced from the mash tun I'd spewed into. The memory brought the taste of bile to the back of my throat. The idea of drinking my own processed vomit was giving me the dry heaves. And yet.

As the golden water of life glugged out of the bottle a powerful drouth overtook me. I licked my top lip. The peat smoke smell stung my nostrils and revived me. Walter and Rudi lifted their glasses and, after a second's hesitation, I joined them.

'I'll drink to that,' said Rudi, holding his glass aloft. 'To sticking it to the man.'

I clinked glasses with them both. 'To sticking it to the man,' I repeated solemnly.

I breathed deeply and threw my head back, a junkie taking a hit on a crack pipe.

Chapter 33

I didn't have time to drive all the way to an Inverness offie and, although Jenny did a roaring trade in wines and spirits, I didn't have the guts to go there.

I went to Dinah.

Steven had come down to the kitchen, half-asleep, hair tousled, yawning and scratching himself, and caught me toasting the deal with Walter and Rudi. Caught me red-handed with the whisky.

That had certainly woken him up. He turned on his bare heel and went back up to his room. I rushed up the stairs behind him.

'Hey,' he held up his arms, 'your bad, your addiction. I don't give a shit.'

He kept walking and wouldn't look at me. Clearly he did give a shit.

'Obviously it looks bad,' I explained, as I trotted along behind him, 'but Steven, I promise you, I wasn't drinking. I was just acting out the ritual, I wasn't actually drinking it. I was sealing a deal with Walter and Rudi.'

Steven shook his head in disbelief, 'Aw, you're such a crap liar! What deal?'

'Well, I'm sworn to secrecy but ...'

'You disgust me,' Steven spat in a contemptuous whisper before shutting his bedroom door in my face.

At least he hadn't slammed it or shouted; Rudi and Walter would have heard, but this whisper was more a measure of Steven's shame for my drinking than his discretion.

The cushion on the chair was old and done, flattened from too many aristocratic arses, so I sat down harder than I'd expected. Now that I had a chance to take in my surroundings, I saw that the inside of Faughie Castle was filthy: everything was greyed by dust, the cobwebs on the lamps dangled and swayed gently in the breeze, high up in one corner the plaster had turned black and peeled off the bare brick. The big fancy velvet curtains looked as if it was only the dirt that was holding them up. Jenny had been right: the castle was a crumbling cowp; it made me itchy to have to sit in it. At least until the whisky kicked in.

Dinah didn't even join me until she'd watched me knock back two large ones. I didn't care. After that she poured herself one, tapped a cigarette out of the pack, put it in her mouth and offered it to me. Good whisky and a cigarette, was there a more wonderful combination?

'Why thank you,' I said, still sucking in my first lungful, 'you are a most generous lady.'

I hadn't had a cig for weeks so I decadently waved my fag end in the air in a regal fashion, 'Milady.'

Dinah accepted my tribute with a gracious nod and laughed.

'So, how come you're a lady?' I slurred.

Unaccustomed to it lately, the drink had gone straight to my head.

'I mean, how does that all work?'

'My full title is Lady Murdina Anglicus of Faughie, of The Most Ancient and Most Noble Order of the Heather,' said Dinah, tilting her chin to match my majestic pose.

'Ah, interesting,' I said, pointing at her. 'You see, normally I'd rate your poshness of voice at a ten but when you said that there you cranked it up to eleven.'

'I beg your pardon.'

'How come you're a princess and I'm a pauper. How did *that* happen? Or am I a pauperess?'

A sneery tone had crept into my voice, whisky did that to me. I'd have to be careful. I was Dinah's guest, and she might not give me any more.

'Oh, it was all a very long time ago,' said Dinah. 'The order was founded in 1687 by King James VII but he was re-establishing an earlier order dating back to 707. There have been Anglicuses in Faughie since well before then.'

'Long time,' I agreed.

'Yes,' she said, tapping her ash, 'too long, perhaps. Regal heritage butters no parsnips nowadays. I'm afraid my ancient and noble family has been brought low by the twenty-first century.'

'Where is your family, Dinah?'

'Gone I'm afraid, all gone. Daddy's dead. My mother left him, and me, when I was tiny.'

'I'm sorry to hear that, Dinah.'

I leaned across and pawed her forearm. I felt a warmth for my new posh pal that wasn't just whisky. Being posh was clearly no safeguard against the vicissitudes. She said more, talked about her dad and her brother and her granny. I remember thinking that she was too posh to use the word 'granny' and that she should really call her 'Graunmama'. I hoped I didn't say that out loud. Over the course of three-quarters of a bottle of Auchensadie and forty cigarettes I got the gist. I was enjoying listening to her posh voice, enjoying the intimacy of what she was saying, but Graunmama sounded like a right cow and somebody needed to say it.

'She sounds like a right cow,' I said.

There was a bit of confusion and then we were giggling for ages, I don't remember why. I remember Dinah crying and me patting her head.

She told me about her son, Robby, or it could have been Roddy, and we bitched off about what a nightmare it was having a son. I was loving that chat. I told her how awful Steven had made me feel about that one teeny toatie nip of whisky. We really bonded over what gits sons were. Hers was older than mine by a few years. She didn't know where he was, out of the country; he had 'specialist tastes' and his trust fund went a lot further in Thailand or wherever.

She was worried he was lying in a drug den. She said, 'horrid', 'a horrid drug den,' which struck me as funny and we started giggling again.

When the whisky was finished, Dinah found a bottle of port. At some point after we'd finished that, I fell asleep in the chair.

It was daylight when I opened my eyes.

I got the impression that Dinah had maybe prodded me or something because she was talking again, as if she had talked all night without stopping.

'It's different for you, Trixie, you're keen to go back to Glasgow.'

How did she know that? I must have told her.

'But I'm being forced to sell. This estate was gifted to my family by the crown more than thirteen hundred years ago, and little by little, in taxes and death duties, the state is clawing it back. We've never really owned this land.'

I nodded, wondering what time it was. It felt early but I was so disorientated and hungover I couldn't trust my internal clock. How the hell was I going to drive?

'Nothing is forever, we can only hope to take care of it for the next generation and, in that regard, I've failed.'

Jesus, she could drone on. I needed to get back to Harrosie before Steven woke up.

'And with all this trouble over the machair, I'm worried that Knox MacIntyre might pull out of the deal.'

I nodded again.

'I'm sorry, Dinah, I have to go. But thank you for a lovely evening.'

Chapter 34

Luckily the car started first time. There was still half a packet of Extra Strong Mints in the glove compartment and I unrolled the wrapper and put them all in my mouth at once. It was only 6 am when I made it back and no one was out of bed yet.

Steven didn't come down to breakfast, which was a stilted affair where I pretended to be sober and the Claymores pretended to believe it. When they had taken the tosgs out of the shed and left there was still no sign of life from Steven.

After eating a handful of parsley and brushing my teeth for twenty minutes, I made up a tray of tea and toast and took it up for him.

'Morning, Steven,' I called through the closed door, 'I've brought you up breakfast.'

I was giving him notice, clear warning that, whatever he may or may not be doing, he might not wish to be doing it when his mother walked in.

'I'm just going to bring it in.'

As I slowly turned the door handle there was suddenly a loud snoring. I listened for a few minutes as it settled into a regular rhythm.

Schnaaaw pheo, schnaaw pheo, schnaaw pheo.

I let out a loud exasperated sigh and then walked away, clumping my feet conspicuously down the hall. The snoring abruptly ceased. I clumped back up the hall again and as I reached his room, surprise surprise, the snoring started up again.

Schnaaaw pheo, schnaaw pheo, schnaaw pheo.

These snores were too consistent. What Steven was forgetting was that I'd been watching him and listening to him sleep since he was moments old. He'd never been that style of snorer. He'd always been more of a nose whistler and snuffly lipsmacker who broke out with the occasional explosive snort. I pictured him behind the door, his eyes open as he dragged the long breaths in, past his waggling, vibrating soft palate.

So this was how he wanted it: this ridiculous fake snoring. It was eloquent; I had to give him that.

It was the smell of moussaka that finally lured Steven down the stairs that night for dinner. When he'd been a wee boy he'd always loved the gorgeous cinnamon smell. I never really under-stood it – moussaka was basically Greek cottage pie – but Steven couldn't get enough of it. Once, when he was about nine, as I laid the hot fragrant tray on the table, he leaned over it and, on opening his mouth to speak – probably to compliment me on my cooking – he accidentally salivated. Everyone gasped. A puddle of wee boy dribble pooled on the surface of our meal, making the fluffy topping, that I'd worked so hard to perfect, sag in the middle. I'd never been more proud. My moussaka was that good it literally induced dribbling. It became a well-established family legend and even now proved to be a powerful tool for enticing my son to the table.

God, I was good.

We exchanged a quiet smile as I put a generous portion on his plate. Steven knew I wouldn't tell the Claymores about his slavering – these family things were sacred – even though my moussaka prowess would have impressed the hell out of them.

Rudi wielded a bottle of beer and as it hovered in Steven's direc-tion they both sought my approval. I nodded. One, just one. He was only sixteen but at least he was doing it in front of me and not on a dangerous island out on the loch. Of course, everyone complimented me on the moussaka and then we played cards and blethered and laughed all evening. Steven acted as if my misdemeanour had never happened.

I had to keep my guard up. I had fallen off the wagon quite spectacularly last night, and all because of a toatie wee nip. I couldn't do that again. It had to be zero tolerance. One drink was one too many. At least I hadn't got drunk here, in front of the Claymores, in front of Steven.

It was a shame. I liked Dinah. Some parts of the night, the bits that I could remember, had been fun. But when I thought about it, the bits that I remembered were mostly the smoking and drinking. After how difficult it had been for me to give up cigarettes I couldn't believe I'd smoked last night. I could still taste the tar in my saliva and feel the carcinogens coursing through my veins. Never again. Dinah and I were a bad influence on each other. I needed to stay the hell away from her.

Chapter 35

The next morning, Steven was late coming downstairs. The Claymores had already left for another day of peat cutting. If it hadn't been legally dodgy I'd have asked Rudi if Steven could go with them. I could see he was bored. We had breakfast, just the two if us, in the kitchen. It was a lovely sunny morning, maybe the council would get the machair back today; I'd get paid, Steven would get work as an extra, and all would be well with the world.

After his toast, Steven took Bouncer for a walk out past Fenton's dairy farm, now his daily ritual. I daren't bring up the lovely Morag; Steven would tell me in his own sweet time – if ever. Whatever he got up to behind the milking shed with Morag was preferable to him hanging about the machair with Jackie and his rebel rousers, but I knew that if I said anything that would be exactly where he'd go.

I had a huge mound of sheets still to be washed. Just me on my own, putting on a boil wash and listening to Faughie FM. Just like the old days. Except that in the old days I'd been desperately lonely. Now that I had a house full of rufty-tufty men and a film star next door and my son living with me, I was glad of the quiet.

Whisky didn't make you happy, it was the little things: your son actually speaking to you and the smell of clean meadow-fresh sheets ready to be hung on the line. On the fabric conditioner box it described the fragrance as Orchid and Diamond. I'd never known a meadow to smell of orchids, never mind diamonds; as far as I knew diamonds didn't even have a fragrance. I was emptying the machine, sticking my head inside the drum to get the full effect of the decadent aroma, when I heard the kitchen window rattle.

I looked up and saw Walter.

Arms full of washing, I nodded at the back door and he walked in before I'd even got up off my knees.

'Who else is in the house?'

He was usually so calm and polite but he seemed agitated.

'Nobody,' I said, struggling to my feet, 'just me.'

Walter nodded, 'Bring it in. Now,' he said into his phone, and then cut the call.

What was going on? Walter took the laundry basket out of my hands, to help me I assumed, but then he took out one of my good white sheets and laid it on the floor.

'Sorry about this, Trixie, but it'll save your floor getting dirty.'

'Walter, is everything ok?'

'Yes, yes, I ...'

He listened hard and we both heard the sound of a diesel van drawing up at the front of the house.

Walter sprinted through the hall to the front door and opened it.

'Back door! Back door!' he hissed, and I heard the van reverse.

Tyres scrunching the gravel, van doors opening and banging closed, multiple hurried footsteps, and then heaving and grunting noises. Walter opened the kitchen door and ushered the Claymores in.

Ewan, Colin, Dave, Will and Danny carried it in, supervised by Rudi.

'Put it there on the sheet,' he instructed them.

Walter's eyes were glittering.

From the bog stench of it this had to be something they'd dragged out of the peat. It overwhelmed my meadow-fresh orchid and diamond fragrance, no contest. It was about the size and depth of a blanket box, an antique one, dark wood and ornately carved. A blanket box or a coffin for a midget. I didn't want any coffins in my kitchen.

Walter hadn't requested my permission and I supposed I only had myself to blame. That was the way of it when you got involved with criminals. One minute you were letting them use your tosg and the next minute they were dragging midget coffins into your kitchen. As they laid it down on the sheet the box oozed mud.

My heart was beating too fast.

'What is it, Walter?' I asked although I wasn't sure I wanted to know.

'That's what we're about to find out. Have you something to open it with, Rudi?'

Rudi slid a jemmy out of his belt and set to removing the lid. It popped easily and surprised us all. I jumped behind Dave, the biggest of them, and keeked out from over his shoulder.

'Be careful!' Walter snapped.

From where I was hiding I couldn't see what was inside the box but by their reactions it wasn't what they were expecting.

'Could you lift it out of the box and lay it on the sheet please?' Walter asked.

There were no volunteers.

'Och, for god's sake, I'll do it myself,' he said, reaching down.

This galvanised Will and Ewan to come to his aid and between the three of them they lifted it up out of the box.

When I saw it, I nearly screamed. Will dropped his end and Walter, not strong enough to keep it up, let it flump on to the sheet. As it splattered onto the floor it left a greasy impression on my good Egyptian cotton, like the chalk mark round a body at a murder scene.

I couldn't fathom what we were looking at. It was about three feet long and two feet wide. It was, or rather it had been, some kind of organism. It looked a bit like a seal: it had a tail flipper at one end, which might have signified a seal except for the fact that it had no head. And it wasn't that the head had been cut off, no, the grey slimy skin was continuous, a smooth rounded area where a head should have been. Some kind of foul mutation as yet unrecorded by science. Walter kneeled down on the floor right next to it.

'Can I borrow a knife please, Trixie?'

I shook my head. I didn't want any incriminating bog monster DNA on my kitchen utensils.

'It won't bite,' he laughed, 'it's a sealskin bag, that's all it is.'

I wasn't convinced and made no move to help him but Rudi produced a sgian dubh from his sock and handed it over.

'Thank you, Rudi,' said Walter, as he stabbed the knife in the swamp-thing and proceeded to gut it. Inside the sealskin there was another sealskin, and inside that it was covered in black sticky ectoplasm, the stuff of horror movies. As he split each layer and lifted out the next he left a pile of cast-off skins like a gruesome game of pass the parcel.

'They really knew how to waterproof in the old days: pine resin, plenty of it, to be had around Inverfaughie, pitch, tar, and of course the sealskin itself is completely waterproof.'

Although we stood watching this, fascinated and horrified in equal measure, Walter was really only talking to himself. I got the impression it was to calm his excitement and steady his nerve as he hacked through layer after layer of waterproofing and into the thing.

'This is the marvellous thing about the peat, it pickles and preserves. You know, you can preserve anything if you get the conditions right.'

By now elbow deep in what looked like an ancient mummified womb, Walter pulled out a rolled-up piece of something. He stood up, shook the slime off his arms and spread open the thing on the kitchen table. It was some kind of skin with writing on it, but it was greasy and most of the letters were too smudged for me to make out, and what language it was written in I couldn't have said.

'Remarkable!'

Walter held it up to his nose and inhaled deeply.

'Quite remarkable! Lambskin coated in wax, I think I can still smell the beeswax! Here, what do you think?'

He held it out to us, inviting us to sniff. I declined, as did everyone else. If the rest of them felt like I did, and I was pretty sure they did, it was an anticlimax. We were clearly not as enthralled by this discovery as Walter, but it took a moment before he noticed.

'Well?' he said, still laughing, 'what did you expect: a treasure chest full of gold doubloons?'

'Kind of, yeah,' Danny admitted shyly, and the rest of them agreed.

Walter laughed some more. 'Thanks for bringing it down for me, you've done a great job boys, I owe you all a pint.'

'But Walter,' said Rudi, 'all these layers of sealskin and wax and tar, why would they have gone to all that bother? It's got to be something valuable.'

'Aye,' agreed Walter, 'it must be.'

'Come on, put us out of our misery, what's the manuscript all about? What does it say?'

'You know,' Walter chuckled, 'I'm sorry to disappoint you all, but I really don't have a clue.'

Chapter 36

The monster/manuscript fiasco had made me and the Claymores partners in crime. Worried that Steven might sense this, I overcompensated in trying to make him one of the gang.

As we sat down to dinner, I remarked that with seven men and one gorgeous lady, anyone looking in the window would take us for Snow White and the Seven Dwarves.

That started a competition to find dwarfish nicknames for everyone. Steven instantly became 'Droopy', as in droopy drawers, because of his jeans always hanging off him and of course Rudi, as he was the oldest and had his trademark big red nose, would have to be Doc. They were all arguing and Dave suggested that I be the one to allocate the names.

'Why don't you make up some for us, Trixie? Excuse me, I mean Miss Snow White,' he said, bowing his head with a chivalrous sweep of his eyelashes.

When they'd first moved in I'd thought of them purely as the Claymores: a homogeneous horde of musclebound manhood, but that changed as I got to know them. They revealed themselves, through their wee habits, as individuals. I thought back to what I'd first noticed about each of them. Danny always went out running. Colin was mad for soup, he was always asking for it, and Ewan had requested after-dinner mints. Will stood out as the best fighter amongst them, but Dave was the tallest and broadest.

'Right, ready for the naming ceremony?' I asked.

Everyone put down their cutlery and leaned in. As I pointed at each one I called out their nickname.

'Droopy, Soupy, Sprinty, Minty, Mighty, Fighty, and Conk.'

They laughed. Conk was a surprise, even to me. I hadn't said it to offend Rudi, he was such a sweet man, it had just fitted the rhythm and leapt out of my mouth before I had a chance to filter. Steven laughed along but I could tell he was annoyed.

'I'll do it,' said Steven, clearing the table after dinner and carrying the dishes through to the kitchen, where I followed him.

'Hi hooooo!' I sang, hoping he'd take it up and give me a responding call.

He rolled his eyes, 'Leave it out, Snow White.'

'Such cynicism in one so young,' I sighed. 'Cheers, Droopy.'

Not so long ago he would have happily danced around the kitchen with me and we would have screamed with laughter. Steven had been such a lovely wee boy. What happened? When did the lovely wee boy become such an uncomfortable inbetweener?

As he bent down to fill the dishwasher I got an eyeful of my son's bum cleavage and had to look away. When he'd first started wearing these droopy trousers I'd taken loads of photos: something to tease him with when, years from now, he'd have a more mature perspective on this ridiculous fashion. The gusset sagged at knee height, the waistband was lower than his hips. He had to walk with both hands in his pockets just to hold them up.

'You know they were talking about your droopy jeans on a radio show the other day.'

'Yeah? And were they saying how sweet my peachy arse looked in them?'

Steven did a seductive little wiggle, forcing me to look away again.

'Eh, no. Not really. They were saying that the trend began in prisons in America. Aye, apparently it was a way of men signalling to each other, without the wardens knowing, that they were available for sex.'

'That's not the way I heard it,' he replied calmly. 'I heard it began in America; with kids who were so poor they had to wear their big brothers' hand-me-down trousers.'

'I don't get it. What's cool about being poor?'

'I didn't say being poor is cool, that's not what I'm saying.'

Oh dear, it wasn't going well.

'Wearing baggy trousers is a way of signalling that you have a big brother. The signal being: don't mess with me or my big brother will f–'

'Enough.'

'– you up.'

'Thank you, Steven, I get the idea.'

'Well, you did ask.'

'Yes,' I was forced to admit. 'But it's not true, is it?'

'What isn't?'

'It's not true in your case. You're an only child, as far as I know. You don't have a big brother.'

I was being pedantic but I couldn't halt my tongue.

'As far as *I* know, that's true,' said Steven putting down the dish towel, 'but there's always Jackie. He's a bit like a big brother, isn't he?'

'I think that's stretching it a bit far, Steven, even for you.'

'Well, just because you can't get on with him doesn't mean I can't.'

Ouch. He must have read the pain on my face.

'What?' he asked, smiling innocently, his arms extended in a mock surrender. He leaned towards me and moved his head, snake-like, in an ugly taunt.

'I said *get on with*. Not *get it on with*. That would be inappropriate.'

I was stunned into horrified silence. As I watched Steven's peachy arse walk out the kitchen I realised that I'd bred a monster.

Chapter 37

I was back at Dinah's place.

Not to drink, to stop her from drinking. She had called me at 8 am, crying, and havering disjointed nonsense about her half-brother having died from some recessive gene syndrome.

'Isn't Knox MacIntyre flying in today?' I asked her. 'I heard that on the radio.'

'The marriage was consanguineous, you see,' she sobbed.

'Dinah, make yourself a strong pot of coff–'

'Robin, my beautiful brother, I miss him so much.'

'Ok, I'm coming over.'

In 50 minutes Dinah was due to personally walk Knox MacIntyre around the estate. The state she was currently in she couldn't walk the length of herself. I made her drink a mug of coffee that I brewed to rocket fuel strength and then stood over her while she changed her clothes, washed her face and brushed her hair. I was running around emptying ash trays and throwing wine bottles in a black plastic bag when the line of Range Rovers processed slowly up the drive.

Me and Bouncer and Dinah's dog Mimi scooted out the back, through the servants' entrance, before Knox MacIntyre arrived. The rain had stopped, although there were plenty of dark clouds and there was a bracingly fresh wind off the loch. I let the dogs off the lead and they ran around while I waited.

I heard Dinah's signature hacking cough before I caught sight of her between the gorse bushes walking towards me. Dinah acted surprised, smiling and waving. I'd promised her I'd be here for her if it all got too much with MacIntyre. I told her to bring him down and I'd do what I could to take the heat off her. I was a trained medical sales rep, I reassured her, I knew how to handle businesspeople.

She introduced me to the small dark-haired man.

'This is Trixie, my friend from the village.'

'Sure,' said the wee man, 'we can give her a job.'

Or at least that's what I thought he said. He spoke in an American accent and pronounced the word as jaab. Confused, I looked at Dinah. What had made him say that? Dinah laughed, whether at my confusion or to cover her own embarrassment, I wasn't sure.

'Oh, that's very kind,' she said. 'Trixie, this is Mr MacIntyre.'

'Pleased to meet you, Mr MacIntyre.'

It was all I could do not to curtsey. What a thrill to meet him like this. I felt my breath come in short gasps. Not because I was excited to meet someone famous, the famous were ten a penny in Inverfaughie these days, and not because he was rich, either. True, he was the richest person I'd ever met, a billionaire, rich beyond even winning the lottery. Nor was it because he was powerful; he had the power to change life in Inverfaughie forever, but that didn't impress me much. No, I was excited to meet him because I could not wait to tell Jenny.

As the three of us stood there in the damp windy field with the dogs running around our feet, I tried to take in as many details about Knox MacIntyre as possible. While Dinah and I were talking he held a pair of expensive-looking binoculars to his eyes, pointing them at the loch and the hills above. He was quite a small man, barely five feet tall, and up close his hair was very obviously dyed a blue-black colour but there was something else odd about it. He had an extreme comb-over beginning at his right ear. He had grown the rest of his hair long and it seemed to be swirled on top of his head like steel wool. He was pleasant enough looking; even on a cloudy day like this he had two rows of the most sparkling gnashers I'd ever seen. As I was committing to memory his country gent ensemble – green wellies, waxed coat, tweed waistcoat – at the edge of my vision I noticed something. Gusts of wind shook the gorse and alerted me to four men at various points around us, at a distance of about fifty feet, very much focused on us. We were surrounded.

'Dinah, those men ...'

'Mr MacIntyre's security.'

Of course, these must have been the people in all the cars.

'Nothing to worry about,' said Dinah, 'they're here to protect us. I'm just showing Mr MacIntyre round the estate. Mimi, stop that!' she said, and laughed, a high-pitched embarrassed spurt.

Mimi had her front paws on my knees and her nose at my jacket pocket. Dinah's clever little dog knew that I usually kept dog treats in that pocket but I'd been in such a foul mood when I'd left the house I'd forgotten to replenish my supply. I clawed out the small broken bits of biscuit that were left and offered them to the dogs.

Mimi forcefully stuck her wet nose in my curled palm.

'There you go girl,' I said, patting her.

When she realised it was just a couple of old broken Gravy Bones that had been gathering fluff in my pocket, she turned up her nose. Bouncer similarly sniffed and turned away.

'You dogs are fussy today,' I said, embarrassed by the slight.

'What you need is some of these bad boys,' said Mr MacIntyre, abruptly joining us.

He thrust a small clear plastic bag of what looked like bran flakes towards me. 'Something we're working on right now. My own dogs love 'em,' he said as he threw a few flakes into his mouth.

He swallowed them and then showed the bag to Dinah. She smiled her approval, although it was obvious, at least to me, that she was as baffled as I was.

'Slimming aids for dogs,' he said. 'Now, don't laugh.'

Dinah flashed me a pleading look.

'It's a problem we have in the States these days. A third of us are clinically obese and our best friends are also suffering. Here, try one, they're delicious.'

He offered the kibble to Dinah and she delicately took one flake from him. Next he was holding them out to me.

'They won't spoil your figure, you'll actually lose weight eating them. They're negatively calorific, a simple fat-binding molecule teamed with a great bacon flavour.'

I tried to think of a way out of it. Pretend to be allergic? But to what? I didn't actually know what was in them. Before I had the chance to change my mind I took one and popped it in my mouth.

The taste hit my tongue like a bullet. Although it was only the size of a bran flake, I felt it was only polite to make a show of eating it so I chewed for a bit, then I chewed some more, and finally I swallowed.

'You're right,' I said, 'they're delicious.'

Dinah put her hand to her mouth, coughing, perhaps discreetly spitting it out but she nodded enthusiastically.

Knox MacIntyre laughed, 'See? I'm calling them Bacon Flakes until the ad agency comes up with something better. Three key selling points: veterinary medicated canine weight loss, a tool for motivation and discipline, and a great-tasting treat. Can't lose, huh?'

'Oh yes,' said Dinah.

'Absolutely,' I agreed.

Knox MacIntyre dropped his voice and with a mischievous look he bent his knees. As he crouched on his haunches at dog height we got a bird's eye view of his elaborate hairdo.

'Let's see what these little guys think of them, shall we?'

The little guys thought they were great: Bouncer and Mimi gobbled them greedily. They barked and bounced and jumped on Knox MacIntyre, shouldering each other out of the way to get at the treat. He laughed and tormented the dogs by letting them have some and then lifting the bag out of range. As the dogs fought to reach them, a strong gust of wind blew the bacon flakes out of the bag and swirled them into the air. At the same time, as if in slow motion, the wind picked up MacIntyre's comb-over. His hair lifted and stood momentarily at the side of his head as if it was hinged, before flopping impotently to the other side to sweep his shoulder. What happened next was no one's fault, an elemental force of nature.

Mimi and Bouncer went feral. A pack mentality set in. A feeding frenzy had been unleashed in them that would not be quelled by a gust of wind or the fact that the biscuits were now landing in his hair and on his naked scalp. To get the remaining treats, those delicious fat-binding miracles of modern science, the two dogs rushed him, knocking him off his feet. Dinah and I watched, speechless, as the four security men rushed towards Knox MacIntyre, laid flat out on the wet grass, mud spattered up his country gent outfit, while Mimi chewed on his fuzzy hair curtain and Bouncer slobbered and licked bacon flakes from his cold baldy head.

Chapter 38

'Well that takes the firkin biscuit, it really does,' said Jenny, 'excuse my language.'

I had expected her to laugh at this story but she wasn't in the mood. Of course I'd asked her right away how the meeting with the minister had gone but she didn't want to talk about it. That suited me; I just wanted paid. I couldn't be bothered getting bogged down in all the political machinations. This long drawn-out tussle over a field was getting really boring now and, comparatively, my Knox MacIntyre story was fascinating.

'That big fat titan of capitalism actually feeding people dog food,' said Jenny, shaking her head.

'He didn't feed me, he invited me to try them. You're making it sound like chunks of braised horse, it was only a toatie wee biscuit. You wait, all your fancy customers will be in here asking for them.'

'I'll not be stocking them.'

'And he didn't look like much of a titan lying in the mud.'

'Och, away, I don't believe you. You're only saying that to cheer me up.'

'I'm telling you, Jenny, he was lying in the mud while Bouncer licked his baldy head; I doubt Mr MacIntyre will be offering me a job now.'

'Och, that's all he's good for, that one. He's been going around saying that to everyone. He thinks Highlanders are that desperate we'll sell our dignity and work for anybody. He's offered to employ all the mill workers.'

'Well, is that not good news?'

Jenny looked at me as though she was about to say something and then, shaking her head again, turned back to filing her paperwork. I'd popped down to the shop directly after breakfast to give her the skinny. The hilarious comb-over malfunction/dog-slobbering incident I was offering was gossip gold, but she didn't seem interested. She carried on sorting her papers and making notes. Why had I even bothered coming down here?

'Oh and I can exclusively reveal,' I said, by way of a teaser, 'that I've been invited to Brenda's place for lunch.'

That should prick up her ears. The last time I visited the Ethecom hippies Jenny was gagging to hear the details. But that was back when she didn't know Brenda. Now that they were working closely on resolving the machair issue, Jenny had, no doubt, already discovered all of Brenda's secrets.

'She's networking on Mag's behalf. She suggested that I come over for lunch and bring Steven. A kind of playdate thing. I think the boys are a bit old for that, but Steven's getting cabin fever sitting about waiting.'

Jenny shot me a look and then went back to her work.

'He's pissed off about not getting a job on the filum and he's fallen out with me again. We had a ridiculous argument about his trousers.'

Still no response, was Jenny even listening? Normally she loved hearing about Steven.

'You know he wears those baggy jeans?'

I carried on – the way young people dressed was a pet peeve of Jenny's.

'Now he's threatening to get a tattoo. He's only saying it to wind me up. Then he said he was going to get the lyrics of some song tattooed on his hip. I don't know it: "Avanti Popolo", is that what it's called? Something like that. Anyway, I says, well that's quite a long title, and he says, not as long as "Supercalifragilisticexpial-idocious". So I says, and you'll like this, that would be something quite atrocious.'

Jenny finally broke her silence.

'Saw that coming,' she sighed.

'Och, lighten up, Jenny. What's wrong, have you and Walter had a lover's tiff?'

'He's in Glasgow; he's down there visiting one of his professor pals. He's obsessed with that manky old manuscript he found in the peat bogs.'

'Aha! So that's why you're so down in the mouth; you're missing him.'

'Indeed I am not.'

'You're worried that he's off in Glasgow snogging some other woman.'

'Believe me,' she said wearily, 'I wish that was all I had to worry about.'

'Och, spit it out woman! Get it off your chest, for god's sake, you'll feel better for it. I've never seen you so miserable.'

Jenny gave me another of her intense looks and then came out from behind the counter, walked right past me, closed the door and flipped the Open sign to Closed. Jenny never, but never, closed the shop during business hours.

With a grim expression she walked towards me and I braced myself. I felt sure she was about to give me some dreadful news: she had the big C, it had to be something like that. It was inoperable, late stage, too late for treatment.

As I saw her, my lively, funny, wee friend, walk towards me, I wanted to embrace her; to tell her that I'd suddenly realised how important she was to me, how grateful I was for her friendship, and how much I was going to miss her. But I knew I couldn't. That wasn't in the rules.

'Trixie, I'm afraid I have dreadful news.'

The rules were that you had to obtain permission for that kind of self-indulgent uncontrolled weeping. I'd have to hold it together. I took a big breath and pulled myself up.

'We've lost the machair.'

'Jenny, I'm so sorry, I ... What?'

'You can't tell anyone, but it's a done deal. We've lost it. We're announcing it at the public meeting tonight.'

'You've lost the machair?'

'No,' she said sharply, 'I haven't lost it, *we've* lost it. Westminster has sold it from under our feet.'

Chapter 39

This was all off the back of the council meeting with the minister: not confident of dealing with international shysters like Global Imperial all on their own, the voluminously trousered Scottish Labour M.S.Ps had called on their big brothers in Westminster. Either that, Jenny surmised, or Westminster had spotted the opportunity and muscled in. The London-based minister Tobias Grunt had helicoptered in and, at a big press conference, assured everyone that he had a put together a package that would have the situation resolved within the day.

He met immediately with Brenda and Jenny, inviting them to join him for a power breakfast in the conference facility, also known as the lounge bar and function suite of the Caledonia Hotel. The meeting was apparently very successful, with Tobias, 'please, call me Toby', listening intently to everything Jenny and Brenda were able to tell him before paraphrasing it back to them, checking and double checking that he'd got everything right. Toby invited them to stay to lunch, where they sat down with Miss Yip and some other G.I. heavy-hitters that had flown in from stateside.

But it was all just window dressing.

It soon became apparent that Toby Grunt had very little interest in Global Imperial and none whatsoever in Faughie Council. He now held secret meeting after secret meeting, except that, in

Inverfaughie, nothing was a secret for long. Behind closed doors he started the horse trading with Global Imperial and, enter a new player, Mr Knox MacIntyre.

Global Imperial was not really important in this deal, except for public relations purposes; they were spending money but not a huge amount, and they'd be gone in a matter of weeks. In the scheme of things they were, as the minister had put it, 'small beans'. On the other hand, Mr MacIntyre had been ready to invest billions of dollars.

The construction of his proposed hotel and polo complex would provide employment for the whole town and beyond. Local people would take up hospitality roles but additionally there would be sought-after jobs in tack cleaning, horse grooming, and manure shovelling. The council argued that there was an abundance of space for multiple polo fields to be located elsewhere on the Faughie estate, but, countered Mr MacIntyre, the machair, once it was flattened and levelled out, would be an ideal size and shape for polo. The international players and spectators, while stomping the divots between matches, would be able to enjoy the views of the Scottish loch and hills beyond. This was the charm of Faughie Castle, and the machair was the unique selling point, the cherry on the cake. Without it, the resort wasn't a viable option for Mr MacIntyre. Even if the polo fields were to be located elsewhere, he believed it would be unseemly for his guests to look out of Faughie Castle and be forced to witness the vulgar spectacle of cattle grazing. Sheep and cows were unsightly. 'Jeez', he was widely quoted as saying, 'those things go to the toilet everywhere!'

Jenny and Brenda were relieved to discover that Tobias Grunt was horrified, but not for the reasons they imagined. Over and above the inequitable tax advantages they dished out to sporting estates, the government had spent years wooing Mr MacIntyre, visiting him in the US, showering him in bogus honours and blandishments and cajoling him to invest in Great Britain. They were not about to give up on him now, especially as the latest news was that MacIntyre Holdings had acquired a similarly picturesque area of land – with full planning consent – in New Zealand.

Great Britain craved inward investment like a crack-head craved crystal meth, and Great Britain would pimp its firkin granny to acquire it, or at least that was Jenny's bitter assessment. The minister's duty was clear: for the sake of Inverfaughie's survival, for good relationships with a global investor and the tax revenue Great Britain might hope to reap, he issued a compulsory purchase order. Ownership of the machair was transferred to MacIntyre Holdings that very day. MacIntyre Holdings, as a goodwill gesture to aid local employment and development, agreed a short-term lease in favour of Global Imperial.

A generous compensation would be paid to local farmers, Toby Grunt told the slack-jawed Brenda and Jenny, he would absolutely insist upon it.

'Surely there must be something that can be done?' I asked Jenny, but she only shook her head.

I felt slightly nauseous when it dawned on me that only an hour or so after he had bought and sold the wee village, Knox MacIntyre had fed me firkin dog biscuits. It wasn't such a funny story any more.

Chapter 40

'Tidal lift. All the energy you need right there, in Loch Faughie,' said Mag, speaking with his mouth full. 'Stuart Wilkie.'

'He's from King's Lynn, where we used to live,' explained Brenda, filling in the gaps. 'Stuart's an inventor. He was our neighbour.'

'Stuart Wilkie has a fantastic idea for harnessing the vertical lifting of large vessels. Compress the air, then drive air motors. Easy. Very efficient,' said Mag as he gulped another mouthful, 'and it's storable.'

'The energy is harvested when the tide lifts the vessel on the upstroke,' said Brenda.

'And the downstroke,' said Mag.

'And the downstroke and, would you like some more rice, Trixie?'

I'd expected I might bump into Jan at Ethecom, but he was apparently away transporting a vehicle all that day. Brenda had made us a delicious vegetable curry lunch, all lovingly home-grown no doubt, but Steven embarrassed me by mostly just flicking it around the plate. Brenda was polite enough not to notice but Mag addressed the issue directly.

'Don't you want that?'

Steven didn't answer, staring off into the distance. I knew this tactic. This situation was so excruciating for him that he was pretending he wasn't actually here. He was concentrating hard, trying to teleport himself away from the mortification of being set up on a playdate by his mum.

'It's good food, it'd be a shame to waste it,' said Mag, gently lifting Steven's plate and setting it on top of his own recently emptied one.

I was grateful Steven was able to maintain his dissociated expression. If he allowed his true feelings to surface his sneer would likely wilt the flowers in the vase. For Steven, being a 'midgie raker,' that is to say, someone who rakes through bins, wears second-hand clothes or eats leftovers, was a source of shame so great the only solution would be suicide by ritual disembowelment.

'If you don't want it I'll eat it,' said Mag, blissfully unaware of his ignominious social blunder. 'The goats would eat it, those goats'll eat anything, but curry gives them windy pops.'

What teenager says 'windy pops' for god's sake? I thought. Mag had no sooner put a forkful of curry into his mouth than he coughed it back out again, spraying it into his hand. I thought he was choking but he was giggling. He'd thought up a joke that cracked him up so much he could hardly tell us for laughing.

'It makes the billies bilious.'

Not so much a joke as puerile word play but, for Brenda's sake, I managed a smile. I didn't want Steven mooning around friendless but even I could see that this wasn't going to work. He laid his head on his arm and hid his face. I was about to rebuke him for his rudeness but Mag wasn't finished with the witticisms yet.

'It makes them fart like billyo!'

Steven's shoulders began to shake. He wasn't laughing *with* Mag.

'So, taking it to the court of European Justice, you say?' I asked Brenda.

'Eh, yeah,' she said.

We'd already filled the long awkward silences with an extensive discussion on the machair situation. There really wasn't anything left to say on the subject.

I'd decided against going to the public meeting, it would be too depressing. The only loss to me personally would be the machair as a handy walking area for Bouncer and once I'd moved back to Glasgow that would no longer be an issue for me, but I knew how gutted everyone in the village was going to be. I felt sorry that Brenda and Jenny had to deliver the bad news but I was well out of it. I knew it wasn't rational but I had a vague feeling of guilt. I wasn't responsible; I hadn't done anything to make them lose their machair.

Brenda stood up, 'You didn't see the place last time you came, will I show you round?'

'Yes, that would be fantastic. Come on, Steven.'

Mag rushed out ahead of us, nearly knocking me off my feet in his enthusiasm.

'Mag, would you look where you're going, for goodness' sake!' Brenda shouted after him.

In complete contrast, Steven dragged his curmudgeonly teenage carcass out to the yard, one petulant foot after the other.

'Has Mag taken a stretch?' I asked his mother.

I was baffled. He was at least a few inches taller since I'd last seen him.

Brenda scoffed, 'He's not growing that fast, thank god. No, it's his latest invention. Mag, show Trixie and Steven your electric shoes.'

As she put the words 'electric' and 'shoes' together, there was no hint of mockery in Brenda's voice. On the contrary: she seemed proud of her madcap inventor son.

With dainty fingers Mag pulled the legs of his jeans out and up, as if he were about to curtsey, and revealed a pair of red 4-inch platform shoes. This was bizarre enough, but then Mag's feet began an energetic toe-tapping dance.

'Jeezo,' I said, trying to remain calm. 'And how does electricity come into it?'

Steven was clearly horrified, as was I, and for the same reason:

When Steven was wee, every night I used to read him a different story from the *Hans Christian Anderson Bumper Book of Fairy Tales*. Until, that is, we hit upon 'The Red Shoes'. To cut a long story short, a wee girl is given a pair of red shoes. She loves them so much she refuses to take them off, even for church. After a while the shoes control her; she can't remove them and they wear her to exhaustion. She begs a woodsman to cut her feet off, but as she hirples along, now footless and dragging her bloody stumps, the red shoes continue to torment her, still dancing with her amputated feet inside.

It was an image neither Steven nor I could get out of our heads. So much for our comforting beddybyebaws ritual. It would have been more reassuring to read my five year old excerpts from *The Exorcist*.

We put the bumper book away after that. Steven crawled into my bed every night for a week, and I was grateful he did. Then, as now, the idea freaked us out and Mag's jiggling dance macabre was a very powerful reminder of those other terrifying red shoes.

'Is electricity making him dance?' I asked.

'No,' laughed Brenda, 'just the opposite, he's doing it to generate electricity. Mag,' she called, but Mag was too far gone. 'Mag!' she yelled, and grabbed his shoulder, 'show Trixie and Steven how it works.'

The horror show finally ended when Mag lifted his foot to show us the right sole. Brenda talked us through it. A large section of the sole had been cut away and replaced with what looked like some kind of dynamo. She explained that Mag had bought the retro shoes in a charity shop because the hollow platform sole was roomy enough to accommodate the inner workings of the mechanism.

'He designed this himself but he originally got the idea from the guy that invented the wind-up radio.'

'Trevor Baylis,' said Mag in his high excited voice, still with his foot in the air. 'But it doesn't have to be a dynamo. I have another pair where I'm experimenting with electrowetting. It's a simple hydrophobic liquid, just oil and water. When I walk on it I'm forcing it over electrodes, creating a current I can store. I'm getting slightly better results with that. You can charge your mobile off this battery,' he said, directly addressing Steven. 'I can get ten watts just from walking.'

'Or dancing,' Brenda smiled. 'Mag wants to open the first electricity-generating gym.'

'It's curr-razy that gyms use electricity,' he squawked, 'when they could easily be adapted to be generating it. Customers won't pay membership; the gym will pay them. It's the future.'

Mag looked to Steven, maybe hoping that, as he was of the same age, he might agree, but Steven was off somewhere else, in his head at least, teleporting again.

Chapter 41

'Come and see our new chickens,' said Brenda.

As we walked towards the chicken coop she elbowed me, darting her eyes towards the boys and smiling. Steven was asking Mag if his shoe battery would charge a Nokia.

The chickens, with their fluffy golden feathers, looked like an old-fashioned illustration on a soup tin. Brenda let them out to run around the yard.

'Look,' said Steven in a shocked whisper, 'they've already plucked those ones!'

He was right. Steven pointed an accusatory finger at a group of chickens still huddled together at the back of the coup. Baldy and featherless with bumpy naked flesh, some of them had patches of blue or green on their body with stubby little wings poking out. They looked like some kind of mutation experiment gone wrong.

'That's sick, man.'

I had to agree. Getting your feathers plucked must be like getting your legs waxed. Brenda and Mag both simultaneously exploded into laughter.

'We haven't plucked them,' said Brenda when she managed to stop laughing, 'they're rescue chickens from a battery farm.'

Brenda explained, between snorts of laughter, that stress

made their feathers fall out. When the chickens were no longer productive enough the battery farm wrung their necks so, to save them, she adopted them.

'I know it looks funny,' she chortled, 'but I knit them tiny jackets. It keeps them warm until their feathers come back. Usually they make a full recovery; you can see how well these other guys are doing, and we get quite a good egg yield.'

'Hey, Mum,' said Mag, 'Steven just asked me if you were a pheasant plucker.'

Mag laughed hard. He wasn't laughing with Steven and clearly this was payback for earlier.

'Or maybe,' said Mag slowly, teasing, 'it was a pleasant ...'

Brenda gave Mag the hard stare, 'Yes, thank you, Mag, I think we all know where you're going with that. Would you like to see our workshop, Steven?'

Steven didn't answer immediately but if I knew my son he would – and with the right answer. For all that he was a huffy arrogant git with me, he was reliably polite to other adults, especially women. His dad and I had instilled good manners in him, I could be proud of that.

'That would be super, thank you, Brenda.'

I had to swallow a laugh.

Steven had spent the afternoon rolling his eyes and mouthing words like 'freak' and 'weirdo' to me. He didn't care if Mag saw him.

'Mag, can you take Steven round to the workshop please? And this recycling's starting to pile up again, could I ask you two big strong lads to take it to the processor on your way there?'

'I certainly shall Brenda, soooper,' said Mag, as he and Steven carried the bags away.

'And it's Mum to you, mister!' Brenda shouted after her cheeky son. 'He's only showing off because Steven's here, but they seem to be getting on alright, don't you think?'

I made a noncommittal noise.

'Mag so needs a friend. I suppose they both do.'

I was slightly offended that she put her weirdo son in the same category as Steven but as we were her guests, I let it go.

'I didn't mention it before,' she continued, 'but some of the village kids have been picking on Mag.'

'Really?'

What a surprise.

'Yeah, he's an easy target I suppose: an outsider, English accent; that doesn't go down well.'

Brenda omitted to mention her son's weird screechy voice, his obsessive nerdiness or his electric shoes, but she was probably blind to these eccentricities.

'That's a shame, I'm sorry to hear that, Brenda. Things'll get easier, it just takes time, I'm sure you remember the nightmare of the teenage years, I certainly do, but if he makes the effort to fit in, eventually they'll come to accept him.'

'Mag will never fit into the herd; he's just not made that way, but I know what you're saying, Trixie: eventually they'll accept him, because they'll have to. Mag is a visionary, a genius. A few years from now they'll all be working for him. He'll be inventing: manufacturing and creating work for local people.'

'Absolutely,' I said.

'Two nights ago a crowd of boys from the village chased him. They were on foot, Mag was on his bike, thank god, so he got away easily, but I don't want him going down there alone any more.'

'Och, that's what boys do, chase each other, it's just high jinks.'

'It's murderously high jinks, Trixie, they were throwing rocks. What if one had hit him?'

I had no answer for that and could only show Brenda my one-concerned-mother-to-another sympathetic face.

Of course Mag was a target for bullies. Highland kids were no different and no more tolerant than kids from anywhere else. More importantly, if Steven was seen publicly with Mag he'd be tarred with the weirdo brush. I didn't want anyone throwing rocks at my boy.

'Help ma' Boab, is that the time?' I said, 'I'll need to get back and get the dinner on for my Claymores.'

Brenda and I walked to the workshop to pick up the boys. As Brenda pushed the door open I saw that Mag and Steven were both riding bikes and they seemed to be racing each other. They were both pedalling fast; their legs were a blur, but they weren't going anywhere.

'Static,' explained Brenda, 'to generate juice for the arc welding.'

A small electric bulb flared in front of Mag's bike and as he raised his arms in victory Steven sagged forward on his bike, exhausted.

'Ok, that'll let us weld some more. Let the welding commence!' squealed Mag.

Considering how knackered he had been seconds before, Steven dismounted fast and rushed to pull on a welding helmet.

'And gloves!' yelled Brenda.

Both boys grabbed for the one pair of heavy gloves at the same time, giggling and struggling with each other. Steven wrestled them from Mag but I didn't like the way this was going.

'Come on, Steven, we need to get home.'

I heard a muffed whine from beneath the welding helmet, 'But Trixie, let the welding commence.'

'*Now* Steven, come on.'

Brenda took us back to the cottage to pick up our coats. Steven was still dragging his feet but this time it seemed to be because he didn't want to leave. As we walked we encountered Ethecom's herd of goats and had to walk right through the middle of them. I suppose Brenda was trying to spare us any more embarrassing misunderstandings and took pains to tell us about the goats.

'This breed is called LaMancha, from Mexico, but originally from Europe, they're great milkers. These are all does, that is: girls, but we're keeping a few bucks to increase the herd.'

'This is Charlotte Wilson, she's my favourite,' said Mag, stroking one of them, 'she looks like a girl in school, same moronic expression.'

Steven laughed too and pushed forward to stroke the goat.

'Mag, what have I told you? No names.' And then discreetly she said to me, 'Don't want him getting too fond of them.'

The goats smelled awful, but I bent down and patted Charlotte politely like a good guest.

And suddenly I was pitching forward with tremendous force. I put out my arms to break my fall and landed in a heap in the dirt. Someone had kicked me, hard.

Brenda rushed to help me up.

'Oh, are you alright, Trixie?'

'I'm fine,' I said.

'Get away,' Brenda yelled, 'shoo!'

Still face down on the ground, I turned to see the culprit. A nasty-looking goat had its head down and was moving towards me. As I pulled up onto all fours my bum presented the goat with an enticing target. I looked down and saw between my legs that it was getting ready to butt me again. Steven and Mag found this hilarious. The two of them had finally found something in common to laugh about: me. My clothes were filthy and my dignity was in tatters, I had nothing left to lose.

'Bring it on.'

I flipped onto my side and lifted my foot in the air, fully prepared for a scrap with a farmyard animal.

'Come and get it, goat!' I snarled.

'Oh no,' said Brenda, 'don't do that, he'll think it's a game. Mag...'

'I'm on it,' yelled Mag, darting into the house, 'I'm all over it!'

'I'm so sorry, Trixie,' said Brenda offering me a hand to pull up on, 'that goat's got problems. He's the runt. None of the other goats likes him, he keeps trying to mount them.'

I stood up and brushed the dust off my clothes. Now I was on my feet I saw that the goat was much smaller than the rest of them.

'All of them?'

'Yes, females *and* males, he's not fussy. His testicles haven't descended yet: cryptorchidism, that's part of his problem, and the vet costs a fortune. It shouldn't stop him impregnating the does, he's certainly trying and, going by his behaviour, his dangly bits must be up there somewhere, but time will tell.'

Mag burst out of the front door of the cottage with two enormous supersoakers over his shoulder.

'Stevo!' he yelled and threw one of the water guns into Steven's waiting arms.

With this activity, the goat looked at me and put its head down looking like he might be ready to charge me again.

'Let him have it!' Mag screamed and lunged into a forward roll. As he rolled he seamlessly blasted the goat with high-pressure water from the toy gun.

Brenda rolled her eyes, 'Oh dear,' she said, 'too many action hero movies I fear.'

Steven immediately joined him. Later he would claim he was only doing it to defend me, which was sweet, but he was no longer the distant too-cool-for-school dude he'd affected to be earlier. Tormenting a goat was too much fun.

The goat swiftly altered course. As I stood braced for attack, a wet, astonished goat ran past me followed by two gun-toting teenagers.

'Get him Stevo!' yelled Mag.

Chapter 42

There was someone at the counter when I walked in so I lurked at the back of the shop.

'Ah, it's yourself, Trixie,' said Jenny, rather more pointedly than necessary, 'I'm just finishing Morag's order. I'll not be a minute.'

It was Morag Fenton. I couldn't see her face, but I knew her from the coil of beautiful burnished copper hair that rolled in thick waves down her back.

I leaned awkwardly round her so that I could address her face to face.

'Hello' I gushed, smiling and nodding.

'Hello.'

Morag smiled nervously.

'Well done getting the part in the film. Jenny and I saw your audition, which we thought was terrific. We knew you were going to get it, didn't we, Jenny?'

Jenny didn't back me up.

'Thanks,' Morag mumbled.

'Acting in a Hollywood movie! Your parents must be proud, and getting to kiss Tony Ramos, I bet your mum's jealous, eh?'

Morag looked at Jenny and then gave a confused noddy shake of the head that was neither yes nor no. She lifted her Ethecom canvas bag and turned to leave.

'I'm Trixie McNicholl, by the way, Steven's mum.' I'd hoped that this would clear Morag's confusion, but she was no more friendly. She mumbled something polite and generic and scooted out the shop.

'What's her problem?' I asked Jenny.

'Well, for starters,' said Jenny, tippy-tapping away on Computer, 'she doesn't have a mum.'

'Oh no.'

'Dropped dead four years ago. Massive stroke. Overworked. Dairy farming isn't the cushy number it used to be.'

'Poor woman. Poor Morag.'

'Och, Morag is a grand wee soldier. She stepped right into her mother's shoes and she'd hardly even started the secondary school. Her mother had her well trained,' Jenny stopped typing, spoke slowly and did her dramatic face, 'almost as if she knew. She's only fifteen but Morag practically runs that farm now. She'll make a terrific farmer and a good wee wife for some lucky man some day.'

'Well she didn't seem that impressed when I told her I was Steven's mother. I hope they haven't fallen out. I'm pretty sure Steven's still seeing her; he sneaks away up to that farm every morning on the pretext of walking Bouncer.'

'Och aye, he's still seeing her; twice I've driven past them out by the lighthouse, hand in hand, love's young dream the pair of them. And talking of romance: you and Jan were conspicuous by your absence at the public meeting – were you off on a lover's tryst?'

'Jenny, how many times do I have to tell you? There's absolutely hee-haw going on between me and Jan. But anyway, sorry I didn't make the meeting, bit of a plumbing emergency,' I lied.

'Well, you were missed. It was noted,' said Jenny sharply.

'Brenda said it was difficult.'

'Difficult? There was nearly a riot.'

'She told me. She says you're thinking of taking it to the European Court of Justice?'

'I'm not holding out much hope there, too long-drawn-out,' said Jenny. 'Some people preferred the general strike idea. No government likes popular revolt, it gives the peasantry ideas. Jackie says it would embarrass them and give us international press coverage.'

I was surprised that Jenny would bring up Jackie's name with me. 'What's he going to do?'

I had a vision of Jackie, like Enjolras out of *Les Mis*, striking a heroic pose at the barricades, waving the flag for freedom.

'Is Jackie organising a strike?'

'I don't know. We couldn't vote. The meeting broke up before we could. There were strangers there, outsiders, probably spies and agents provocateurs, who knows. They tried to start a fight, stirring up factions, trying to fragment opinion. It turned quite nasty, actually; I thought there was going to be a lynching. We had to close the meeting before anything kicked off; folk had brought their kiddies. Divide and conquer, that's what they're up to. The whole thing's a shambles. When we shut the hall Jackie and some of the others were so fired up they wanted to storm the machair.'

'Hmmm,' I pondered. I was naturally excited about Jackie leading the charge, I'd have paid good money to watch him take back the machair, but at the same time I was worried he might hurt himself. 'Is that not a wee bit risky?'

'Of course it is!' said Jenny, as if I was an idiot. 'Not to mention stupid and pointless, I told him that. It's exactly what they want. Then they can make arrests and portray us as dangerous extremists. Brenda talked Jackie and the others out of it, eventually, but now he's taken the huff with me.'

So, I thought, with a small delicious butter-cream satisfaction, now I wasn't the only one Jackie wouldn't speak to. Now, like me, Jenny would know the cold chill of being ignored by him.

'But Jenny, how will you live without the radiant glow of Jackie's smile in your life?'

'I'll manage, somehow,' she said dryly.

'But seriously, I hope you two make up.'

And I meant it. She was my only Jackie source.

'The whole village knows about my relationship to Jackie,' I said. Jenny shrugged.

'And before you say anything, I know that's my own fault. I shouldn't have got drunk and shot my mouth off at the ceilidh, but you don't know how hard it is to live here, to see him and be ignored by him every day. It's humiliating.'

'Whoa there,' said Jenny, suddenly businesslike, 'no crying at the counter please, it makes the mags damp, smudges the ink. Now, what can I get you?'

I had embarrassed her. I shouldn't have been surprised – villagers always closed ranks against outsiders – but I was a little shocked by the brutality of the brush-off. I fumbled in my bag while I decided how to respond.

'Eh, I'm just returning the DVD, a bit late I'm afraid.'

'Och, we'll not worry about that,' said Jenny, her voice softening a bit. 'Did you watch the film?'

She seemed to be indicating that she was willing to chat so long as the topic moved away from the subject of Jackie. I grasped the opportunity to return to more amicable ground.

'No, we never got around to it, is it good?'

'Aye, it's old but it's good. *Passport to Pimlico*, but of course ...'

Here it comes, I thought. Now she's going to do that really annoying thing of telling me how the film ends and, as usual, I'm just going to let her.

'... the person I'm most annoyed with is that knob-end Walter.'

This was the last thing I'd expected to hear.

'I mean it this time: finished, finito, good night Vienna.'

I gulped air. Was she finally giving up the pretence that she and Walter were just good friends? Not only that, but she was actually confiding that she'd chucked him. This was huge. This was proper girl talk. Jenny was sharing. With me. Real, intimate, heartfelt stuff.

'Knob-head said he couldn't come to the meeting, and do you know why?'

It was Jenny's prerogative to insult him all she liked, but I had to be more circumspect. Apart from the fact that I genuinely liked Walter, if I slagged him off she'd probably end up forgiving him anyway and then I'd be the bad guy. She'd tell Walter the unpleasant knob-based names I'd called him, which would cause awkwardness.

I resolved to stay sympathetic, no matter what.

'Did he get stuck in Glasgow with his professor pals?'

'No, he went to Italy,' she said flatly, 'at a time like this, in the midst of the biggest crisis this village has ever known. Walter and his professor pals jumped on a plane to Florence, or "Firenze" as he called it on the phone. Knob. I told him he had to be here but he said the meeting in Florence was much more important. FFS. How can one of his fusty history meetings be more important than the future of our village? Crumbling ancient history, how can that be more important?' She moaned, 'Our history's being made right now. That knob can't see what's right in front of his eyes.'

It was my job to be supportive, not to bring up the fact that this was the complete opposite of what she'd said the last time we discussed Walter's history obsession.

'What's happening right here, right firkin now,' Jenny said, banging the counter, 'New history. That's what's important.'

Chapter 43

'No way, hers is blonde, guaranteed,' said Steven.

'Think about it,' said Mag, 'that bright blonde colour is out of a bottle, it's got to be.'

'Nah, she's a natural.'

'Are you kidding? Her eyes are brown, and look how dark her eyebrows are. And her skin is sallow.'

'You are so full of it,' scoffed Steven.

'I'm telling you, I can confidently predict that hers is dark and rich.'

'Rich?'

They had forgotten I was there. If I kept ironing, kept my head down and kept quiet, I could keep earywigging on their conversation, puerile though it was. I was in the kitchen, they were in the lounge, but I had left the door open a crack and I could hear everything.

'I mean plenty of it. A big healthy bush. Just the way I like it,' squeaked Mag.

Steven packed up laughing. I had to stifle a giggle too. They were discussing a young actress on TV.

'So what colour are Morag's?'

'Hey!' said Steven with a warning snarl.

'Ok, well then, take Charlotte Wilson, for instance, hers are indubitably red. She's got red hair on her head, ergo red pubes.

Hot Asian girl who works for G.I. – black hair on her head: black pubes. When they've dyed their hair then it's down to skin tone and eye colour. I can tell the colour of any woman's pubes just by looking at them,' Mag boasted.

'By looking at their pubes?' teased Steven.

'I wish,' said Mag ruefully.

Mag had become a regular visitor to Harrosie. They took it in turns: one day Steven would cycle over to Ethecom and help Mag on his inventing projects, and the next Mag would come to Harrosie. I didn't mind. After what Brenda had said about the kids in the village picking on him, I preferred it when they were where I could see them. Mag talked absolute nonsense, but it was sometimes entertaining nonsense and he didn't seem to notice or mind that I was often within earshot. Like most sixteen-year-old boys, Mag and Steven spent a lot of time discussing the anatomy of girls. If it wasn't pubes it was most likely breasts..

'H ha h ha h ha, a foam dome! That's brilliant, Stevo,' Mag was slapping his thigh and screaming with laughter.

'You've honestly never heard that before?' said Steven incredulous.

'Never, but it's brilliant. That's what Charlotte Wilson wears, h ha h ha, a foam dome. Or rather, two domes filled with high-density foam.'

'You fancy Charlotte Wilson; you're always talking about her.'

'I do not!' said Mag, outraged. 'Oh! Oh! Oh!'

Mag couldn't contain his excitement and slapped himself repeatedly on the chest, 'I've got a brilliant one, wait for it: a bresticle receptacle!'

Mag collapsed screaming and laughing again, but Steven maintained his composure. If I knew Steven and how competitive he could be, he'd be desperately trying to top Mag's suggestion. I put the iron down as quietly as I could and keeked through the kitchen door.

Steven nodded and grinned, 'Did you just make that up?'

'Of course!' screeched Mag.

'Quality,' says Steven, 'but bresticle isn't an actual word, and

173

technically you said *a* bresticle receptacle. Technically, there are usually two. Is it a technical bresticle receptacle?'

'Are you sceptical?' said Mag, generously feeding Steven the line.

Steven nodded, 'I'm sceptical about the bresticle receptacle.'

'I wouldn't worry, it's an ethical bresticle receptacle.'

And so it went. I tip-toed back to the ironing board and left them to it.

Although Mag was an oddball, Steven seemed to recognise that there was a lot he might learn from him.

Mag was always coming up with new schemes; he saw opportunities in everything and his enthusiasm and inventiveness were breathtaking. For instance, at the back of our garden the boys had found an abandoned nest of three raven chicks that had fallen out of a tree. Mag insisted that they keep them in our shed and both boys took great delight in caring for the chicks. Mag read up everything he could find about the breed, *C corvus corax*, he informed us, and, realising that the birds could be trained to follow certain basic commands, came up with an audacious plan to sell them as pets to the highest bidder on a Goth website.

He reckoned, and he was probably right, that affluent middle-class young Goths might pay good money for a black sinister-looking bird to sit on their shoulder. A raven might fulfil the role of witch's familiar: a shape-shifting vampire, it would look cool, attract black-lipped Goth girls and, best of all, scare the shit out of the Neds who harassed them. After all, it was only fair: Neds kept Rottweilers to tear Goths' throats out. Why shouldn't ravens peck Neds' eyes out? Luckily Brenda managed to talk Mag out of it and the birds were eventually returned to the wild.

Steven obviously enjoyed Mag's company, but I was still nervous about them going about together in public, being seen by the village kids. It had to happen; it was bound to happen sooner or later, and it did. One afternoon, when my hands were covered in flour and I was just getting ready to put an apple pie in the oven, my worst fears were realised.

Chapter 44

'Am I speaking with Trixie McNicholl?' said an American male voice.

'Yes, this is she,' I said grandly.

Another tourist looking for accommodation that I'd have to disappoint, no doubt.

'Thank you, Ma'am. We have a white male Caucasian, blue eyes, sandy-coloured hair, sixteen to eighteen years old, approximately five feet ten inches, a hundred and twenty-five pounds. We believe he may be your son. Can you confirm?'

I never drove so fast in my life. I screeched up to the front door of Faughie Castle and jumped out to be met by a tall, slim, very serious-looking young man. I thought I recognised him as one of the security guards who had rushed to Knox MacIntyre's side the other night.

'This way, Ma'am.'

'Where's Steven? I want to see my son,' I said, halfway between begging and demanding.

'Please don't worry, Trixie,' said Dinah.

Dinah walked towards me smiling and holding out her hands in greeting.

'Well, where is he?'

'He's here. He's quite safe but I'm afraid there's been an incident.'

'I'll kill him. What happened?'

Dinah laughed, 'That's exactly the way I am with my Roddy: once I know he's safe I want to kill him. Please, Trixie, sit down and I'll explain.'

Dinah's laughter could have wound me up but it actually had the opposite effect: if she was laughing things couldn't be all that bad. I took a deep breath, sat down, and relaxed a little. I felt my teeth, my buttocks and finally my blood vessels gradually unclench. Dinah's wee dog, Mimi, came to me and as I stroked her I felt my blood pressure return to almost normal.

'Can I offer you tea? I hesitate to offer you something stronger.'

I shook my head and Dinah and I shared a wee smile.

'Trixie, this is Mr Galbraith. You've already met, although I don't think you were introduced. Mr Galbraith and his colleagues are security experts, part of Mr MacIntyre's retinue. An hour ago they detained six boys and a man within the grounds of the estate. Your son, we think, is one of them. They're fine, all of them, they're down in the kitchen where another of Mr MacIntyre's staff is, I believe, offering them soup and crackers, but I'm afraid they haven't been very co-operative. The gentleman who is with the boys refused to give his name, or any information, and the rest of them followed suit. I thought I recognised your son, I saw you with him in the village the other day, and that's why I asked Mr Galbraith to call you. Thank you so much for coming, Trixie, I...'

'Did you say you were detaining them?'

'Eh,' Dinah gave an embarrassed wee laugh and suppressed a bigger cough, 'yes, I'm afraid so.'

'Can I ask why?'

Dinah looked at the security guy.

'It's standard practice, Ma'am,' said Galbraith, 'when security has been breached.'

'Right, but why are you detaining them? I mean, what have they done?'

'These are private grounds; any encroachment on the estate is trespass and a security risk. Additionally we suspect criminal damage.'

Dinah interrupted him, 'But we won't press charges. These are difficult circumstances, you understand, with feeling running so high in the village ...'

'You suspect? What evidence do you have?'

'Several of them were carrying tools or weapons,' said Galbraith.

'Honestly, it's nothing to worry about, Trixie,' said Dinah, 'Mr MacIntyre feels this doesn't need to become a police matter, that's why we called you. We hoped you could talk to them, explain the situation.'

I'd talk to them alright. What the hell was Steven doing with tools and weapons? Thank god she wasn't going to have him charged.

Dinah dropped her voice to a whisper now, 'Although the sale of the machair has gone through, Mr MacIntyre hasn't actually bought the castle yet, we're still in negotiations.'

'I understand. I'm so sorry my son has caused you this trouble, Dinah.'

'Please don't worry about it at all, I know what teenagers are like. Roddy was the same at that age.'

'I'll speak to them,' I said, 'don't you worry about that.'

Mr Galbraith walked me down the dingy corridor to the kitchen and as I approached I heard a man laughing. This didn't sound like a person who was worried about being arrested; this was the insouciant belly-rumbling chuckle of someone without a care in the world. It was a laugh I'd only heard a few times before but I knew it well enough.

Chapter 45

'Hello Jackie,' I said, my voice squeaking with the effort of controlling it, 'think this is funny, do you?'

Jackie had been laughing with Steven, but their mirth evaporated as soon as they saw me.

'We'll be right outside if you need us, Ma'am,' said Galbraith as he and his CIA Secret Police-type associate walked out of the kitchen.

'Thanks lads,' said Jackie giving them a sarcastic thumbs up. 'Appreciate the hospitality.'

Steven stifled a snigger.

Jackie and Steven were standing together obviously relaxed and enjoying themselves. Four boys I didn't recognise sat at the opposite end of the long kitchen table. Mag was sitting with his legs hugged tight to his chest up on the counter as far from the rest of them as it was possible to get.

'Are you here to spring us, Trixie?' said Jackie, causing Steven to giggle.

I ignored him and spoke directly to Steven, 'What the hell were you doing?'

In reply Steven put his head down and sulked.

'We didn't do anything, Mrs McNicholl,' whined Mag.

I ignored Mag and turned my beam on Jackie, 'You should

be ashamed of yourself, getting kids involved in your anarchistic carry on.'

'Och, it was just high jinks, nothing to worry about,' said Jackie.

'Jackie stopped them, Mrs McNicholl!' said Mag, his voice high with indignation. 'He came to help us.'

'I wasn't speaking to you,' I barked towards Mag.

'Well I'm speaking to you,' Jackie boomed back.

Stunned by his masterful authority, my gas was instantly at a peep. Everyone's was.

'Steven and his pal got chased in here by these hooligans,' Jackie continued, nodding towards the four boys sat at the other end of the table. The boys looked nervous and did nothing to deny it.

'It's true, Trixie,' said Mag, 'we had to run for our lives. If it hadn't've been for Jackie – we'd've been dead men.'

'They said you had weapons and tools.'

'That wee psycho did,' said Jackie, pointing to one of the boys, 'he was running through the woods with a tomahawk.'

'It missed my head by inches,' Mag squealed.

I looked at Steven but he refused to return my glance. I sat down and took three deep breaths. Then I took a few more. Then I stood up again and leaned into the face of Tomahawk Boy.

'Listen, Geronimo,' I said between gritted teeth, 'if you as much as look at my boy again I will personally chop up your goolies for firewood, got it? What's your name?'

Geronimo sat staring straight ahead, as did the other three stooges. They'd probably never encountered a Weegie psycho before, especially a Weegie psycho *mum* whose child they had threatened.

'Micky Smith's your name, eh?' said Jackie, 'Live out Annacryne way. I know your faither.'

Micky Smith was a small overweight kid with shockingly bad acne, the kind of acne that, although he couldn't have been more than seventeen, had left him with deep permanent craters in his face.

I felt sorry for his mother. I imagined her in pregnancy, giddy with anticipation, joyful when she delivered a healthy son, a cute pink-cheeked bouncing boy that grew into a bright-eyed clear-skinned schoolboy who, with the cruel onslaught of puberty, became a festering gargoyle of boils, suppurating sores and pus-filled carbuncles. A face that, literally, only a mother could love.

'Mr Robertson had a big spade,' said Micky, suddenly finding his voice and pointing at Jackie. As his face muscles worked to speak, his sores wept a little – it was painful to watch. 'He said he was going to stove my head in with it.'

'Well, lucky for you he didn't,' I spat, 'and you're lucky you're not all being arrested.'

'But we didn't do anything!' wailed Mag. 'Not fair!'

'I don't mean you, Mag, or Steven, or … Jackie, why were you in the woods – '

'That's my business.'

' – with a spade?'

'He told them he was ferreting,' said Mag, 'you know, trapping rabbits.'

'But,' I said carefully, I didn't want to say something stupid, 'don't you need a ferret for that?'

Steven and Jackie smirked again.

'Jackie told them it had escaped. He said his ferret is a free man, a Faughian, a Scot, a European, and not subject to American imperialism. He's going to sue for loss of ferret income.'

Everyone sniggered at that, even Micky. Clearly, despite the conflict with the tomahawk and the spade, they all admired Jackie's rebellious stance.

'Still and all,' I said, maintaining my serious tone, 'this is private land.'

'No such thing in Scotland,' said Jackie. 'The Land Reform Scotland Act of 2003 provides that we can all enjoy access rights, here and anywhere else for that matter.'

'Dinah could have had you arrested for criminal damage, and with good reason: you had tomahawks and spades after all,' I insisted. 'Just lucky I was able to talk her out of it. It wasn't easy, you know.'

'The only reason they didn't call the cops is because they don't want any bad publicity, not when the deal hasn't gone through yet.'

Jackie might be right.

'You, Micky Smith,' he said, 'if your tomahawk had hit that boy you'd be getting arrested now for murder. You'd get ten years at least. How would a good-looking bitch like you cope in prison?'

Micky Smith gulped, the others wriggled, scraping their chairs on the kitchen floor.

'Watch your back, laddie, because I'll be watching you.'

'Sorry, Mr Robertson,' Micky squeaked.

'I don't need your apology.'

'Sorry, Magnus, sorry Stevo.'

'That's more like it. Play nice, boys, eh?'

Jackie winked at me. I wasn't sure if it was an inclusive us-adults-together wink or he was showing off his reconciliation skills.

This wasn't the first time he'd saved Steven's neck and it probably wouldn't be the last. I didn't know what Jackie was doing in the woods, but when I thought about the damage that tomahawk could have done, I thanked god he was.

All the while I was processing this I looked at Jackie. Instead of turning away, as he usually did, he smiled. He walked over and gave the back of my chair a wee encouraging pat. There was no physical contact between us, he had only briefly touched the wood on the back of the chair, but my body surged with heat and relief.

Maybe he had finally forgiven me. Maybe now we'd move on and build a more lasting relationship. I really hoped so. This rapprochement, if this was what it was, was long overdue.

'Anyway,' said Jackie, 'they can't hold us here. I was only staying until you came. Dinah told me they'd called you; I didn't want you worrying.'

I smiled. 'Thank you so much, Jackie,' I gushed, 'I hardly know how to thank you, I ...'

'Come on lads,' he said briskly, 'we don't want to outstay our welcome. Who wants a lift? You can all pile in the back of the van.'

I knew Steven wouldn't want to come home in my car. I was glad he was going in the van with Jackie and the rest of them. Not that I had any warm feelings towards Smith and his cronies, but it was probably safer for Steven and Mag to at least have the veneer of friendship with these village thugs. Jackie had the right idea: throwing them together and making them 'play nice'. Keep your friends close and your enemies closer, that's what my mum Elsie always used to say, and she and Jackie had a lot in common.

As they were standing up to leave we could hear Dinah's heels clip-clop down the corridor.

'Has everything been sorted out?' she said, addressing both me and Jackie.

Jackie ignored her and stood by the door.

'Thank you so much, Jackie,' I repeated.

He smiled and gave me a mock military salute as he led the boys out. I turned to Steven but he hurried past me towards Jackie. I should have been frustrated by his rudeness but I was too happy to care. Steven was safe and Jackie liked me again, that was all that mattered.

'Handsome, isn't he?' said Dinah as she watched Jackie and the boys being escorted off the premises by the security guards. 'What's his name?'

'Jackie Robertson,' I said, my voice betraying my pride.

Dinah stood leaning in the doorway facing down the corridor but now swung round to face me, her arms folded.

'Oh,' she said flirtatiously, 'I think someone's been smitten.'

I laughed. I looked down and suddenly realised that my hands were spotted with white splodges of dried flour. I'd rushed out of the house in such a hurry I'd forgotten to wash up and now as I picked at each stubborn flour plaque I wondered what Dinah would think if she knew I'd tried to kiss Jackie that time. She'd probably think I was sick.

'You like him, don't you?' she teased.

'Actually it's a bit more complicated than that.'

'Oooh, complicated! I love complicated. I thought I sensed a tension between you two.'

'Well, there's certainly been plenty of tension, but not the kind you mean.'

'Oh, poo!' Dinah pouted. 'Don't be a spoilsport, Trixie, why ever not?'

'Because,' I said, preparing to say out loud the words that had puzzled and hurt and frustrated me for so long, 'because Jackie's my father.'

Chapter 46

After that bombshell, Dinah made tea and insisted on hearing my complicated family history. I told her how I'd inherited Harrosie and moved here, how the gardener had offered his services, how I'd fancied him, thrown myself at him. How I'd tried to snog him before discovering the awful truth:

That the man from whom I'd inherited was actually my grandfather – Jackie's dad. That while working here as a chambermaid my mum had had an affair with the sixteen-year-old son of the house, Jackie, of which I was the result. That, because of a bitter family feud, Jackie's father had passed him over and left the house to me. That Jackie, although he knew I was his daughter and knew that I was unaware of this, didn't have to guts to tell me. Hence me chucking myself at him. That, because he was so bitter, Jackie refused to acknowledge me, and, because I was so hurt, I'd drunkenly tried to out him at the ceilidh. The whole thing was a humiliating mess but I was glad I was finally able to talk about it. When I got to the bit about trying to snog Jackie I thought Dinah would be shocked, but she was confused.

'So,' she said, 'am I missing something?'

'I don't know, I ...'

She put her hand over mine, talking gently but firmly.

'If I've got this right you inherited Harrosie from your grandfather–'

'Well, when I say I inherited it, it's a bit more complicated than that. My grandfather never owned Harrosie outright, he owned a lease on it. I'll never be able to sell it, but in as much as he left the lease to me, I inherited it. That's what pissed Jackie off I think. He grew up in Harrosie, it had been his home until his father threw him out, he probably assumed the lease would come to him.'

'Yes, but your grandfather was entitled to bequeath the lease to whomsoever he chose. You were not involved or even aware of his decision so you certainly didn't steal anything, you did nothing wrong. Secondly, regarding the kiss: if a handsome man like Jackie is kind to a lonely woman she's going to want to snog him; that's a scientific fact. *You* didn't know he was your biological father. *He* did, however, and he might have mentioned it to you before you embarrassed yourself. Here too, you did nothing wrong. And thirdly, when you told the people at the ceilidh that Jackie was your dad you did nothing more than tell the truth; a truth he should have been proud to acknowledge.'

Dinah put her arm around me and looked into my face, 'You did nothing wrong.'

I stared into my tea not trusting myself to return her look. Dinah got the message and stood up and went to the tap to drip a little cold water in her tea.

Everybody loved Jackie, everybody in the village, including Walter and Jenny. My own family: Steven, Jackie's grandson, thought he was great. Even my own mother liked him enough to bear his child.

'Thanks, Dinah,' I said, 'you're the first person who's seen it from my side.'

Dinah sipped her tea and screwed up her face. She must have put too much cold water in it. She walked out of the kitchen, came back a moment later with a bottle of Auchensadie and poured a stiff measure into her tea cup.

'Top-up?' she offered, waving the bottle.

Without lifting my head I gave one short definite nod and she poured a generous glug in my cup.

'There's another thing we have in common,' said Dinah, 'we're both living in the houses we were conceived in.'

'Yeesh, I've never thought about that,' I said, 'I'd rather not dwell on my old mum doing the mattress mambo with Jackie.'

'I had always thought that Faughie would be the place I would die,' said Dinah, staring into the bottom of her mug.

'Inverfaughie won't be my final resting place,' I said slugging my whisky-tea.

Dinah pulled a twenty packet of cigarettes out of her back pocket.

'Want one?' I shook my head. Even if I was unable to resist the whisky there was no way I was going back to smoking again. It was frightening.

So as not to tempt me, Dinah shifted to the other end of the table, sat down and lit up. She dragged so hard on her cigarette you would think it owed her money, sucking down every last molecule of the deliciously moreish nicotine. From this distance I liked the smell of the cigarette smoke. It reminded me of long-ago nights out in pubs and clubs, the exotic hypnotic romantic smell of immortality and youthful decadence, and I felt the haunting pangs of self-denial. Dinah had set out a plate of posh biscuits and I teeth-tore the wrapper off one.

But up close Dinah smelled quite differently. Up close her smell made me think of old pubs when they first opened in the morning. Her perfume had damp gothic top notes, the sweet decay of dead lilies, and when she'd leaned into my face I'd caught a whiff of rotting gums and guts. No wonder she had such a worrying cough.

I devoured the Fortnum & Mason biscuit. I scrunched up the wrapper and casually stuffed in it my jeans pocket. I'd show it to Jenny later and see if she could source an order from somewhere.

'I'm even more worried now that MacIntyre might pull out of the deal,' said Dinah.

I nodded, understanding her anxiety.

'I know how you feel. I'm stuck here until Global Imperial pay up what they owe me. I suppose we're both in the same boat: we both need cash and we're both depending on rich Americans to decide our fate.'

'You make it sound terribly dramatic. I suppose it is. And what will be your eventual fate, Trixie?'

'Glasgow, my home town, that's my destiny. I feel about Glasgow the way you feel about Faughie. I made a mistake coming here. I don't have any of your happy childhood memories of this place.'

'But that's all they are: memories. My family are gone, there's no one here who needs me.'

I couldn't disagree. Dinah's family had enjoyed the grace and favour of ancient monarchs but there was nothing left for her here now.

'But you, Trixie, you still have your business.'

'Och, away, I'm only running the B and B to raise the deposit for a flat in Glasgow. Believe me, Dinah, I'd do anything to get out of Faughie.'

Chapter 47

It was on the news, not the *Chanter* or Faughie FM, but the real news, the 6 o'clock news on the telly. Lead story: that's how big it was. I jumped in the car and headed for the shop to hear it straight from the horse's mouth, but the horse had bolted. Jenny had cantered off to give an international press conference with the best legal minds in Europe.

Jenny, Walter and Brenda, on behalf of Faughie Council, were disputing the compulsory purchase and subsequent sale of the machair by the Westminster government on *a non domino* grounds: that is to say, it wasn't the government's property to sell in the first place.

'Oh, and listen to this,' said Betty Robertson, who was minding the shop and hosting a small Highland gathering of Inverfaughie residents, 'the remote village is now at the centre of the greatest legal challenge to the Westminster government since that raised by Mahatma Gandhi.'

Jan was there, Jackie too, and all the usual suspects from Faughie Council. My stock was rising: both Jan and Jackie greeted me with smiles and a friendly nod when I walked in. The two men were standing more or less side by side. I tried to move in beside them but got stuck behind a display of tinned berries that Jenny had assembled in a giant stepped pyramid on the floor. In the packed-out shop, Betty was all of a twitter, reading to her eager audience the latest press headlines and updates from Jenny and Walter.

'Oh, Jenny's just heard from the Catalan parliament,' said Betty, scrolling down and reading from her tablet, 'they're backing us 100 per cent.'

The crowd burst into applause. This whole kerfuffle had been brought about by the manky old manuscript Walter had pulled out of the peat bog. I already knew, because Jenny had moaned so much about it, that he had taken it to a pal of his in Glasgow. What I didn't know, until I heard it on the news, was the impact this prehistoric bit of lambskin was likely to have on life in Inver-faughie. Walter had taken it to his pal Professor McRitchie, who had immediately called upon the services of some of her colleagues at Glasgow University and was able to arrange for the document to be translated and carbon-dated. When the results were in, Walter and Professor McRitchie had set out on a whistle-stop tour visiting academics in the fields of science, law and history, in Brussels, Florence, Rome and finally London. Such was the authority the manuscript had acquired that on arriving in London, they were ushered into an immediate meeting with the Prime Minister and his advisors.

The best legal minds in Europe were in complete agreement: 'The Faughie Accord' as the manuscript was apparently called, legitimately established Faughie and the lands pertaining to it as a sovereign state. This agreement predated the Act of Union of Scotland with England by some fifty years. This meant that Faughie was independent of Scotland, and therefore independent of Britain. If this was the case, Faughie's machair was not under Westminster's jurisdiction.

Not surprisingly, the Westminster government took a different view. They couldn't dispute the authenticity of the document, but the Prime Minister's ministers argued that, within the prescription and limitations of Scots law, as Faughie had not operated as a sovereign state or even been recognised as such for many hundreds of years, the accord was unenforceable. Walter demanded on our behalf that the matter be referred for adjudication to the Court of Justice of the European Union.

No one in the shop knew yet what 'Faughie and the lands pertaining to it' might mean, but everyone had an opinion. Was it just the machair? Might it include Inverfaughie? But even if it extended as far as the entire Faughie river system, it could never survive as a sovereign state, could it? Independence for the wee village was a cute idea but it wasn't workable, was it?

In between text communiqués from Walter and Jenny, playful discussion of *what if* scenarios broke out in corners of the shop. The notion that we could be standing in a country independent of any other seemed so absurd that few people seemed to take it seriously. If anyone was taking it seriously, and I suspected that Jackie and some others might be, they disguised it beneath flippant banter and jokes.

'Oh, and this just in,' said Betty, obviously enjoying her role as town crier, 'this one's from Walter. "We demand our entitlement to a fair hearing as laid down by Article 6(1) of the European Convention on Human Rights."'

Everyone cheered. The mood was of good-humoured rebellion and every bulletin was met the same way.

'He goes on to say,' said Betty doing a pretty good impersonation of Walter, 'I remind all Faughians that we are not, nor have we ever been, subject to the laws and control of the United Kingdom. Furthermore, conforming to Westminster rule may be misinterpreted as acceptance of such laws and control, and may be injurious to our case. Until we are able to establish our own fair and equitable legal system, I strongly recommend that all citizens of Faughie should recognise only one law: that of natural justice.' Among the noisy clapping and yelling a woman at the counter asked Betty, 'What does that mean?'

'Hold on, hold on,' said Betty, lifting her arms and lowering them slowly in an attempt to calm things down, 'before anyone gets any ideas about looting and pillaging, it means that we should conduct ourselves in a reasonable and dignified manner.'

This appeal to our collective sense of decency had a sobering but not dispiriting effect.

'Yes, but it won't stop us celebrating,' said Bobby Fenton, who no doubt saw this potential resolution to the machair dispute as a reprieve for his grass-hungry milkers. 'How much does Jenny charge for a bottle of that champagne?'

'I'll happily sell you it, Mr Fenton,' said Betty, 'but you can't open it in the shop, Jenny's only licensed as an off sales.'

'You heard what the man said, Betty. Walter told us to disregard UK law, natural justice: so long as I'm harming nobody I can do what I like. We all can. Everybody,' Bobby yelled, 'we can do what we like. Who wants to chip in for champagne?'

Chapter 48

Well, that was it. When Bobby popped the cork out of Spor's Finest Premier Cru, the genie came fizzing out of the bottle. It made the TV news that night as a last, feelgood, comedy item: the quaint formerly law-abiding village flouting the law and apparently getting away with it. Inevitably, the story went viral. Within days news programmes around the world picked it up. Using Spaghetti Western angles and a suitably moody soundtrack, Inverfaughie was framed as a remote outlaw bolthole, with Faughie's tidy white cottages as disreputable saloons.

But unregulated consumption of alcohol was the least of it. There were more important things happening: Knox MacIntyre had left for London, vowing to get the machair back. He maintained that the machair was legally his and that his plans for the polo resort were going ahead. When he left in his private helicopter, Jackie and some of the farmers turned out to give him a send-off of boos, whistles and jeers. Jenny tssked and said it was unseemly and bad for business. The cows were back on the machair and now sharing it with the film crew – Faughie Council had agreed a new deal – so long as G.I. toed the line. This was great news: I'd finally get paid and could put down a deposit on a flat in Glasgow.

While the case for independence was being tested in Luxembourg the sovereign country of Faughie was declared to be an area of nearly one hundred square miles encompassing the loch, the coastline and a few surrounding villages.

Walter announced that as Faughie was now beyond the control of the Scottish or Westminster parliaments, Faughie needed its own. As our sitting M.S.P. Malcolm Robertson was sadly deceased, Inverfaughie's democratically elected councillors should act as a caretaker government. As a replacement M.S.P. was no longer necessary or indeed valid, an interim leader would be sought from amongst Faughie Council members. A ballot would be held as soon as it could be organised.

Surprise surprise, a few hours later Jenny announced that she was withdrawing from the M.S.P. election campaign with immediate effect and running as a candidate for interim leader of Faughie.

These were huge historical events for Inverfaughie, and for Britain, but the story was complex: too many strands and possible outcomes, too many unanswerable questions. The media continued to represent Faughians as lawless Mexican banditos – it was a simpler and more amusing narrative.

Independence for Faughie was hard for the people of Faughie to believe in. No matter how often Walter proclaimed it they were scared to believe it. It didn't seem real. Everyone seemed wary and self-conscious, as though expecting a hidden camera crew to jump out and reveal the giant hoax. Everyone was bracing themselves for the reaction shot when they'd have to laugh sheepishly at themselves. Independence was a challenge to the imagination. If it was in a book it would seem too far-fetched, like something out of a Hollywood film. But like when the movie first came to Inverfaughie, everyone quickly got used to the idea and found ways to turn it to their advantage.

Walter insisted that as we were not British and needed to establish ourselves as such we should pay no further tax to the Westminster system. People were quick enough to take up that initiative, although Brenda strenuously encouraged everyone to open a credit union account and put money aside against future tax bills. The immediate effects were all positive. Business was brisk. Customers came from Inverness and further south to take advantage of the bargains. With no pesky tariffs like VAT or alcohol duty to worry about, sales of everything rocketed, especially salmon and whisky. Bobby Fenton's first naughty spurt of champagne quickly became a torrent of unregulated liquor. With whisky production and sales now untaxed, Faughie was experiencing a liquid gold rush. After only two weeks the tweed mill had sold its entire stock and was once again running at full strength, three shifts working round the clock, barely keeping up with demand. Even Global Imperial were happy. *Freedom Come All of You* was famous before it was even released. As word spread, tourists from around the world added Inverfaughie to their essential Edinburgh–Loch Ness–Skye itinerary. The village was heaving. Inverfaughie, much touted by Jenny as the ancient capital of Faughie, was where, for a price, tourists could have their passport stamped in the official state capital passport office, which was, coincidentally, Jenny's sub post office and shop.

Unfortunately, I wasn't in a position to cash in, not right away at least. Of course if I didn't have the firkin Claymores clogging up the house I could have turned my front room into a shebeen and made a fortune selling moonshine. The tourism boom was passing me by, but once the movie left town, I'd be able to hike my prices up and make a killing like everyone else.

Traffic now was a nightmare. With the increased tourism it was nose to tail in and out of the village all day every day. Bouncer and I were actually quicker walking down there but if I needed to pick up my order I was forced to take the car. Getting parked involved sitting like a mug in the motor for upwards of an hour until a space became available. Even then, boy racer tourists would sometimes screech forward, execute a handbrake turn and nick my spot.

Shopping had lost all its glamour. Gone were the days of the long lazy browse, the slow perusal of Jenny's weird and wonderful stock, the sneaky read of her gossip mags while she was in the back, the bartering of news, gossip and advice, the occasional cuppa across the counter when the shop was quiet. The shop was never quiet now. Any time I went in there now I had to stand in a long queue and Jenny never had time to chat. She was too busy raking it in: selling tourist tat and stamping bogus passport visas. I wouldn't have minded, but she never had any free time in the evenings either. The shop was now open till ten every night except when there were Faughie Council special committee meetings. Jenny had dropped hints that I might want to join the special committee but she hadn't insisted. I managed to dodge that bullet.

I wasn't impressed with the way things were going; what with the traffic and the drunks and tourists everywhere, independence wasn't shaping up to be all that.

Chapter 49

Steven didn't answer when I knocked on his bedroom door and then I heard him in the bathroom further down the hall. The door was wide open, he must be decent. I walked straight in.

Decent was not what was in there.

Steven sat on the toilet with his head hung low, repeatedly wiping his arms and hands. He had only a towel around his waist, still dripping from the shower. When I walked in he looked up, his expression quickly turning to hooded guilt.

'Where's Mag?' I asked, suspicious.

'What?' said Steven.

He looked confused, shell-shocked.

'Eh, he's at home,' he mumbled into the hand towel, 'up at Ethecom.'

I opened my mouth to ask him what was going on when my attention was caught by the water lying in the bottom of the shower. There were wee blobs of dark red dancing in the water. Each of the blobs was surrounded by a watery pink halo. They were dissolving and colouring the water pink. I looked at Steven's clothes, lying in a pile just to the side of the shower. His favourite baseball boots, his baggy jeans and top were all spattered with blood. Lots of it. My eyes frantically surveyed his body but there was nothing amiss. No cuts on him. I didn't understand; that amount of blood must surely mean a nasty gash at the very least. Steven looked into my face.

'We killed Micky Smith,' he said.

'What?'

'We slaughtered him. It was kinda, I don't know, satisfying.'

'What?' I repeated.

Steven doubled over laughing.

'We didn't slaughter *that* Micky Smith!' he squealed in delight.

'Well, how many Micky Smiths are there?' I asked feebly.

'Look,' Steven said, his laughter subsiding, 'not the humanoid Micky Smith, the goat Micky Smith. The one who butted you. Ha ha! You thought I'd murdered the humanoid!'

'I never did! And anyway, why does the goat have the same name as the – humanoid?'

'Mag names all the goats. He said that one looked like Smith: wee, fat and ugly. Take away the tomahawk and you can't tell them apart. He got picked because his balls haven't dropped, he's useless for siring. I wish we had slaughtered the humanoid but we had to make do with the goat. We butchered him good. We dragged him into the shed to have his throat cut. He struggled, he knew it was coming.'

I felt my stomach heave.

'Please Steven,' I pleaded, 'I don't want to know.'

'Aye, you'll want to know this: Brenda gave me a shoulder joint for braising. She said we could make curry, and she gave me the recipe. We've got a pressure cooker, haven't we? Brenda says that'll make it tender and energy efficient. I thought I'd cook it now for tomorrow night's dinner, let it rest and soak up the curry flavours, the guys'll love it.'

I lifted my head. A free meal and I didn't have to cook. I was starting to feel better. 'See?' I said, trying to reinstate some sense of normality, 'I told you you'd like it up here. You'd never get an experience like that in Glasgow.'

Steven nodded. 'Fair doos, you're right.'

And that was a first, Steven telling me I'd got something right.

'Mag is training Jan and me. Jan is crap at it but Mag says I'm a natural,' he continued, 'he says by Christmas I'll be slaughtering beasts on my own.'

'Christmas? Do you want to come up for Christmas?'

I didn't know how to break it to him, but by Christmas I'd be long gone, never to set foot in Inverawful again.

'I'm not coming up,' he said, 'I'm staying.'

'Sorry?'

'I'm staying here, I'm joining Ethecom; I decided today.'

'What? What about college?'

'I'm not going to college.'

'But didn't you say you wanted to improve your options for uni?'

'I'm not going to uni either.'

My mouth fell open. 'Steven, what are you saying?'

'I'm saying I'm not going to sixth form college, or university. I'll learn all the skills I want in Ethecom, I'll learn more important stuff here. I'm becoming a member.'

'No you are not. Your dad will have something to say about this. You're going to uni like we all agreed.'

'Mum, I'm sixteen, I can make my own choices.'

'You're not going to get yourself stuck in this wee backwoods village, I won't allow it.'

'They've offered me an apprenticeship.'

'Ethecom are paying wages?'

'A share of the profits.'

'What profits?' I screeched. 'They don't have any money!'

'Mum, listen to yourself. You used to say money isn't everything.'

'I was only saying that because we didn't have any! Money isn't everything, but everything's money, and if you don't have it, you're stuffed. You'll learn that soon enough when you don't have mum and dad to pay for everything.'

His face contorted as he spat the words at me, 'I don't want money. I want something better, something real, I want ...'

'Money's the realest thing there is–'

Steven hunched forward on the toilet seat, flexed his fists and roared.

'Will you just shut up!'

At such close quarters, in such an echoey bathroom, it was painful on the ears. I think it frightened us both. Steven had pumped himself up so much the towel around his middle was straining and threatening to come loose. With what seemed like a tremendous effort of will, he brought the volume down to a quiet murmur, which only made it more sinister.

'Stop it!' he whispered. 'Just. Stop. Trying to convince me. I'm joining Ethecom. I've made up my mind.'

Chapter 50

I wasn't relishing the prospect of having to sit through yet another meeting but I knew Jackie would be there.

I got there early, I even managed to get a seat, and waited for the show to begin. I'd never been to a hustings before and I was pretty sure I wasn't going to like it. Apart from Jenny there were three other candidates: Calum McLean, the fly fisherman from the last meeting, Dr Andrew McKenzie, our public-spirited GP, and – of course, she just had to get her oar in – housewife, committee member and rose-grower extraordinaire: Betty Robertson. Or as Walter was calling her, Mrs Elizabeth Mason Robertson.

Betty led off the husting and man, could that woman hust. She spoke for forty minutes, without notes, and the way Betty told it, we were all going to be millionaires. She'd had her hair done and wore a beautiful pale blue suit that she must have bought special. She spoke much slower than she usually did, which I found soothing and almost made me forget about the total hash she had made of the original machair negotiations. It was Betty Robertson who'd got us into this guddle in the first place. She had some cheek standing for Interim Leader.

Calum McLean was nervous; he kept forgetting his lines and having to stop and squint at his notes, but his policies seemed a lot like Betty's in that he was keen not to let any foreigners into Faughie. Dr McKenzie was brief, informative and self-effacing;

he hadn't quite got the idea of politics and clearly wasn't going to fare very well. Jenny was the popular candidate. When she stood up to speak everyone cheered, mostly because she was introduced by Walter as 'Ms Jennifer Haddock Robertson'.

'As is the tradition in Inverfaughie, I'm using my middle name to distinguish me from any other candidates who share the fine Robertson name,' she said, nodding graciously to Betty.

'My mother was a Haddock. From Peterhead,' she said, with great dignity, 'I come from a long line of Haddocks.'

This was met with good-natured laughter; she already had everyone on side. She went on to remind us that she had been the councillor to open a dialogue with the Scottish government, she had been in negotiations with the Westminster minister; as council representative she had gone with Walter and spoken to the world's media about Faughie's newly established independence. She had proven credentials as an international stateswoman.

There was then a debate. Between the candidates and the audience there was no shortage of raucous and passionate banter. I had no idea politics could be so much fun. It was obvious to everyone who was going to win. Despite a feisty performance from Betty, Jenny gently and respectfully wiped the floor with her. It was like putting a girl guide up against Nelson Mandela. I should have brought popcorn. Then they took the vote. We put our hands up and Jenny won hands down. Even Dr McKenzie voted for her.

'Cheers for voting for me, everyone,' she said, by way of an acceptance speech, 'I'll do my best. So, it's quite simple: to win our independence we have two tasks: convince the European Court of Justice, and convince the people of Faughie. Some of us will be called to Luxembourg to give testimony: you farmers, businesspeople, ordinary members of the community, Ethecom. I'm counting on everyone to stand together to present our case but we can only prove that it's the will of the people if we ask the people. And it has to be legally binding. The world will be watching and we have to be squeaky clean. We have to be seen to be scrupulously democratic. I move that we organise a full and formal referendum asap.'

When the meeting ended, I had to ram my way through the crowd, apologising as I rammed, to get to the door before Jackie left.

'Hi Jackie!' I yelled, still trapped behind two particularly mulish farm wifies.

'Trixie,' he replied, his head down, but he waited for me.

'Good meeting, eh?' I said.

'Aye.'

Outside the hall we stood and looked at each other; or rather, I looked at Jackie while he stared at the ground. After a few moments of this Jackie slowly moved off and, not knowing what else to do, I followed. He was escorting me to my car. This was sweet and gentlemanly but I realised that once we got to the car, having done his duty, he would excuse himself. There was no time for pleasantries; I had to dive right in.

'Steven says he's going to join the Ethecom community.'

Jackie didn't say anything at first, perhaps expecting me to continue, but when I didn't he spoke.

'Is he now?'

I was pleased and relieved to hear a note of disapproval in his voice.

It had occurred to me that Jackie might not necessarily be on my side. He might selfishly think it was a good idea for his only grandson to live nearby: a family member to look out for him when he got old, but thankfully that didn't seem to be the case.

'He's been invited to join as an apprentice. They're not even paying him a wage.'

Jackie screwed up his face, disbelieving, 'Huh?'

The concept of working and not being paid was obviously as alien to Jackie as it was to me.

'I know!' I said, 'it's exploitation. They want a strong young lad for the heavy lifting. If the Ethecom hippies want to farm medieval style, well, that's their business. Let them break their own backs but my son is nobody's donkey. Steven has a place in sixth form college to go to in September and next year he's off to university.'

'Hmmm,' said Jackie, in what sounded like agreement.

'So you'll back me up?'

'Hmmm.'

'If you could speak to him, Jackie, remind him that there's a wider world out there. Tell him not to squander his life here.'

Jackie stopped when we reached my car.

'Is that what you think I've done? Squandered my life?'

'No! I ... Look, Steven's clever, he's got the chance to go to university, to have a career in whatever he fancies, a few weeks ago he was talking about studying architecture. It's different for you, Jackie, you were born here, you didn't know any different.'

Jackie sighed heavily, gutted probably by my impression of him as a small-town hick. I made a mental note, once I got home, and in the privacy of my own bedroom, to kick my own head in. I really should have learned by now that insulting people wasn't an effective way to win them over.

'Sorry,' I gushed, 'I didn't mean it like that.'

'But I *did* know different. You're forgetting my years in the navy. I've seen the wider world out there. That's why I came back to Inverfaughie.'

'Yeah, but at least you got to see it, you got to make the choice. Steven has hardly seen the end of his nose yet.'

'True,' he conceded.

We stood in silence at the side of my car for a few moments. Anyone passing would have thought we'd lost the keys.

'So you'll talk to him?'

'What difference would it make?'

'He looks up to you, Jackie.'

He nodded and didn't try to deny it.

'Yes, but we must respect his wishes.'

'No,' I said, my face flushing, 'we absolutely must not. It's our job to respect Steven's best interests, not his latest mad notion.'

'Stevo's his own man,' Jackie said, shrugging in the helpless fatalistic way Steven and his pals often did.

'Stevo?' I sneered angrily, that's all I needed: Jackie getting down-with-the-kids. 'When did he become Stevo? You just don't want to do the hard part, Jackie, the thankless task of being a boring sensible grandparent. You only want to be the cool dude big brother figure he admires.'

'I don't think ...'

'I'm not saying it's your fault, Jackie. I know you're new to it, but to be an effective grandparent you need to – to grow up.'

Jackie laughed, chortling away to himself. I smiled anxiously, for such a horribly tactless blurt he seemed to be taking it well.

'Good night, Trixie. Safe home,' he said, as he walked away still laughing.

Chapter 51

Jan had a new job. As well as being the postie, and the guitar tutor, he was now the village bus driver. Ethecom had bought an old Routemaster at auction and were running a bus service to Inverness. Since the village had got so horribly busy they were trying to reduce pollution and traffic congestion.

They'd converted the Routemaster engine to run on filtered chip pan oil and set up deals with hotels around the coast. The tourists loved it; they were always jumping onto the road to take pictures of it and sniff up the smell of fried haddock it left in its wake, but second-hand vegetable oil wasn't the only thing Ethecom were converting. They were obviously using this new service for proselytising. Once they had people trapped on the speeding bus they'd be preaching to the captive audience about their wonderful home-grown, hand-knitted, solar-panelled, eco-gadget, electric-shoe lifestyle. They were becoming a cult; trying to control everything, to run every aspect of village life. I for one was beginning to resent their intrusion into Highland traditions, even if Highland traditions were wasteful and toxic. They had no right to intrude, especially on my family. They were brainwashing my son and I needed help.

The Claymores were no use at all. When I asked Rudi to speak to Steven he shied away.

'None of my business,' he muttered, 'that would be a family matter.'

He was right, of course, it was a family matter, one I wasn't keen to get into with Steven's dad. Bob would blame me and he'd probably be right too. If I hadn't insisted that Steven come and spend the summer with me he'd never have got involved in Ethecom's groovy flower-power love-in.

I phoned Jenny expecting to get her ansaphone and I did. Since she had become Interim Leader she was far too busy to talk to the likes of me. She didn't have time for my problems. No, nowadays it was all committee meetings and infrastructure and tax raising. She'd even delivered a speech about how funding essential services had to be our priority; I was lower down her priority list than ever. I was missing my wee pal. I missed her practical help and sensible advice; most of all I missed her patter. I didn't even bother leaving a message, what was the point?

Two seconds later my phone rang.

'Trixie?'

'Is this what's it's come to, call screening?'

'We are currently experiencing a high volume of calls.'

'You are so full of ...'

'I'm not screening *you*. I called you straight back, didn't I?'

'S'pose.'

'So. What can I do you for?'

'A chinwaggle.'

'Chinwaggle?'

'Aye, you know, you used to be a past master at it.'

'Past mistress, actually, and post mistress, but we'll let that one go. Is it Steven?'

'Och, but with affairs of state and what not, you're far too busy to take time out of your busy schedule ...'

'Can you pop round tonight?'

This put the brakes on my sarcasm.

'What time?' I asked, my eagerness all too obvious.

'Well, I can't until at least after nine. No, better than that: can you turn up dead on nine? That way I can get rid of them. Oh, and can you pick up fish and chips from the Caley on your way? My treat. I'll be too knackered to cook by that time of night.'

I was coming out of the Caley with a steaming bag of two fish suppers – Ali made them extra large but no extra charge: friends in high places – when who should I see lurking in the car park but Dinah.

'Contraband,' she said, 'tax-free ciggies, I'm waiting for a delivery.'

'You'll stunt your growth,' I said, and walked on with a cheery wave. I didn't want to hang about, the chips would get cold and the fish batter soggy if I stopped. I was already gunning the engine when she stuck her head in my window.

'Mmmm,' said Dinah, filling her nostrils with the aroma, 'that smells jolly good! You having a night off?'

'Yeah, something like that,' I said, smiling, ramming the gear stick into reverse.

'Going anywhere nice?'

'I'm just popping up to Jenny's.'

'It's lovely that you're such good friends,' she said, a wee bit wistfully it seemed. 'Well I can see you're in hurry so I won't keep you, but I wondered if you and Bouncer wanted to come over to the castle again some time?'

'I don't know, Dinah, I'm trying not to drink.'

'No, I didn't mean ... We could just walk the dogs, good healthy fun, any time that suits.'

'Ok, I'll see.'

I pulled out past her and gave her the slow arm-in-the-air salute.

'See you tomorrow then!' she yelled after me.

*

'Perfect timing,' said Jenny, when she opened the door. I tried to hand her the bag with our dinner in it but she flitted it away.

'No,' she whispered, 'that's part of my fiendish plan. I'll make myself scarce. You go straight through and plunk yourself down in amongst them. Hopefully you'll embarrass them out the door.'

As I walked into the living room I spotted the first flaw in her plan. There were no spare seats. Every available chair, stool and bit of couch was occupied by wild-eyed coffee'd-up committee members who fell into a shocked hush when they saw me. I smiled and nodded hello to Moira Henderson the distillery guide, Brenda from Ethecom, Andy the superstar DJ, Walter, and everyone else who, unlike me, had been drafted into this elite cabinet. They smiled back and stared until Walter was gallant enough to give me his seat. I sat with the flagrantly fragrantly steaming bag in my lap. People sniffed and looked away. Awkward silence then ensued, during which I noticed the absence of Mrs Elizabeth Mason Robertson.

'No Betty tonight?' I asked, but no one was inclined to answer. They looked, with shifty glances, one to the other. Something was afoot but whatever it was, they weren't telling. I obviously hadn't had security clearance. I wasn't going to let them cow me into silence so I carried on regardless. 'Is this the flag then?' I asked, somewhat obviously.

Draped across the dining table was a huge yellow, pink and green tricolour. I knew from the incessant emails Brenda sent out every day that they'd run a competition amongst the schoolkids to design a flag for Faughie. Michael Robertson's design had won. I remembered that the green colour represented the fertile fields and yellow the broom flowers the area was known for. The acid yellow blossom always made me imagine Inverfaughie as an old lady wearing a vibrant party dress.

'What does the pink stand for then?' I asked and caught Moira's eye.

'Eh, no reason,' she said hesitantly, 'but it's a lovely colour, isn't it? Nice.'

'We chose pink because we couldn't find another national flag with pink in it,' Walter added.

'Yes, that too,' agreed Moira.

'The Anglicus Coat of Arms is obviously what they expect, but it's so obsequious,' said Walter, and everyone nodded. 'The triband flag design dates back to the sixteenth century. Due to its associations with liberty, republicanism and indeed even,' he lowered his voice to a mischievous whisper, '*revolution*, it's perfect for us.'

No one had anything to add to this so there was another round of nodding until the haar of silence again descended and settled on us. I almost asked about the cardboard box full of rosettes made up in the Faughie colours, but I didn't want Walter to go off on one again so I shut up and let the fishy chippy smell do its work.

'Well I suppose we must call it a night then,' said Walter, his disappointment obvious, 'and let you get your dinner.'

As Moira put her tartan cape on, the others took the hint and prepared to leave. Now that she'd heard movement, Jenny came back into the room to find Moira pumping everyone's hand, thanking everyone profusely, even me. I smiled graciously and accepted her thanks. I'd learned that afternoon, from another email update from Brenda, that the committee had successfully agreed a deal with the distillery. Moira and her co-workers' jobs were now safe.

The distillery owners, a multinational corporation, had reported a ten-fold increase in sales, which obviously pleased them, but they were concerned about the effect Faughie's 'political instability' might have on their supply lines. They had calculated that even if all arable land in Faughie were to be converted to barley production for their exclusive use, it would still be nowhere near enough for the amount of whisky they wanted to produce. They would have to import it. The owners, no doubt nobbled by Westminster, had temporarily shut down production and laid off the staff. A delegation led by Brenda had made them an offer they couldn't refuse. Faced with compulsory purchase of the plant and remaining stock, the distillery decided that not only were they happy to retain ownership and restart production, but they were delighted to contribute appropriately by paying a levy on all the water they used.

As Brenda reasoned in her follow-up email, if they could produce Scotch whisky anywhere else in the world, they would have done so long ago. The distinct qualities of soft Scottish water, (peat, mineral content and so forth – I skimmed that part of the email) were what gave Scotch whisky its distinctive taste. I was of course too modest to mention my own personal contribution; perhaps my humble alimentary ejaculation had played a part. But the distillery was open again, the staff kept their jobs and a lucrative slice of whisky profits would now come directly into Faughie council's coffers. The sovereign state of Faughie was going to be pure minted.

Chapter 52

'Have you seen my wee rosettes?' Jenny asked, as soon as she had hustled the last committee member out.

I ignored this and asked a few questions of my own. I'd sensed hot gossip and, like a dog smelling dinner, I wouldn't be distracted.

'What's the story with Betty? Why was she not here tonight? Have I missed an email?'

'She's probably gathering her forces before she makes an announcement. We'll probably get an email in the morning.'

'What forces?' I gasped. Jenny used such thrilling language these days.

'She's setting up the No vote campaign.'

'No to what?'

'FFS Trixie, try to keep up: the no to leaving Britain campaign. She and some of the other committee members feel it won't be in Faughie's interests to go it alone so they're setting up a 'No to Independence' campaign.'

'Oh, right,' I said, 'so does that mean that you're political enemies now?'

'Och, don't you start; the press will soon be working that angle. No, we're opponents. As I've been telling everybody all night, this is good for us. This will actually strengthen our case in Luxembourg.

It lets us demonstrate that we aren't a tinpot dictatorship, as the gutter press are trying to paint us. The referendum will show that, despite a pro-British lobby, we have the majority. We can stand a bit of opposition and, anyway, we need them. If we don't have opposition we don't have democracy. It makes us accountable. Now, can we move on please and you can tell me what do you think of my rosettes?'

'Yes,' I said automatically, 'they're lovely.'

'Not too gaudy?'

'Nope.'

'The folk in the mill are running them up for me.'

'So, anyone wearing one of these is on your side and not Betty's, is that the idea?'

'Well, I prefer to see it as a show of support rather than a divisive measure, and they're not just for voters, the tourists love them as well – they're going like snow off a dike in the shop. The mill is struggling to keep up with the orders.'

'Is this you Keeping It Niche, Keeping It Expensive?' I said, ingenuously.

Jenny laughed, 'Hah! Well remembered, indeed I am; why would I not? I'm getting a cracking mark-up on them.'

'You know,' I said, once we were settled down at the table and eating with our fingers, 'Walter was right. He said that Faughie could be rich beyond the dreams of avarice. Looks like it could be.'

'Huh! Typical idealistic socialist. It's pathetic; that man sickens me.'

Jenny's unexpected vitriol made me laugh so much I nearly honked my pickled onion through my nose.

'That's a bit harsh, even for you. You love Walter.'

As usual she blanked my sneaky Walter-love jibe.

'Och, they're all getting carried away with this small victory,' she said. 'They're forgetting we have to satisfy Luxembourg that we have the means to pay for public services and employees – police, teachers, dinner-ladies; old Joe, the lollipop man, for instance, who's going to pay his wages? Not to mention all the coffin-dodging pensioners we have.'

'You can talk: typical politician; only looking after your own interests. You yourself are foremost amongst Faughie's coffin-dodging pensioners.'

'For Faughie's sake, I told you not to mention coffin-dodging pensioners!' she said, and then spoiled it by laughing.

She was on great form. Despite working in committee meetings every night, sometimes until one in the morning, and still opening the shop first thing, it was obvious Jenny was thriving on the buzz of running the country.

'So, what's the word on the street?' she asked. 'How does Faughie think we're doing?'

'I'm sure I don't know! You know a lot more people than I do, you ask them.'

'They won't tell me, they talk behind my back but they'll never say it to my face. That's what you're here for: to tell me what they're saying about me. I need to be able to respond. You're my eyes and ears out there.'

I giggled but carried on licking my finger and dragging it across the paper, gathering the delicious remnants of fish, chips, grease and salt, and sooking it off my finger.

'Seriously, I can take it.'

I stopped licking.

'Well, nothing terrible. Since you announced your middle name at the election I've heard people referring to you as Captain Haddock. You know, as in ...'

'Aye, I get it: Tintin. Well,' she reflected, 'an alcoholic beardy sailor, I've been called worse things.'

'And Walter is Captain Birds Eye.'

Jenny snorted.

'But I haven't heard anything bad.'

'And the Claymores, the filum people?'

'Nope, everyone seems happy enough.'

'Good. So remember: keep your eyes open and your ear close to the ground.'

'Yes sir!' I gave her an exaggerated salute. 'So, now that you're El Presidente, d'you not think –'

'Interim Leader. And I might get voted out at the referendum.'

'– it's time you did the decent thing,' I continued, 'and made an honest man out of young Captain Birds Eye.'

'Pfffff.'

'No, hear me out: apparently unmarried politicians aren't popular with elderly voters. People might think you're gay.'

'Hah! Let them, probably get me a few more votes.'

'It's probably worse for Walter; a spinster looks like a career woman but an old unmarried man just looks sad.'

'Walter isn't sad.'

'I know that! I'm just spindoctoring. Think what it would do for your popularity: a fairy-tale happy ending for two of Faughie's most popular pensioners.'

'Forget it, Trixie.'

'Everyone loves a wedding.'

'Not going to happen.'

'I don't know why you and Walter bother keeping up this silly pretence, it's obvious you love each other, everyone can see ...'

Jenny thumped her fist on the table. 'Enough!' she yelled.

I think we were both a bit shocked.

'I'm sorry, Jenny. I didn't mean to wind you up, it was only a bit of banter.'

'I know,' she said.

I started folding up my fish paper.

'I'm sorry,' she said, 'tired, stressed, whatever, I'm overreacting. Don't go home, I've hardly seen you in ages.'

'Ok,' I said, in awe of what I'd just heard. Was Jenny actually admitting that she missed me?

'I keep everything so tight, you know?'

She balled her fist and held it low on her stomach.

'Walter says I'm so secretive I owe myself a shite.'

I didn't really know what that meant, but I laughed anyway.

'For years I wanted him to marry me,' she said, 'I dreamed of it: my big day, my big white dress.'

It took an effort of will for me not to slap the table and shout: Yes! I knew it! Instead I gave up ironing my chip paper with the flat of my hand and watched it slowly unfold itself as though it were alive.

'Well if you've dreamed of it why not go for it? What is it they say? *Carpe diem*: seize the day. Neither of you is getting any younger, why don't you just carpe the firkin diem and get hitched?'

'And play Darby and Joan? Can you honestly see me in a lavender anorak? Och, I'm too busy for that nonsense, I'm too busy carping the firk out of every diem.'

'But what about your big white dress?'

'You're new here, Trixie,' she sighed. 'You don't know. The gory details.'

She said it in such a doom-laden voice I wasn't sure I did want to know the details, especially not gory ones. I was still reeling from the revelation that Jackie was my father. That hadn't exactly had a positive effect on our relationship.

Jenny sighed again, a big heavy sigh.

'So,' I said, as gently as I could manage, 'when you say "gory"?'

Chapter 53

'I was engaged once, you know,' Jenny began, 'not to Walter, to Bernard. He was handsome, a decorated soldier, and had only just come home to a hero's welcome. He asked me to dance at the ceilidh in Bengustie hall. They would always play a slow smoochy one, the last dance of the night, the "moonie" it was called. Bernard asked me to dance the moonie with him.

'He was twenty-two, a grown man, and he couldn't dance, not properly, but he had all the moves. He did it slow and in time to the music so that nobody would see. He slid himself across me, right here, and oh my god. I felt it. I felt it right through his clothes and my clothes. It was one of the most exciting things that ever happened to me, I mean *ever*,' she stressed like a teenager, 'including being elected Interim Leader. He walked me home that night. We were engaged two weeks later.

'That's what you did in those days. In a small village you knew what your options were and Bernard was a catch. His family were respectable and they had a good bit of land out by Gaffney.'

'Out where Walter lives?' I asked.

'Exactly. But more of that later.

'Now, since he'd come back, Bernard was the man of the house. His dad had died on the fishing boats the year before, leaving his widow to look after the farm and bring up Bernard's wee brother, but she wasn't fit for it. Luisa her name was – fancy name, fancy lady. She had a dodgy hip. It wasn't that bad, but she played it up every so often, hirpling around to get sympathy. She leaned on Bernard, I mean, depended on him; used him as a replacement for her husband. Och, not in that way, but he was under a lot of pressure from her and from whatever else was going on in his head. Anyway, Luisa didn't want a common village girl like me for her son's wife. First she accused me of being pregnant and when I assured her I wasn't, she said, 'Well then, what's the rush? The wedding can wait until we've got the harvest in.' And Bernard agreed. He did everything he could to please her.

'Anyway, it gave me time to get to know my fiancé, but the more I knew the less I liked. Don't get me wrong, he was sexy and very charming, that's what had attracted me to him, but at times he could be cruel. Malaya did that to him. Sometimes he would sob in my lap and say he'd never been forgiven for the things he'd done.'

'And what had he done?'

'He'd never tell me but it must have been bad. He was in Malaya.'

'Sorry, Jenny, as you know, I'm not big on history.'

'No, I didn't know much about it either but years later I read up about the Briggs plan: forced relocation, quelling of rebellion and general terrorising of the Malaysian population. It's gruesome reading. Nowadays Bernard would be diagnosed with post-traumatic stress disorder but then they were just medically discharged.

'Luisa didn't want anyone getting close. She didn't want anyone ruining his war hero reputation. And meanwhile his brother – and this is where it gets interesting for you, Trixie – his baby brother, Walter, he was easy to get on with.'

I perked up immediately, 'So that's how you met Walter?'

'You don't meet people in Inverfaughie, you grow up with them. Walter's two years younger than me; we'd been in the same class all through primary, we were friends.

'I don't remember his dad, but Walter must have got his nature from his dad's side. You know what he's like: gentle, easy-going. Bernard was ... There was a sour atmosphere around him. I didn't know what to do. I told my parents but Mum said it was just pre-wedding jitters. They wouldn't hear of me breaking it off, not with a decorated war hero who would inherit that land. Bernard said he'd been having second thoughts too but that we should leave things as they were, give it a few weeks before making any decisions.

'I thought about it, and worried about it, until eventually I decided I had to tell him it was over. I went to see him but his mother said he was out ploughing the haugh and shut the door on me. Walter, he was only fifteen at the time, a kid, was heading out to go fishing in the wee lochan; there was a big pike up there eating all the other fish. He pleaded with me to go with him; he said it was so big it would take both of us to get it in the boat.

'Walter and I were just climbing into the rowing boat, laughing and splashing each other, when Bernard came crashing through the bushes at us. It was terrifying, the look on his face; I thought he was going to murder us. He hauled Walter off the boat and punched him so hard in the stomach it knocked the wind right out of him. Walter crumpled and fell to his knees and Bernard started kicking him in the head and all over his body, anywhere he could land a blow; he wasn't going to stop. Walter curled into a ball; his hands were on his head and I could see the blood spurting out between his fingers. I was screaming for Bernard to stop.

'I was already in the boat so I lifted an oar and whacked Bernard on the shoulder with it. It was the closest I could get. Bernard turned and pulled it out of my hands. I knew that if he used it on me or Walter we were finished. Bernard was crying and screaming that I was carrying on with his own brother. I swore to him I wasn't but there was no reasoning with him.

'Behind him I could see Walter stagger to his feet. Bernard came at me and poked me hard with the oar but it glanced off me and had the effect of pushing me and the boat away from him. Bernard must have heard Walter move and turned back to see him up and running. You only know Walter as he is now, a doddery old man, but back then Walter could run like the wind. He was only fifteen and a skinny big kid and despite the beating he'd taken he managed to outrun Bernard. He had to; he was running for his life.

'When he realised he couldn't catch him, Bernard turned back to me. I was frantically paddling with my arms, anything to get away from him, but I was still in the shallows. He strode right into the water and just as he leaned forward to grab the boat he sunk. We were in deep water now. He had completely disappeared. I peered down into the water looking for him. It's something I remember vividly; it was so strange because, after the screaming and violence, there was suddenly only the sound of birdsong.

'Something grabbed my arm. Bernard pulled me out of the boat and capsized it over our heads. It was dark under there and all I could think of was getting out, but Bernard kept fighting me. We struggled in the water; Bernard was pulling me under. I kicked and punched, I don't remember how I got out from under the boat or out of the water or even how I got back to the village, but I did. All the men ran up to the lochan: my father swore he was going to kill him.

'Bernard wasn't there. Everyone thought he had run away, but they started to search the lochan. While they were waiting for Jock Pirie to bring his boat, my dad found Bernard under a tree in the shallow water.'

Chapter 54

Was Bernard dead or alive? I was hooked like a big pike, caught up in the story.

'There was an inquest,' Jenny continued, which at least answered that question.

'A lot of debate went on about the injuries on Bernard's body and the time it took me to reach home – there was a discrepancy of thirty minutes. I don't know what happened during that half-hour, I have no memory of it; the doctor said I was in shock. I was never accused, it wasn't a criminal case so there was no jury, but you can be sure that I was tried in every house in this village – and found guilty in some of them. The Procurator Fiscal returned a verdict of death by misadventure.

'Luisa never saw it that way, of course, and made sure everyone knew how she felt. At the gala day she caused a terrible scene. In front of the whole village she cursed me for a kelpie and threw fish at me. Believe me, you can wash and scrub as hard as you like but in a small place like this the smell lingers a long time.

'Luisa made my family's life a misery. She told everyone I was a murderess; huh, she wanted them to drown me as a witch. It might have been hundreds of years ago but when it comes to drowning women for witchcraft, this village has form.

'She wore black every day, she even shaved her head to remind everyone of her grief. Of course they felt sorry for her, but they didn't believe I had murdered him. Or at least I hope they didn't. You never really know up here. It got so bad mum and dad had to bar her from the shop. Others thought we had been too harsh on the poor distraught woman and stopped shopping with us in solidarity with Luisa. They bought everything from Inverness. It was a disaster; my parents were on the way to losing their business. That's why I had to go away to London.

'I came back every year for Christmas – she couldn't stop me doing that. The first few years she came and stood outside the shop as a protest. Some years she'd shout at me in the village and some years she'd just blank me; there was no telling how it was going to go, but she never gave up hating me. I think I told you before why I came back?'

'Yeah, your dad died and your mum had flu and you stayed to help, that was it, wasn't it?'

'It wasn't the whole story. I did stay until mum got better but at that time I started receiving anonymous letters. No, not what you're thinking. It wasn't Luisa; they were too eloquent. At first I didn't know who it was. It was frustrating because I would have liked to have replied. The letters were clever and interesting. I wanted to speak to this person.'

'Did you find out who was sending them?'

'It sounds creepy, but the letters started to mention that they had seen me in the village at a certain time or place, so I knew they were watching me.'

'That is creepy.'

'I wasn't scared, I was fascinated. One day I got dressed up and went out, paraded myself around the village, then walked up to the old quarry. I knew that if my mystery correspondent was going to follow me all the way out there they'd have no hiding place. Obviously it was Walter. You knew it was him, didn't you?'

I made a reluctant face but admitted it with a nod. We moved on.

'He was so clever. If he had written, "Meet me at the quarry at such and such a time", I probably wouldn't have gone. He let me decide if we were going to meet. That's Walter.'

'So that's when it started. Wow! Yours must be the longest courtship on record.'

'It didn't start. Nothing started. Remember, there was still Luisa to contend with. She was older, and even more bitter. Walter was a big mammy's boy. He would never confront her, never stand up to her. He said he couldn't make her suffer any more than she already had; it would kill her. I wished it would. He said we couldn't risk meeting again until she passed. She had a bad chest infection and the doctor had hinted that she might not last the year. We'd have to gird our loins and content ourselves with secret billets-doux.'

'Who's Billy Doo?'

'It's French for love letters. We developed a system of dead letter drops, leaving them stuffed in a dry stane dyke up on the Bengustie Road.'

'Like spies.'

'Some letters got lost: strewn across the moors, eaten by a sheep, or maybe blown on to the loch and out to sea. Luisa relapsed a few times but always recovered and five years later, except for sneaky glances when he passed me in the village, nothing had changed. Ours was a relationship of the imagination. I needed more than that.

'I wrote and asked him to meet me in Inverness – there was a history conference on at the college there, he could pretend to go to that. I wanted us to run away. I had the shop and he had Luisa but we weren't shackled to this place, we could leave, I had to convince him of that.

'At the last moment Luisa had one of her wheezing attacks and he couldn't leave her. I think she smelled a rat. I wanted to give up then. I knew I was too young for that kind of abstinence; my loins were fed up with being girded. I cursed Walter for his weakness and cursed his mother for destroying my life. Yet Luisa and I had so much in common: we both loved Walter and we both spent our lives wishing each other dead.'

'So your wish came true?'

'She died two years ago.'

'You're kidding; only two years ago!'

'She was nearly ninety. The old witch hung on as long as she could. I think she suspected. By then both Walter and I were council members. I don't know why we hadn't thought of it years before. Luisa still had all her marbles and she did not like it one bit but she was too feeble to do anything about it. Being council members meant we were able to meet in public, talk, be normal with each other. It was a good way to get to know him. I mean, I knew him through the letters obviously, but all those years I longed to hear his voice, see his wee mannerisms, look into his face.'

I shook my head in disbelief, 'And all those years you made do with pen pal Billy Doo letters.'

'Och now, don't underestimate the power of the written word. I still have all the letters. Sometimes I take one to bed with me. I hold it like this between my hands, as if I'm praying, and then I put my hands between my knees. Sometimes it's the only way I can get to sleep.'

Chapter 55

After a respectful wee while I was eventually able to bring the conversation around to the Steven situation. Jenny's advice was to let him join Ethecom: fill his boots, knock himself out. There was nothing I could do to stop him anyway. I couldn't argue with that but she suggested that *I* should go and work for them as well.

'No, Jenny, you go too far. I'm not working for those firkers!' I squawked.

Jenny laughed, 'Hah, I see what you did there. "Firkers" as an insult.'

'Isn't it?' I asked. 'It was you I firkin learned it from.'

'Hey,' she shrugged, 'Doesn't firkin bother me. I love it when one of my new words take off. It makes me feel influential.'

'Pfffff, not that influential. There's no way I'd work for those hippies.'

'But don't you want to know exactly what it is that Steven's getting into? I'm serious, you should work with Ethecom. You might find out what they're really all about.'

'Oh right. I get it. Be your eyes and ears?'

'No. And yes. Their green technology is a big part of our sustainability argument. They'll be called to Luxembourg to give evidence, so we need to keep them on side. I happen to believe they're a bunch of decent hard-working folk, but I could be wrong. If you think there's something sinister about them then you owe it to yourself to do a bit more research. Get close and you'll find out one way or the other. But you never know, you might like them. You need to make more friends here, Trixie, I can't be here for you all the time, not now I'm so busy, and anyway you need to be putting down roots. Friends and family, that's what binds you to a place. And if you find out anything bad – anything that would be detrimental to Faughie – we can work out a way to shut them down.'

'So while I'm busy spying for Faughie, for queen and –'

'I'm not the queen,' she said graciously, 'just the Interim Leader.'

'– country, my son misses out on a university education?'

'You know as well as I do that nothing will drive your Steven into the arms of Ethecom quicker than his mum telling him he can't. So, encourage him. Join Ethecom yourself, talk it up, that should take the rebellious shine off it for him. Let him get it out of his system. He's got all summer; a few months of back-breaking shit-shovelling will soon make him realise what a cushy option university is.'

'And what if he decides he loves it?' I challenged.

In response Jenny laughed, 'Well then, would it really be so bad for Steven to find what makes him happy?'

I couldn't think of an answer.

*

Me and Bouncer sprachled round to Dinah's fifty-roomed but-and-ben. I'd already promised myself that, no matter what, there would be no drinking today. A walk was be good for the dogs and I was keen to get Dinah's perspective on the Steven problem. Although my wee pal Jenny was older, and arguably wiser than me, she'd never had a kid; she'd no concept of what it was to be the mother of a wayward son. I knew Dinah had personal experience.

Before we started our walk Dinah handed me a pair of mud-spattered green wellies.

'You're going to need these I'm afraid.'

'Why?' I asked, 'it's hardly rained all week.'

'Hmm, you haven't been here in a while, have you?'

'I suppose I haven't. Now that the machair is open again I never come this far round.'

'I think you're in for a surprise.'

The last time I had been down here, when I'd bumped into Dinah and MacIntyre, the field this side of the loch was picturesque with the last of the bluebells, pink heather flowers, yellow coconut smelling broom blossom and random bright red poppies. Since then something apocalyptic had happened. The beautiful wild flower meadow had become a slurry pit. From the castle all the way down to the loch the long grass was drowning in thin brown mud and smelled foul. The dogs didn't like it. I heard the sound of their feet plopping and sucking as they gingerly attempted to walk through it, little Mimi's long fur dragging and weighing her down.

'FFS. What's happened here?'

'You remember your father and his spade?'

I wasn't used to thinking of Jackie as my father so it took a moment.

'Jackie did this?'

Dinah shrugged.

'I can't prove it of course, but he was in the grounds with a spade.'

'But I don't understand, there must be literally tons of mud in this field, how could one man do all this damage?'

'You underestimate your father, Trixie.'

This was getting a bit freaky, Dinah constantly referring to Jackie as my dad. 'I've done a bit of research. Jackie Robertson, better than anyone, knows the watercourses in this area,' said Dinah, 'above ground and below, he knows what culverts and ditches take water to the loch – and how to divert them. Dam an underground stream here, bung up a soakaway chamber there and hey presto: the lochside becomes a flood plain. I'm sorry to say it, Trixie, but your father is the only person with the specialist local knowledge to achieve this. He also had a motive.'

'But they have the machair back now,' I blustered. 'No, it just doesn't make sense, Jackie wouldn't do a thing like this.'

Even as I was saying it I remembered Jackie's improbable explanation for carrying a spade, some story about ferreting, and heard the conviction dwindle and fade from my voice.

Chapter 56

Later, when we were in Dinah's kitchen drinking coffee and she was plying me with biscuits, I asked her what she thought about Steven joining Ethecom, telling her what Jenny's advice had been.

'I agree with Jenny,' she said. 'Roddy always does precisely the opposite of what I want. To annoy me he managed to get himself expelled from some of the most expensive schools in the country, no mean feat, and now he's lord only knows where, doing lord only knows what. The only clue I have is from his credit card bills. I worry about him so. At least you know where your son is, and he won't come to any harm in Inverfaughie.'

'I know, but, och, I'm so stupid!' I wailed. 'Why did I ever ask him to come up here? His dad's going to go nuts. It's all my fault.'

'Now, Trixie, you have to stop blaming yourself. That's classic single-parent guilt. A top Harley Street psychiatrist has assured me that Roddy's behaviour isn't my fault. Teenagers are pre-programmed to be rebellious and horrid. It's all part of growing up.'

I sighed and wondered how much Dinah had paid her Harley Street psychiatrist for that pearl.

'Dr Ramana explained that young people are growing all this new white matter in the frontal cortex,' said Dinah, holding her fists to her forehead and miming a bulging brain. 'It affects their insight, judgement, all that kind of thing. That's why, once they've outgrown the cute little boy stage, we as mothers apparently can no longer do anything right.'

I nodded in recognition and resignation and carried on munching my biscuit.

'The good news is that Steven and Roddy will eventually return to human form. I know how painful it is right now but please: talk to me about it any time, a trouble shared and all that.'

'Thanks Dinah.'

'You're welcome. That's what friends are for. Another bickie?'

'Cheers.'

Dinah buzzed around the kitchen filling the machine to make another pot of coffee while the dogs lay curled up together in Mimi's basket.

'You and Jenny seem to be good friends.'

'Yes,' I said, reflecting on how Jenny had finally let me in on the big secret, 'we are.'

'That must be lovely,' said Dinah.

The big secret that everyone else in the village knew. Well, not *everyone*: not incomers or tourists or film people, and not Dinah, but everyone who belonged.

'Yes,' I said, feeling a tiny wee bit smug and a bit sorry for Dinah, 'it is.'

This smugpity was a novelty, but tainted by Jackie's guilt, it quickly melted. I wanted to reach out to Dinah, to share her troubles and halve them. After all, I was the daughter of the person who had caused them.

'I'm so sorry about your polo field, Dinah, I really hope it wasn't Jackie who did it, but if it was I'd like to apologise on his behalf, on behalf of the family.'

'Thank you, that's sweet of you, Trixie.'

'I'm sure when the groundworks start they'll drain it off, no harm done in the long run.'

'There aren't going to be any groundworks,' Dinah said quietly.

'No, I mean when they start the landscaping ...'

'Mr MacIntyre has pulled out of negotiations.'

'What?'

'Oh, he blustered a lot to save face, but it's over. The council giving permission for the new Bengustie wind farm was the last straw for him. He's following up the New Zealand option. One would imagine that if Faughie remains a tax-free haven it would be the perfect location for a billionaire but he's used to getting exactly what he wants. If that isn't assured he's out.'

'I'm so sorry, Dinah. What are you going to do?'

'What can I do? The National Trust was my fallback, but even paying a much-reduced price they've bailed out too. With the uncertainty over Faughie independence they say they can't fund it.'

'I'm so sorry,' I repeated.

'I don't know where to go next. My agent can't even look for another buyer, not while there's a swamp at the front door. The Environment Agency don't have watercourse maps for this area. They've told us that, as it's likely to be underground, it would take weeks, months perhaps, to locate the source. Whoever did this is holding all the cards.'

'I'll speak to Jackie; I'm not saying he did it, I'm sure he didn't, but if he knows about the waterworks I'll ask if he can put things back the way they were. I'm sure he'll help.'

I was sure of no such thing, but I felt the urge to be optimistic and supportive.

'I hope so, but there was something else I was going to ask you, Trixie.'

'Fire away.'

'I wondered if you could get me some face time with Jenny. We want to tender the estate to Faughie with the same price structure as we offered the National Trust. Given the income they're generating from the whisky water tax, they'll soon be running an operating surplus. We're marketing the castle to them as a parliament building or even a presidential residence. After all, the castle is at the heart of Faughie history: Faughians have fought and died for this castle for hundreds of years; it belongs to the people, don't you think?'

I gulped in amazement at her seemingly unconscious hypocrisy. If the castle belonged to 'the people' then why had her family held it for so long? And if their forebears had already fought and died for it why would 'the people' need to pay for it?

'Do you think you could pitch it that way to Jenny? I'm sure she values your opinion.'

I almost laughed.

'I realise we're in back-scratching territory, Trixie, and I wouldn't be unappreciative of your efforts.'

What the hell was she talking about?

'We could discharge Harrosie. I'm not sure how many years are left on the lease but we'd convert to freehold for a nominal amount. With the boom in tourism we would expect to see the value of property in Faughie rocketing. Predictions of 150 per cent increases in net worth are conservative. I know you're not planning to stay so you'd be able to achieve an enormous profit and finally buy your place in Glasgow. And you'll be mortgage free.'

My ears pricked up at those three words: 'Glasgow', 'mortgage', 'free'.

'Obviously I could only afford to do this once I'd sold the estate. It would be conditional upon Jenny and her committee approving the sale. You'd really have to sell it to her.'

Again I felt the urge to laugh, but this time I also felt a rough grain of indignity beneath my skin. Did Dinah believe for one minute that Jenny would fall for it? If so, she was seriously under-estimating her, but then, all Dinah knew of Jenny was the sweet little old lady who'd sold her dolly mixtures in the shop all those years ago. Did she think Jenny was corrupt or vain enough to want a fifty-roomed presidential residence? And the idea of me trying to persuade her was laughable. Jenny would see through it a mile away. Not only was I indignant on Jenny's behalf, I was also insulted that Dinah had assumed she could buy my loyalty. This was bribery and corruption, bare-faced cash for questions. But in terms of getting me the hell out of Faughie – it was the perfect solution.

Chapter 57

And so I started volunteering with Ethecom three afternoons a week. Steven huffed a bit at first, telling me to get a life. When I replied that I had a very nice life thank you very much, he said, yeah, I mean one of your own, stop muscling in on mine. Charming. Brenda, on the other hand, was pleased to see me. To avoid anything that was too back-breaking, tedious or smelly I volunteered to look after the chickens.

As part of my undercover mission for queen and country I had to pretend I thought chickens were cute. In real life I was terrified of them, especially when they flapped, at which point I usually freaked and ran away. During the day the hens and roosters were let out to run around the yard but at night, to keep them safe from foxes, they were locked up. The hardest part of my job was getting them all back into the coop. As I was so scared I couldn't approach them and the chickens were so stupid they hid in bushes, this was a nearly impossible task. Thank the good lord for Jan. If it hadn't been for him helping me catch the chickens, at night the air would have been thick with the chicken-flavoured burps of local foxes.

Brenda said it was unadvisable to give the chickens names, I might get emotionally involved. That was highly unlikely, but to keep up my cover I called them 'it' or 'that one' or 'hey you'. Jan and I developed a system where I would point to the bush where a hen was hiding, he would approach from behind, frighten it and sweep it towards me. This was where our system was flawed. If the hen did run towards me I'd hold my ground for as long as possible while Jan chased it and rugby-tackled it. If the bird got too close to me I'd panic and run away screaming. The other Ethecom members and volunteers, while peacefully undertaking their pastoral tasks, were sometimes treated to the spectacle of a screeching woman being chased by a squawking chicken being chased by a laughing man. This was exhausting for all three of us and so I began to slowly conquer my terror. Soon I was catching more chickens than I fled from. It all made for a satisfying end to my day's volunteering.

My week fell into a pleasing rhythm: when I wasn't cooking or baking for my Claymores I was walking over to Ethecom with my co-worker Steven, catching chickens and having a laugh with Jan. Either that or I was entertaining a friend at my place.

I'd stopped eating every night with the Claymores and ate instead with Jenny a few nights a week. I knew she didn't have time to cook and I was worried she was burning herself out. Not only was she trying to keep Faughie afloat and Westminster off her back, she was now having to contend with vigorous opposition from Betty and, though she'd never admit it, it was wearing her out. Jenny was getting too thin and scrawny for my liking. She refused my hospitality at first, saying she didn't have time, but I insisted.

'You've got to eat, haven't you?'

She couldn't argue with that.

'Once you're finished all your meetings, come to my house and I'll give you a light late supper. You could be doing with some home-cooked food inside you. It's not charity; call it my contribution towards the Faughie independence campaign. And anyway, painfully thin isn't a good look, not at your age,' I said kindly. 'No one wants a scraggy-arsed First Lady.'

It was all going swimmingly; I was planning pasta carbonara for supper when Dinah phoned.

'Hello, Trixie darling, just wondering if you've had the chance to speak to Jenny yet? Time is quite pressing on this deal,' she said.

The truth was I couldn't bring myself to do it. A few times I'd danced around the subject and then quickly backed off before Jenny had rumbled me. I knew I wouldn't fool Jenny, I wasn't a good enough liar. I didn't know what to do. I wanted the chance to buy Harrosie from Dinah, of course I did, I just didn't want Jenny to think of me as some snivelling corrupt lobbyist. She'd think that inviting her to eat with me had been part of the plan. Maybe it had started that way but now it was the part of my day that I most looked forward to.

'Yeah, we've chatted about it a bit, but I don't think Jenny's terribly interested,' I lied, 'her priority is paying salaries. She's worried about being able to pay Joe, the lollipop man, amongst others.'

That much was true. I remembered this from when the rest of the committee had been so excited about the whisky water tax.

'Really?' shrieked Dinah, so loud I nearly dropped the phone, 'but does she realise the revenue potential to be had from running the estate as a resort? Even a golf resort. With investment in infrastructure, the estate could be an absolute gold mine. I can bring my agent in and we can show her some of the projections. In the first year alone it is predicted to ...'

'Ok, I'll ask her again.'

'Oh golly, that would be terrific! When?'

'When what?'

'When will you see her again? Are you seeing her tonight?'

'Eh, yes, I am. Oops, there's my kitchen timer. I've got to go, Dinah, I've got a cheese soufflé due out of the oven, I'll get back to you.'

That had seemed to satisfy her and I forgot all about it until that evening, when, while the Claymores were playing their customary game of poker in the dining room and Jenny and I were sitting in the kitchen sharing the last of the tiramisu, Steven ushered Dinah in.

Chapter 58

'Hello Dinah!' I screeched and, to cover my embarrassment, ran to embrace her.

She had never come to my house before and as I hadn't invited her, this was the last thing I expected. Jenny was sure to wonder what Dinah was doing rocking up here at this time of night.

I improvised, 'Have you come for Mimi's lead and collar? The one you left in the back of my car the last time we walked the dogs?'

With staring eyes I signalled to Dinah that she should play along.

'Thanks for setting this up, really apreesh,' she whispered, and then in a loud obvious voice she said, 'Yes, I've just popped in to pick up the dog's lead.'

'Right, it's hanging up in the hall, I'll just get it for you,' I said.

Then I realised that if I left the room they'd start talking and most likely find me out: I'd told Dinah I'd already asked Jenny – she'd soon discover I hadn't and, much worse than that, Jenny would find out that I'd plotted with Dinah. Scared of what they were each likely to say, I couldn't leave them alone together.

'But there's no rush is there?' I giggled.

'Eh, no, not really,' said Dinah, fumbling to keep up.

'Och no, I'm sure Lady Anglicus doesn't want to hang about, give her the thing and let her get back home,' said Jenny, with an almost imperceptible wink to me. All this nodding and whispering and winking was making me feel like we were in a bad soap opera. I had no option but to sprint into the hall, find a dog lead, and sprint back again before they had a chance to swap stories.

When I dashed into the hall, Bouncer interpreted my speed as enthusiasm and seeing me reach for his lead bounced around madly. When I made it back to the kitchen I was relieved to meet with no recriminations. Dinah and Jenny were getting along famously.

'Lady Anglicus ...'

'Please, Madam Interim Leader, call me Dinah.'

'Yes, of course, thank you, and you must call me Jenny.'

Dinah had produced a big folder from her bag and was leaning over Jenny, pointing at a graph.

'As you can see, Jenny, the projection is to be comfortably into double figures by year two.'

'Yes, it's a compelling proposition, Lady ... Dinah,' said Jenny.

I made an effort to stop my mouth from gaping. This was not what I had expected at all. This was looking promising, very promising indeed. I had to suppress a yelp of joy when I considered the implications for me: Jenny would ask the Council to buy Faughie Castle, Dinah would sell me Harrosie.

'This is a tremendous opportunity for investment,' Jenny agreed, scrutinising the figures.

And I would buy my flat in Glasgow.

'... I'm sure Faughie Council can help.'

Steven would come with me and go to university, yay!

'... It's in all our interests for this project to succeed,' Jenny continued. 'If we were able to defer payment until we could build on the revenue stream I'm sure the committee would ...'

'Can't you source the finance?'

'I'm sorry.'

The sweet music playing in my head was abruptly ripped from the turntable. Whoa! What just happened?

Dinah looked at me. I looked at Jenny. Jenny smiled sweetly.

'But we'll certainly do everything in our power to help you find a buyer.'

Dinah looked nonplussed by this. It had all been going so well.

'I'd rather hoped that Faughie Council would purchase it from me.'

Jenny held the smile. 'That would also be my fervent wish, but we simply do not have the funds at present. Why don't you have your accountants speak to our accountants and see what they can come up with?'

'But if you don't have finance ...'

'I'm so sorry,' said Jenny.

Dinah's smile faded as the reality sunk in. With a pathetic and transparently false chumminess, she said her farewells and left. I was relieved and keen to see the back of her before she grassed me up. An unpleasant quiver of guilty fear had shot up my back every time she'd opened her mouth. I was glad in a perverse way that Jenny wasn't going to ask the council to buy Dinah's castle.

Jenny let out a big exaggerated sigh as though she'd been holding her breath all night, which only made me feel worse.

'There's something I need to tell you,' I confessed, 'Dinah asked me to persuade you, that's why she came round.'

'Trixie,' Jenny said gravely, 'you should have come to me immediately.'

'I know, I feel awful about it. '

She was so serious I lost my nerve and drew back from telling her the whole truth. There was no need now anyway.

'I'm so sorry, Jenny.'

'If we'd had more notice we could have pushed through authorisation for property sweeteners: rates rebates and such. We really need to keep her on side. If we recognise the Faughie Accord, and we have to for any hope of independence, we have to acknowledge that your pal Lady Dinah owns everything in this village – that's your damn feudal system for you – and we'll have to work with her. Her opinion is going to carry a lot of weight in Luxembourg. But you did well setting up this meeting, good call, thanks a lot.'

I wondered what Madam Interim Leader would think of me if she knew about the Harrosie pay-off, and felt my ears burn with shame.

'Look at you. Blushing!' she laughed. 'You're finally finding your political consciousness. Good on you, Trixie.'

Chapter 59

Later that night, just before she left, I remembered the flooding in Dinah's fields and told Jenny.

'Aw, FFS,' she tutted.

But her eyes lit up when I suggested that this would be a great opportunity to get Dinah on side. Out of filial loyalty I didn't cast any aspersions but Jenny was ahead of me.

'I'd ask Jackie myself but since our wee fall-out we're not on the best of terms. He listens to you, Trixie, could you not ...'

'No, he doesn't!'

'For Faughie's sake, where's that new political consciousness of yours, eh? Blood's thicker than water and it's not as if you're asking him for yourself, it's for the good of the village.'

And it was in exactly those terms that I put it to Jackie when I pitched up at his house the next morning.

'Don't know anything about it,' he said, shaking his head and stirring his tea.

This was the first time I'd ever been in Jackie's house. I'd hung about outside once or twice but I'd never actually been invited in. His garden was all trim lines of perfect vegetables and well-behaved flowers standing to attention. I'd half expected to find a dishevelled bachelor pad inside, an insight into the real Jackie. But the inside was like the outside, except even more regimented, if that was possible. I'd forgotten that Jackie had been in the Navy. That must have been where he'd learned such fastidiousness. Instead of the neglected threadbare country cottage I was expecting, everything was superclean and tidy and the décor was trendy and minimalist, which was even more of a surprise. A bit of clutter might have given it a lived-in feel but there was only a powerful atmosphere of stylish pristine loneliness.

'No one is saying you did it, Jackie; I told Dinah it wasn't you and I'm sure she believed me,' I said diplomatically. 'It's in everyone's interests to find a buyer but no one's going to buy it while it's under water. The environment agency can't fix it; they don't have watercourse maps for the area. You're the only person who can rectify the situation quickly. Please, Jackie, I'm asking you, for Faughie's sake, can you fix it?'

'Maybes aye and maybes naw,' he grudgingly mumbled into his tea.

'It would mean Faughie Council could find a new buyer, it'll mean jobs and …'

'But that doesn't mean I did it.'

'No, of course it doesn't,' I said, unable to look him in the face. I noticed he couldn't look at me either.

*

At dinner that night the Claymores were discussing yet another stushie in the village: a crowd of drunk lads had had a pitched battle with another group of boys down at the harbour. Street brawls and drunkenness were regular occurrences now. Yes, everyone was getting rich off the back of it, but Faughie was beginning to understand the real price of cheap unregulated alcohol. Walter had sent an email just the day before requesting that all alcohol suppliers sign up to a voluntary code of conduct. With no regular police presence in the village except for the occasional visit from a squad car from Inverness, drunks rampaged freely. It was pointless reporting it – by the time the police arrived they had usually sobered up and left the village.

'Aye, but these guys weren't drunk,' said Rudi.

'How d'you mean?' I asked.

'They were acting it. You can see it in their eyes,' he said, waving two fingers in front of his own eyes, 'those guys were stone cold sober.'

The village was a wild crazy place to be these days, especially after dark. Referendum fever had taken over. Every available wall space was covered in posters, pro-independence or pro-union. The campaign had now outgrown the small village hall and, seeing as the weather was good, a kind of unofficial Speakers' Corner had been set up at the car park of the Caley hotel. When I drove past I could always tell by their flags and banners, either Union Jack or Faughie Tricolour, which side was currently pontificating.

Betty was tireless in her activism. Every day she held some kind of soap-box rally with celebrity guests flown in from London. Walter and the rest of the council were baffled as to where her funding was coming from but there seemed no limit to her budget. Betty's nice dresses and ladylike demeanour played well to the old folk in the village, who were after all the biggest portion of eligible voters. Jenny was concerned about this but she was spitting mad about the treatment her own Yes campaign was getting from the media.

Every day the press reported another good reason why Faughie should remain within the United Kingdom. If the Yes campaign was to win, pensioners would lose their bus passes, their winter fuel allowance, their pension. Industry would pull out, unemployment would reign, crime would soar, taxes would be ginormous, mobile phone bills would be humungous. According to the News, an independent Faughie might be invaded by Russia. I could understand why the old dears might want to stick with the status quo. The court in Luxembourg had started hearing from Faughians. I was bored stiff with it all and the referendum was still weeks away. Other people were starting to get fed up with it as well; the initial excitement had worn off by now, reality had kicked in and people were sick of the hullabaloo. We were being force-fed a diet of political candy floss, point-scoring debates about what-ifs and maybes in avarious fantasy futures.

I didn't care. Whichever way it went I'd be gone by then, set up in my new flat in Glasgow. Of course, I'd still see it on the news and I'd laugh and just be grateful that I'd managed to get the hell out of it.

Chapter 60

'Mum, Mum!' Steven yelled as he came running up the stairs.

That's how I knew it was serious; he hadn't called me Mum in weeks.

I was turning a mattress, a heavy one, but I let it fall and ran out to meet him on the landing.

'What is it, son?'

'They've set up a border!'

'What border?'

'Between Faughie and Britain.'

I laughed, 'Don't be silly, there isn't one.'

'There is. They've set up a checkpoint on the Inverness road, military police and everything. Walter was right, it actually worked! Non-compliance with Westminster legislation has turned us into what the UK government are describing as a "volatile region", how cool is that? They're saying they can't guarantee the safety of British nationals and are recalling them to within a "safe" zone.'

'And then what?' I asked, still scoffing. 'They release the dogs? I don't believe you.'

'Go downstairs and turn the telly on, it's on every channel.'

'Steven, there is no border, this is ridiculous!'

'Go,' he said, indicating like an air steward, 'put the telly on.'

'FFS! I'm sick of this drama. If it's not the machair it's Knox

MacIntyre or firking independence and now there's suddenly some fictional border?'

'Let's call it the Safe Zone, if that's what you'd prefer. Faughie Council are advising everyone to remain calm and sit tight.'

'Right, that's it; I've had enough of this shite. Pack your bags, Steven, we're getting out of this madhouse.'

'Relax, Trixie, it's a scare tactic. They're not actually stopping anyone coming or going, they can't, they're trying to frighten us into leaving. The rumour is that if we get a Yes in the referendum then they can control who enters their borders – and so can we. Walter says it's perfect. Even Westminster are acknowledging we're separate. The Court in Luxembourg has to find in our favour now. Faughie Council are co-operating fully with the British security services.'

'We'll bunk up at Auntie Nettie's until we can get our own place, unless you'd rather go back to your dad's?'

'Walter says we must do all we can to maintain a good relationship with our British neighbours.'

'How soon can you be ready, Steven?'

'Mum, do you not get it? Britain has just recognised our defined borders; this is huge, and you want to leave just when it's all kicking off?'

'I don't care how or where or when it kicks off. I'm out of here, and you are too, if I have to drag you by the hair. Is this about Morag? You know, these holiday romance things ...'

'Morag?'

Steven did a good job of looking absolutely baffled.

'I know she's your girlfriend, I've seen you at the lighthouse as I've driven past,' I lied, 'and that's great, really, I don't mind. And of course she's welcome to come and visit us any time in Glasgow if that's what you're worried about.'

'Me? I'm not worried. You're the one ranting about us running away to Glasgow like fugees.'

'We're not refugees, or fugees or whatever you want to call it. We're Glaswegian, Steven, and we're going home to Glasgow as soon as I can get the car started.'

'You're Glaswegian, Trixie, I'm not.'

'You're as Weegie as I am! Steven. Listen to me son, we're not from here, we're not Faughian and we never will be; we don't share their weird wee Faughian ways. We've just had the misfortune to land in this fantastical dreamscape and the best thing we can do is get the firk out of here before it turns nasty. I've had enough now, this is too stressful. I just want to go home, and I want you to come with me. Please son, let's go home now while we still can.'

'I know you want to go, I get it, and that's fine, and I'm sorry, Mum, I really am.'

'Steven you're only sixteen, you ...'

He put his hand gently on my shoulder.

'Mum, I'm sorry. I'm staying.'

Chapter 61

Except for the midgies, it was like the fall of Saigon. Near the helipad there was a gale force wind created by helicopters constantly taking off and landing, airlifting Global Imperial's executives and film stars out of Faughie. Tony Ramos, when asked for a quote for the *Inverfaughie Chanter*, said, 'Better to die on your feet than live on your knees', which I seemed to remember a woman character saying in his film about the Spanish civil war. He was neither on his feet nor his knees but on his arse in a comfy seat in a helicopter.

There wasn't room for everyone in the helicopters and they took to the sea. G.I. chartered every boat big enough to carry cameras and equipment through the loch and down the coast. On behalf of the newly instituted 'Faughie Boat-owners Incorporated', or F.B.I., Jackie brokered a deal for him and his mates worth humungous money.

The rest of the tax tourists, holidaymakers, campers, walkers, fishermen, mountaineers, seasonal European farm workers, hotel staff and film crew minions took the Inverness road to the checkpoint, which had been set up fifteen miles outside Inverfaughie. Ethecom volunteered their Routemaster, driven by Jan, to drop people at the checkpoint.

Coincidentally, G.I. had just finished shooting the film. This caused speculation in the papers and in the village about such convenient timing. Clearly the government had held off putting in their bogus border crossing until G.I. had finished – there was obviously too much money involved. Even so, what had taken weeks to assemble was going to take even longer to get out due to the congestion the panic had created. G.I. sought volunteers from amongst its staff to stay. They were tasked with dismantling sets and equipment and protecting it until such times as G.I. could uplift it. Rudi and his merry band of Claymores applied and got the gig, which dismayed me no end.

'Are you mad?' I asked them that night at what, after G.I. had paid me and all their bills had been settled, I'd jokingly referred to as *The Last Supper*. 'Are you lads off your heads?'

Steven hadn't come home yet, he was still up at Ethecom, so I was glad he wasn't around to hear this nonsense. I'd hoped to use the Claymores as an example of people who were smart enough to get out of Dodge.

'There won't be much call for combat performers now the movie has finished.'

'Are you kidding?' said Rudi, 'This is a wet dream for my men. We don't need to *perform* any more. We're doing it for real now.'

'But how will you earn money?'

'There's plenty of work on the farms.'

'But are you not frightened that you'll be trapped here after the referendum?'

'Nope, are you?'

Rudi and I came to a new arrangement. The Claymores could stay until I was ready to go. No sense in shutting down my revenue stream before I needed to, and I had yet to convince Steven to leave.

Since the machair dispute had been resolved I'd stepped up my flat hunting. I was now registered with every estate agent in Glasgow and spent every spare moment poring over home reports, looking at photos and taking virtual tours. My old neighbourhood was now well out of my league, but there were other flats in other neighbourhoods. The difficulty was in securing a mortgage. The mortgage advisor I'd spoken to on the phone had expected me to be working – financial security had tightened up considerably since the last time I'd bought a flat. Now they were looking for proof of earning, an employment contract. So I registered with every employment agency in Glasgow, but the thought of returning to my old job as a medical sales rep was giving me the heebie-jeebies. If I examined my conscience and looked down deep in my soul, I really didn't want to go back to that huckstering.

I was going to miss being a landlady. Landladying had suited me very well. I enjoyed making up the menus and experimenting with new recipes. I'd learned how to run a business and my baking and cooking had improved no end. Of course, the cleaning was boring, but also satisfying and I was my own boss, that was the best part. If I could uproot Harrosie and take it with me to Glasgow I would. I now started looking at bigger properties but there was a huge gap between a deposit on a two-bedroomed flat and a deposit on a B&B.

Chapter 62

After the initial panic, the queues dwindled at the checkpoint until there was no waiting and it became a drive-thru. In all the telly coverage the government were keen to emphasise that everyone who wanted to leave had ample opportunity. I wanted to leave. I had ample opportunity.

So many people had left I'd expected to find a ghost town, movie prop tumbleweed rolling across the Caley car park, but the village was still quite animated. I'd been sent an email inviting all citizens of Faughie to the launch of the new market.

I'd been to a farmer's market once before in Glasgow. Until then I'd had no idea that farmers spent so much time producing chocolates, soap, candles, tea-cosies, cufflinks, rat catchers, sun catchers and dream catchers. And who knew farmers were good at face-painting? Everything was priced at three times what it cost in the supermarket. How did that work?

This market had none of the froufrou fripperies of the Glasgow farmer's market. This was all about old-fashioned hunks of meat, actual blood-stained limbs, naked and raw, without so as much as a sprig of plastic parsley to cover their modesty. And wildly, hilariously misshapen produce: an apple that was almost perfectly oblong, an oversized tomato skewed to one side like a Tam o' Shanter, a tiny turnip shaped like a wee dog's willy. Some of these fruit and veg were far too interesting to eat. Everyone crowded round these stalls giggling and taking pictures on their phones. Why did you never see fun stuff like this in supermarkets?

Walter, Jenny and Brenda got up on their soap box, which was actually a few shoogly wooden pallets, to formally declare the farmer's market open. Jenny seemed nervous, probably from all the cameras trained on her, so she gave quite a formal and mercifully short speech. She asked that sellers charge no more than a reasonable mark-up and that buyers report any instances of profiteering. Going by the prices I'd seen so far, they were comparable to Asda, if not cheaper. Walter backed her up and, true to form, made all sorts of political and classical allusions. He started comparing the setting-up of the market, 'by the people for the people', to the 1970s work-in by the Glasgow shipyard workers.

'Sadly we're all aware of the recent increase of unruly behaviour and public disorder in our village. This is partly due to an unwise quantity of strong drink taken, but also, I believe, to the presence of agent provocateurs in our midst, whose chief aim is to stir up division amongst us. I hope you'll join me in sending them this message: Faughie is for the benefit and enjoyment of everyone. Jimmy Reid put it so well in his entreaty to the shipyard workers when he said, 'There will be no hooliganism, there will be no vandalism, there will be no bevvying ...'

Everyone laughed. It was funny to hear Walter use such informal language so passionately, but everyone quickly sobered when they caught the sense, and felt the weight, of what he was saying.

'... because the world is watching us, and it is our responsibility to conduct ourselves with responsibility, and with dignity, and with maturity.'

He said more but I couldn't hear him over the noise of a wee low-flying aircraft that was headed towards the loch. As it flew over, some of the TV news crews that had been avidly following the speechifying suddenly packed up, jumped in their vans and sped off. I thought no more of it until later that evening.

I was back at my post, in the kitchen making dinner, contemplating the hopelessness of my situation and cursing my inability to leave Steven in this wee blighted village when I heard the jeers and laughter. The Claymores were watching the telly in the lounge.

'Trixie, come and see!' Dave shouted, 'you're going to love this!'

I rushed into the lounge wiping my hands on a tea towel. Dave paused the live TV, rewound and replayed.

They were covering Inverfaughie on the six o'clock news. This was no longer a novelty. Faughie often made the news these days, and never in a good way. The wee plane that I'd seen earlier was now on the telly dropping cardboard boxes in the field next to the lighthouse field. That's where the camera crews had scooted off to. External No campaign sympathisers were dropping food parcels for the starving people of Faughie.

'Shameless propaganda,' said Rudi, tutting, 'the whole thing's a set-up.'

'But it's funny,' said Ewan.

It was funny. It was hilarious watching them dodge the cardboard boxes falling out of the sky.

'That's Keek!' I squealed in delight, 'and Bell Boy behind him, that's him, see? That's the back of his head!'

'That guy doesn't need a food parcel,' said Ewan, as we watched Bell Boy waddle across the field to retrieve a box.

'C'mon, be fair,' said Dave, 'you don't know what's in them, could be diet shakes.'

'Yeah, a WeightWatchers' mercy mission,' said Ewan.

Bell Boy ripped open the box to show the camera what was inside: packets of rice and pasta and a few tins.

'Just a protein shake for lunch and I'm full all the way to dinnertime!' said Ewan in a high camp voice.

Dave's was even camper: 'Then I have a fish supper and six pints!' he squealed.

Everybody laughed at the banter, but the biggest laugh was yet to come. They'd seen it before me so they were all waiting for it.

'There's your pal,' said Dave.

On the screen a headscarved welly-booted peasant woman smiled for the camera. As the wee plane flew above her she shielded her eyes and looked up. She waved and then gave an affectionate salute as she watched it soar away into the distance. For a few moments she stood still, as though she was waiting, hoping that it might return and rescue her. Betty Robertson, dressed like a refugee with not as much as a smear of lipstick on her, turned back to the camera with a wistful sigh, still clinging to her food parcel as the shot dissolved.

I laughed so hard I thought I'd wet myself.

'What a ham,' said Rudi in disgust.

'It's not ham, it's diet shakes,' said Ewan.

'Och, you all have a good laugh, go on, laugh it up, but people all over the world are watching this,' said Rudi, sooking the fun out of it, 'they don't know Betty Robertson, they think this is real. You mark my words, this isn't good. Not for us, not for Faughie. Not good at all.'

Chapter 63

Of course Rudi was right. A few nights later they started trailing a documentary, 'Inverfaughie, the Inside Story', which was going to be on telly the following Thursday. The village was buzzing with it. The trailer promised to reveal the scandalous goings-on of the committee members as well as showing spectacular views of almost everyone's house. We could not wait. Ali organised a big screen in the function suite of the Caley, offering hot pies during the adverts, and sold tickets in aid of the Yes campaign. You had to hand it to Ali Karim – the guy was a marketing mastermind. Even though you could watch it at home for free, tickets sold out within the hour.

Meanwhile, back at Ethecom, we had a crisis. What Jan hadn't told me when I'd first volunteered, because if he had I'd have run a mile, was that our chickens were being bitten by red mites. That's why they didn't want to go into the coop at night: the bugs were waiting for them. The poor wee chooks couldn't get a decent night's kip for those blood-sucking pests feasting on them, leaving them drained, knackered, and with infected wounds under their feathers. No wonder they ran away from us; I wouldn't have wanted to go in either.

Jan was a gentleman; he insisted that he be the one to go into the coop and dust the birds with home-made chemical-free insecticide while I watched from the door.

'Don't come in!' he yelled at me. 'It's hoaching with red mites in here.'

He'd said this in all seriousness and I had to bite my cheeks not to laugh. If I did he might get all sensitive and self-conscious. Other people teased him about his wholesale adoption of the Scottish vernacular with his thick Dutch accent, but I enjoyed it.

'You're awful rough,' I tutted, 'can you not be a wee bit gentler?'

As he gave each chicken a liberal dusting with mite powder he grasped their feet and tipped them over his knee until they were dangling almost upside down.

'The powder has to cover all their feathers,' he said as he struggled with Jacqueline, who was flapping her wings.

'C'mon, Jacqueline,' I said in a sing-song tone, 'you're ok, nearly there. That's it, good girl.'

'Jacqueline's a cute name for a chicken,' Jan admitted, 'though if Brenda finds out you're naming them she'll not be pleased.' But on hearing me call her name, Jacqueline stopped flapping.

'That's brilliant,' said Jan, obviously impressed with the hypnotic effect of my honeyed chicken tones. 'Aye, Trixie, you're right, it calms the birds.'

He next scooped up a lovely wee white chicken.

'Och, be gentle, Jan, she's my favourite. Good girl, Ellen, there, just a wee minute, that's it, all done.'

Next up was Holly, a gloriously golden-feathered hen, who was smart enough to make for the door. Intercepting her escape, I bent down and gathered her into my arms, snuggling to try to relax her.

'Baaalk, baaalk,' said Holly.

'It's ok, sweetheart,' I soothed, 'it won't hurt, it's just a bit of powder; it'll make you feel better, get those nasty bugs off.'

While Holly buried her head in my chest, Jan took the opportunity to dust her feathers, accidentally brushing my fingers, and my bosom, as he stroked her. I suppose I could have moved my fingers but she was settling.

'Shhh, there now, Holly, don't worry, you're my favourite too.'

'Baaalk,' she replied, but her body no longer felt so tight.

Jan smiled, 'You shouldn't have touched her. You'll probably have mites on you too now.'

'Och, it's ok, they'll wash off.'

'But it's a bit more complicated than that, Trixie. Even if you don't mind the mites crawling on your skin, which is pretty gross, by the way, you don't want further contamination of the hens, do you?'

'No, of course not. The girls have been through enough.'

'I knew you'd say something like that, but,' and here Jan hesitated and shifted his weight, 'if you want to prevent further spread we'll have to wash together; co-ordinate our decontamination strategy.'

I was still stroking Holly, calmed by the fact that her heartbeat had slowed.

'Ok,' I said, 'I'll co-ordinate. I have no problem co-ordinating.'

Jan cleared his throat.

'Just so's you understand: to be completely thorough, we'll need to completely strip off and put all our clothes in the wash.'

'Aye, I can do that,' I said, feeling a sudden rise in temperature all the way to the roots of my hair.

'Really?'

He seemed more surprised than me by the turn things had taken, but Jan softly raking his fingers across my breast had awakened an old familiar sensation, a confusing but not unwelcome signal my body had all but forgotten, now radiating south towards my nether regions.

'Yeah, what else?'

'Eh,' he hesitated again, 'so: to ensure eradication we shower.'

'Together?'

'Aye, I think it's for the best.'

Jan held his breath and waited for me to speak.

'Yup,' I said, nodding thoughtfully, 'I can see that makes good hygiene sense.'

Now on more solid ground, Jan became quite enthusiastic. My eyes were drawn to his twinkly eyes and full lips as I watched him whisper.

'We'll have to soap up; get a good lather going and wash each other, intensively; the soap has to get everywhere.'

I caught my breath and tried to clear my head. I tried to put my misgivings and my throbbing loins to one side, but, after all, what could be more natural? We were two lonely people with a raging sex drive, some scabby chickens and a good excuse to soap up.

*

Ach, it came to nothing. Before we even got to Jan's cottage, walking quickly, but not too quickly, the game was up. Steven and Mag were waiting on his doorstep, after him to help lift their new wind turbine onto the truck.

It was a prototype and they were anxious to get it 'planted', tested and take a reading. They were setting up Faughie's own power grid against the day Westminster turned off the lights. Everyone seemed convinced that day was coming. As Mag argued in his squeaky voice, even if it never came, supplying Faughie with free renewable power would show the world and the Faughie committee that with a bit of ingenuity – trademark Magenius, patent pending – it could be done. Now that they didn't need Dinah's approval they had placed water turbines all down the river, which were showing great results. From welding bits of scrap metal together, Steven and Mag had fashioned a unique, and apparently 40 per cent more efficient, wind turbine. As the three lads enthused about the innovative rotor blade design, I felt my loins cool and my excitement fade. I was grateful when Brenda showed up and offered me a bath at her place.

My lust for Jan was probably only momentary; more to do with the exciting times we were living in. I hardly knew the man – how could I fancy someone I hardly knew?

Chapter 64

I was dying to run the whole confusing episode past Jenny, but of course she was away in Luxembourg. Jenny, Walter, Brenda, Moira Henderson and Dr McKenzie had been airlifted out to go and tell the Luxembourg court how wonderful it was living in a free Faughie. They were wined and dined and two days later came back as conquering heroes to a tremendous fanfare. Like everyone else in the village, I'd received a text asking me to turn out and welcome them back, but I hadn't time for that kind of staged nonsense. Some of us were too busy doing real work, like keeping Faughie in fresh eggs, to hang about the helipad waving stupid wee flags.

The next time I saw Jenny was at the grand showing of the documentary in the Caley. The place was stowed out, a noisy festive atmosphere with everyone dressed up for the occasion. On walking in I quickly mapped out who was positioned where: on the left at the front Betty Robertson was sitting laughing with some of her No camp, affecting social blindness. The blindness was mutual. I was just as happy to blank her. On the same side at the back Jackie was on an all-male table with his mate Spider and some fishermen. He saw me straight away and nodded: a perfunctory nod without warmth, a clear warning not to approach; he would acknowledge me but he wasn't rolling out the red carpet.

Turning to the other side of the room my heart sank. The Claymores were crowded round one table – there wasn't space for me. Steven had got in before me and had sat at an Ethecom table. No sign of his burd, but maybe Morag wasn't the political type. More likely, she had an early start with morning milking. Steven didn't look like he was missing her; he was laughing and chatting away as he sat with Mag, Brenda and Jan. Awkward.

Seeing me falter, Jan stood up and offered me his seat while Brenda smiled and waved me towards their table. As I reluctantly approached I found that I couldn't look at him. I could not bring myself to be gracious: to smile, thank him and acknowledge his kindness. I couldn't see his face, but I hoped he'd understand and not be hurt by my rudeness. A few seconds later, though she didn't realise it, Jenny rescued me.

She and the committee top brass had been allocated the top table: front and centre. Jenny signalled to me that there was a spare chair at their table between her and Walter. As this was not official committee business, more of a social outing, they both kept their guard up. Even now Walter and Jenny wouldn't be seen publicly enjoying themselves together. Relieved to find somewhere I could finally relax, I hardly minded that they were using me as a decoy.

Jenny seemed nervous.

'Are you ok?' I asked.

But she only had time to nod distractedly before the lights went down.

The first three or four minutes of the documentary provided a historical context through a montage of old black-and-white photos and film stock of Inverfaughie. People milking cows, threshing barley, cutting peat, heaving nets, gutting fish, their bright young faces prematurely lined with the back-breaking work. What struck me most was that although things had changed and most of that hard manual labour was now gone, thank goodness, the village of Inverfaughie was completely unchanged. All of the buildings still looked exactly the same, still in exactly the same place.

There was footage of Faughie Castle having what looked like a garden party. An incredibly dapper young man was playing croquet on the lawn with his guests. I looked around but couldn't see Dinah anywhere; then I remembered she'd told me she'd been summoned to give evidence in Luxembourg in a few days' time. She was probably packing. I quickly texted her telling her what channel it was on in case she wasn't already watching.

The footage exploded into full colour with a 1979 TV news item on how remote Highland villages were coping during the Winter of Discontent. Not well, as far as I could see: it looked cold and miserable. Considering we'd soon be heading into a Highland winter and might be cut off from the national grid, I was suddenly grateful for Mag and his wacky renewable schemes.

Squeals of pleasure burst from tables as people recognised themselves or family members from 1979, jumping up and pointing at the screen, ridiculing their long hair and loon pants. This dissolved into contemporary shots all around the village and people cheered when they saw their own house.

The stunning views of the yellow broom, green fields, purple mountains and mist rolling across the loch painted an idyllic picture of Inverfaughie. I caught Jenny's eye and gave her a wee reassuring wink. The documentary wasn't the hatchet job some people had feared after all. Until recently, Inverfaughie had rarely been on the news. Now they were making documentaries about us and everybody was a celebrity.

But even before they went to the first advert break the documentary had begun hinting at a more sinister side to life here. They showed committee members caught on camera entering or leaving Jenny's shop. It must have been shot secretly; there was the sound of the camera shutter whirring and then a blurry freeze frame with the person's name stamped on it as if from a top secret dossier. Most damning of all was Walter's shifty expression as he checked the coast was clear before slipping into the shop. I felt like I was attending an espionage briefing on an undercover gang.

During the first ad break, I saw Jackie go across the room seeking out Steven as avidly as he'd avoided me. Of course, I was glad that Steven and Jackie got on so well, but it wasn't fair. When Jackie found him he squatted down at his seat and the two of them went into a huddle. Nodding their heads, they had a handshake and a manly hug, before moving swiftly into a hetero backslap. What was this all about? I'd investigate after the film. Jackie better not be involving my son in any of his illegal activities.

During the adverts and while the pies were being passed round, Jenny shifted in her seat and tutted a fair bit.

Walter leaned across me to whisper to her.

'Will you relax woman?'

She shook her head. No, she couldn't relax.

And then the adverts were over and we began to see the story the documentary really wanted to tell. The celebration of Inverfaughie's pastoral joy quickly turned sour and became more like a Hogarth painting with drunkenness and violence everywhere.

This was hardly an accurate representation. Yes, there had been drunkenness and violence, but not from Faughians. There simply weren't enough young people in the village to make that much trouble. These were tourists who'd come for the unlicensed drinking and party atmosphere; a cheap out-of-season debauched Spring Break.

And to be fair, it hadn't lasted long. The mayhem on the streets had been a brief but regrettable period while Faughie businesses adjusted to the huge influx of visitors and increased demand. Due to Walter's sobering influence it wasn't like that anymore, but the documentary made out that this once unspoilt village was now being exploited by greedy tax dodgers. As everyone in the room began to understand how they were being stitched up, the cheering turned to boos.

Having established that Inverfaughie had now become a modern-day Sodom and Gomorrah, the documentary's focus now turned to the evil committee members, and especially the committee's evil Interim Leader, Jenny Haddock Robertson. There was footage, again secretly shot, of Jenny selling a bottle of whisky to someone in the shop: shoogly close-ups on her smiling face, the exchange of bottle for cash, cash going into the till. This overlaid with a cynical kerrching sound effect. It was so obvious it was laughable. There was a dizzying sequence of drunks being sick, Jenny smiling, taking cash, kerrching, drunks having sex, Jenny smiling, taking cash, kerrching, drunks starting fights, Jenny smiling, taking cash, kerrching, pitched battles by gangs of youths in the car park, not one of them from around here but waving Faughie flags, each of them clearly displaying their Faughie rosettes, kerrching, kerrching, kerrching.

The voiceover asked the question, 'Who is Jenny Haddock Robertson?' And this was where the hatchet job really kicked in: how she'd lived in London mixing with rock stars – it was true, she actually had met Jimi Hendrix! There was a picture of them at a club called The Scotch of St James. Admittedly it was primarily of him, stiffly posed with other rock icons, but Jenny's cheeky young face gate-crashed the photo, muscling in and making a V-sign above their heads. Jackie and a few of his pals old enough to remember who Jimi Hendrix was whistled their respect.

How she'd dabbled in drugs – a series of photos, presumably taken at a party, of Jenny with a dodgy-looking perm, lingering on a photo of her with a giant spliff in her hand. Predictably there were catcalls, some good natured, but there were loud tuts from random oldsters and all of the No tables.

Dave from the Claymores shouted, 'Busted! Somebody call the cops!'

Some people, but by no means everybody, laughed.

'You look baked in that one,' I whispered to her, 'although, to be fair, it's hard to tell if it's the effect of the perm lotion or the mareewhaana.'

But nothing would cheer Jenny up. She must have sensed what was coming next, and she didn't have long to wait.

The story of how her fiancé had died in mysterious circumstances was illustrated with newspaper clippings from the *Inverfaughie Chanter* and national press showing a photo of the war hero Bernard. How they had argued and he had drowned, how there were no witnesses. How she had left town under a dark cloud of suspicion. How his mother had always accused Jenny of his murder.

'It's a damned lie!'

Walter had pulled himself to his feet and yelled, spittle flying from his mouth.

No one whistled or laughed or shouted anything.

Then the adverts came on. A cliffhanger break in the documentary. There was a noticeably more muted atmosphere during this ad break.

'We'll sue,' said Walter, 'this is a clear case of defamation, they won't get away with this.'

Jenny kept her head down and shook her head.

'Excuse me please, Trixie,' said Walter, as he reached under the table and across my lap.

There was a moment of unsavoury groping under the table until Walter's hand re-emerged, now grasping Jenny's, refusing to let her go.

As everyone went to the loo, got the drinks in or finished their pies, Jenny silently struggled to break free. I would have liked to have stood up and moved away but both Jenny and Walter had gripped the arms of my chair, anchoring their weight with their free hand, effectively holding me prisoner. I could only watch helplessly as they put their all into this wrestling contest, their flabby old cheeks wobbling with the strain, until finally Jenny succumbed and her arm went limp.

She put her head down but allowed Walter to lovingly entwine his hand in hers. Their relationship, no longer repressed, was now on top of the table for everyone to see. It was wonderfully romantic. Or it would have been if I hadn't been stuck between them like a forty-year-old gooseberry.

When the lights went down for the final time Jenny tried to pull her hand away from Walter but he held on tight. The last section of the documentary was no kinder or more truthful. It showed Betty's Robertson's play-acting charade during the propaganda food drop, to wild applause from the No tables. It suggested that the committee had links to terrorist organisations, citing a radical book shop that sold pro-IRA pamphlets and T-shirts from which Walter had ordered books. It showed messages of support sent from separatist groups around the world, including some with a history of violence like ETA. It even showed footage of Walter's 'there will be no bevvying' speech and used cutaway shots to make it look like people were scared of him. As if. It was so ridiculous: first Jenny as a murdering drug addict and now Walter as a feared despot.

As the credits rolled some people hissed and booed and before anyone had time to leave, Jackie walked quickly to our table. Steven suddenly materialised beside me as well. What was going on?

'We've talked about it and we think now's the time. I'm going to make a statement,' Jackie whispered sternly in my ear, 'but only if you're ok with it. Stevo said you would be.'

I looked to Steven who nodded and made a reassuring face. I nodded.

'Sure?'

I looked at Steven and nodded again.

'Ok, let's stand together then.'

Jackie took my arm as I got to my feet and Steven stood on the other side of me.

'Please friends, before you go, I'd like to make a wee announcement.'

This stopped everyone in their tracks.

'There's been a lot of unpleasant accusations made in that programme. We all know what gossip is like in this wee village and how quickly nasty rumours fly around. Lots of things are said, and maybe a lot more should be said.'

Jackie looked quite pointedly at me when he said this.

'But we can't let our community be divided. We must stand together. So we, and when I say we, I mean me and my family: my daughter Trixie and my grandson Steven ...'

After all these months under his nose my dad had finally acknowledged me. I may have gasped, but if I did I was the only one – everyone else seemed to be aware of our family ties.

'... my family stands here by our friends Jenny and Walter, who we know to be honourable people. And I hope you'll all join us in celebrating them as a couple.'

Again, no surprise. Most people stood and clapped, there were no more jokes or banter, no more whistles or catcalls, just supportive applause.

Jenny seemed almost overwhelmed. She looked like she might cry. I must have been close to tears myself because she gave me a secret wink and I took a big breath.

The evening had suddenly taken a tremendous turn for the better. Everyone in Inverfaughie now officially knew that I was Jackie's daughter. It didn't seem that big a deal. I never imagined this – if I had, I'd probably have thought I'd feel euphoric. What I felt instead was calm; a quiet satisfaction that something had finally clicked into place.

It was a big night too for Walter and Jenny: they were finally out of the closet and Jackie's endorsement had turned the documentary's hatchet job into a victory rally.

But of course there were no cameras there to record it. I remembered what Rudi had said: the whole world would have been watching telly. The problem was that they didn't know Jenny, or Walter. The rest of the world didn't know that film for a damned lie.

Chapter 65

The following Tuesday Jan asked me out. It wasn't a date as such – technically he merely invited me to attend a public meeting, so I suppose, in one sense, he asked everyone in the village out – but I went anyway. If I'm honest, I wondered if this informal 'date' might lead to something else, a right good soaping, for instance.

Jan and Mag were giving a talk on Faughie council's newly adopted policy of renewable energy. Energy was a hot topic in the village now. Since the checkpoint had been established there had been a 'problem' with fuel deliveries. Without diesel to operate their generators, the TV news's massive OB unit trucks lay like beached whales by the side of the roads.

Mag's part of the talk was complicated and boring but the good thing was that when it was Jan's turn to talk, it was perfectly permissible to stare at him; in fact, it was the polite thing to do. He began, in his mesmerising Dutch/Scottish accent, by talking about a time, two and half million years ago, when humans first started using tools. Jan held us spellbound as he acted it out: the first man to tentatively smash something with a rock, to use the flint edge to cut.

'That first man changed our future.' said Jan. 'He could not know it then, but from a modern perspective we can appreciate that this was a huge step in human evolution.'

I certainly could.

'That primitive man believed he was only bashing something with a stone, but if he could see what this would eventually lead to: the iron age, the wheel, electricity, space exploration, the digital age; if he'd understood the significance of that first small action, you can imagine how excited he would have been.'

I could; I was very excited.

'You and I are the descendants of that primitive man. And, credit where credit's due, we learned fast. Let's face it: who dares wins, right? We were resourceful. We were the smartest, the fastest. We carved out empires showing the rest of the world how to use the technology we'd created. Yes! Finally the chance to make some real money! And we've been making it ever since. We've fished, and farmed, chopped wood, mined coal, drilled for oil. We've been bringing home the bacon, earning an honest buck, we've used it up and thrown it away, we've even polluted the air we breathe, but we've created huge wealth. Huge! Multimillion-pound wealth. Billionaire wealth.

'For whom? Are you wealthy? I'm not. Nearly every penny of mine that comes in goes straight back out again on petrol, electricity, the supermarket. Somebody somewhere is making money, but it certainly isn't me. And now I no longer have the forests, I don't have healthy rivers and seas, I don't even have clean air to breathe any more.

'I've been ripped off. And now everything is wasted, rubbish.

'But you know what? It isn't. This planet is just like us. We get ill but then, if we rest up and take care of ourselves, we get better again. That's what the Earth does. We've learned that we don't need to chop down trees, we can pollard; prune the trees and still have all the wood we need. We can fish so long as we throw the wee ones back. We can grow food and, if we manage it well, it'll keep on growing and providing for us. We've already got everything we need to make all the energy we want and more, ten times, a hundred times more. Sunshine, water, wind – these things never run out.

'So now we're at the next big step in human evolution. Now we realise that we can't keep using everything up and throwing it away any more. We know it's possible to work *with* the planet. We have the technology, not to make more money for global corporations and billionaires, but to secure the future for our children. Ladies and gentlemen, we're all still that man with that rock; the difference is that this time we have the experience, knowledge and technology to understand its significance. Pioneering renewable energy here in Faughie, leading from the front, shining a renewable beam to light the way for others to follow, isn't that exciting?'

I kicked off the applause. Who knew renewables could be this thrilling?

I wasn't the only one. Jan was asking for scrap metal donations and volunteers to help install the wind and water turbines, and, in a heightened barn-raising atmosphere, all the men were putting their hands up. I put it down to Jan's charisma and the blitz spirit provoked by that awful documentary. There was a newfound sense of community in Faughie or maybe it was only me who was newly finding it. I probably had Jan to thank for that as well. While Jan continued to captivate his audience, I suddenly saw Steven squeezing past the people in my row to get to me. As he slowly made his way towards me, he frequently apologised for bumping people and, once, for standing on Moira Henderson's foot. He looked mortified. I was surprised: Steven never drew attention to himself like this, but I was delighted that he was so keen to sit with me.

'Thanks for coming,' I whispered, 'I think you've missed the best bit though.'

'Did you not see me?' Steven asked, not taking the trouble to lower his voice.

'Shhh! See you where?'

Steven could barely restrain himself. 'I've been standing at that side door waving for the last ten minutes!'

I was baffled. I hadn't seen him, but not only that: why was he waving? He handed me a note. It simply said: 'Urgent – meet at my house. Tell no one. J.' I laughed. Jenny's message was all very cloak and dagger and quite unnecessary, probably. It was so cryptic I wondered if the note would self-destruct in the next five seconds.

'Can I at least stay till the end and say goodbye?' I asked. 'Jan asked me to come; I don't want to be rude.'

Since it had first been suggested I couldn't stop imagining the soaping up.

'Up to you,' said Steven huffily.

Right, so, it was up to me. I'd stay to the end. I turned my attention back to Jan's lovely talk. It had to be something pretty serious for Jenny to summon me like this, she'd never done that before.

'But it does say urgent. If you want to risk the security of Faughie that's up to ...'

'Oh for god's sake, let's go then!' I hissed, and then we began squeezing past everyone in the row.

'Sorry. Excuse me. Sorry. Oh, I'm so sorry,' I said, much too loud.

I'd stood on Moira Henderson's other foot.

*

Steven escorted me as far as Jenny's house and then doubled back to the meeting. It was Brenda who opened the door.

'How was Mag's presentation?' she asked me.

'Terrific.'

Whatever this emergency was, it must be serious. She was an incredibly supportive mum; I'd never known Brenda to miss any of Mag's events.

'I couldn't get away. We've just been working flat out,' she explained in an apologetic tone.

I nodded my understanding.

'Affairs of state,' she muttered, lifting her eyebrows.

Brenda led me into the living room where Jenny sat at the dining table, still with the Faughie flag draped across it, punching numbers into a pensioner's supersized calculator.

'If we take off what she'd pay the UK in stamp duty and inheritance tax I can get the asking price down by nearly 37 per cent,' said Jenny without looking up.

'What asking price?' I asked.

Jenny lifted her head, only now noticing me in the room. She turned round to face me.

'Listen: we're going to Faughie Castle and we need you to come with us.'

'Why?'

'We're going to make an offer and we need you to persuade Dinah to accept.'

'Oh. Right,' I said.

This took me a few seconds to get my head round. This was exactly what I'd been after. If the committee bought the estate from Dinah I'd get my part of the bargain: Harrosie. Mine to sell to the highest bidder. I should have been pleased, and I tried to be, testing out an unconvincing smile, but I was too busy trying to stop an infestation of toatie wee imaginary beasties crawling over my skin.

Jenny wanted my help but she had mistaken me for a noble person. How ironic this whole horrible pickle was. Little did she know, but Jenny, dear selfless trusting Jenny, was actually pushing me towards feathering my own sleazy cash-for-questions nest. And what if my double-dealing ever came to light? How would Jenny and Walter and Steven and Jackie, and everybody in Inverfaughie feel about me then?

'C'mon Trixie,' said Jenny, 'Now is the time for all good women to come to the aid of the party and all that.'

Brenda and Jenny had no idea of the treachery they were encouraging me towards. How could I tell them?

'You said there wasn't the money to buy her estate,' I complained, 'I remember you talking about Joe, the lollipop man, and having to fund his wages. And now you're going to just give all the money to Dinah Anglicus?'

'It's our only option,' said Brenda, entering the fray. 'As expected, Dinah's been called as a witness. Dinah Anglicus owns 93 per cent of Faughie. She'll have the loudest voice in Luxembourg and, as things stand, she's indicating that she won't support our case.'

'No, I'm sure she'll ... Did she actually say that?'

'She did. It's not in her best interests,' said Brenda, matter-of-factly. 'So, despite fierce opposition from Betty and her followers, we've got authority to purchase Faughie Estate. In the long run it'll be useful revenue for funding infrastructure. It's not ideal, but we need to buy the estate now for the influence it buys us in Luxembourg.'

'Yeah, but where's the money coming from?'

'We're borrowing most of it,' said Jenny. 'At extortionate rates, but what can we do? Our hands are tied. We're going to make her an offer. She can't refuse.'

'An offer she can't refuse? You're going to threaten her?'

'Huh! I wish. I'd be a more effective Interim Leader if they let me threaten people.'

'You know,' I told them, playing Devil's advocate; playing for time, 'Faughie Estate has been in her family for hundreds of years. She told me her family fought for it.'

'True,' said Jenny, 'in-bred, over-privileged, silly wee tart.'

'Well,' I argued, 'if her family fought for it hundreds of years ago and she's still sitting on it, is it not about time we had a rematch? There's only one of her; there are a lot more of us, and the odds are on our side this time.'

'Yup,' said Brenda, 'Walter lent me a book, *The Poor Had No Lawyers*, and the author, Andy Wightman, makes exactly that point. I must say you're coming out of your shell, Trixie. I've underestimated you.'

You certainly have, I thought sadly, you poor principled naive fool, underestimated what a cheating, lying, low-life scum-bag I am.

'So, you'll help us then?' Jenny asked.

What was I supposed to do? I could see the pragmatism of their position: to have a chance at independence they needed to buy the estate, but incurring huge debts to bribe the landed gentry seemed well dodgy. That was politics, I supposed. At least Brenda and Jenny were doing it for the common good, for Faughie. Who was I doing it for? I would personally profit while Faughians would be bonded slaves to the debt.

'No. You go and ask her if you want but I can't be involved, it's too difficult, too – complicated.'

'But we need you!' wailed Brenda, 'Trixie, you're the only person in the village on first-name terms with her. I understand it goes against your principles, and I commend them, but we have to be practical. If you won't come we'll go without you but we'd rather you came. Please, Trixie, it might make all the difference.'

Just tell them, I told myself, they'll understand. It comes to the same thing anyway. It won't change anything, they'll still have to buy the estate. Just tell them.

I cleared my throat. Fluid in my body was flowing to all the wrong places. My mouth was dry and my hands were sweating.

'Well ... let the record state that I personally am not in favour of this course of action.'

'But you'll come?'

'Are you sure it's what you really really want?'

'FFS,' said Jenny exasperated, 'what are you, a firkin' Spice Girl?'

'No! Of course it's not what we want,' Brenda sighed, 'but it's the only chance we've got.'

'Ok,' I said calmly, 'then I'll do it. I'll do it for Faughie.'

Chapter 66

Dinah was absolutely delighted to see us. Embarrassed, I think, by the boxes stacked up in her fusty main room, she ushered us through to the kitchen where she immediately set about making tea.

'I've packed everything away, so I'm terribly sorry, I can't even offer you a biscuit,' Dinah apologised. 'I know you like those Fortnum and Mason ones, Trixie.'

'Och, please don't trouble yourself, Lady Anglicus,' said Brenda, 'we're very grateful that you were able to see us on such short notice.'

'Please, do call me Dinah.'

There were nice, slightly awkward, smiles all round.

I was surprised to see Brenda and Jenny so out of their depth. They had skilfully handled prime ministers, academics and the international press and yet here they were practically doffing their caps. Nerves probably, but if I knew Jenny she'd find her stride once they got down to discussing business.

Dinah turned from us to pour the water into the teapot and Jenny took the opportunity to swivel her eyes at me, signalling that I should open the discussion. Dinah passed us our tea cups and we all politely sipped. Now that the tea ceremony had been sorted, a bashful silence descended. Jenny began giving me the evil eye again, right in front of Dinah. Dinah reciprocated by also staring hard at me. I was getting it from all sides.

'Well, Dinah, the good news is that Faughie Council has found a way to buy the estate. As you've probably worked out from our late-night eleventh-hour appearance, the ladies are here to make you an offer.'

'Oh, I'm so pleased!'

Another round of smiles, this time more genuine. When no one else spoke, Dinah was forced to, 'Might I ask what you are offering exactly?'

'The full asking price,' said Jenny testily.

'Oh, splendid! I must say I am relieved.'

As the tension broke we gave up the tea party pretence. Brenda whipped the papers out of her briefcase and spread them on the table before Dinah.

'You'll see from our calculation that if we waive the inheritance tax and stamp duty you would normally pay the UK government, we can discount the price nearly 37 per cent.'

There was a moment's silence while everyone assessed Dinah's reaction. Other than sipping her tea, Dinah made no reaction so Brenda took a breath and ploughed on, 'We'd make an initial payment of 20 per cent of current market value,' she said, pointing at a spreadsheet, 'if you care to look at the payment schedule.'

Dinah let Brenda burble on for a few minutes but I could see she wasn't comfortable.

'Forgive me,' she said coyly, 'I'm not terribly au fait with the terminology. Eh, could you explain what "payment schedule" means exactly?'

Brenda and Jenny seemed mystified. I was a bit confused myself. Even I could hazard a guess; surely the phrase was self-explanatory? All three of us were reluctant to embarrass Dinah by stating the obvious, but again, somebody had to take the lead. Brenda and Jenny looked at me.

'Well, if I'm understanding things correctly,' I piped up, 'it really just means what it says: it's a schedule.'

Jenny and Brenda nodded along.

'That is to say, a eh, a ....'

'Timetable.'

'A timetable, thank you, Brenda, a timetable for when Faughie will make the payments to you, eh ...'

'The payments,' Dinah repeated, flatly.

'Yes,' said Brenda rescuing me, 'this green figure is the forecasted revenue over the five-year period and the red figure is the payments we'll make to you; effectively, what'll be going into your bank account.'

'And this is a projection?'

'Yes, an extrapolation on the revenue we hope to generate.'

'Not an actual, confirmed amount?'

'No-oh, but ...'

'If I could just stop you there. I must say I didn't expect an equity-release scheme. I'm not drawing my pension quite yet.'

So much for Dinah not knowing the terminology, but everyone obliged with a smile for her wee joke.

'Well,' Brenda blustered, 'this plan may share some of the features of equity release, but –'

'But unlike equity release I can't continue to live here.'

'Well –'

'And you intend to pay instalments from the revenue you "hope to generate"?'

'Yes, but we're fairly confident –'

'*Fairly confident* butters no parsnips with HMRC, I'm afraid. I understood you'd come to offer me the asking price, a much-reduced asking price as it is. Can't you find financial backing? A mortgage even?'

'We have a mortgage. That's where we raised the 20 per cent down payment.'

'So you'll be servicing that debt too?'

Brenda took on the look of a naughty schoolgirl in front of the headmistress.

'Yes.'

'As well as all manner of start-up costs, wage bills, running costs.'

'Yes.'

Dinah folded her arms.

'But,' Brenda pleaded, 'I'm sure within the five-year projection ...'

'What if I can't wait five years?'

'Dinah, we're not finished, hear us out,' said Jenny. 'Tell her, Brenda.'

'We're authorised to offer you a 3 per cent stake in the business,' said Brenda, obviously reluctant to give it away.

'Three per cent? Please. You might as well offer me cashback or a free Parker Pen.'

Brenda looked stumped. I thought toffs found it vulgar to talk about money; Dinah wasn't so much vulgar as downright snarky.

'The percentage is negotiable,' said Jenny, leaving Brenda to sulk. 'We'll go back to the committee and ask them to reconsider, perhaps 5 per cent might be more appropriate ...'

'Five per cent of promises? Hmmm, I'd have to think about that.'

Jenny once again stepped in.

'What would seem an acceptable percentage to you then?'

Dinah couldn't hide her smile. Maybe this was what she'd been waiting for: a bigger slice of the pie. She shook her head, trying to shake off the tell-tale smile.

'This piecemeal payment plan, it's not what I had in mind.'

'Look,' said Jenny sighing, 'let's cut to the chase: Knox MacIntyre's gone, he's not coming back, is he? This might be the best offer you get. You call it piecemeal but owning a stake in a multimillion-pound business, well, I call that a damn good pension. And it's tax efficient. It's also something to leave your son.'

Dinah received the last comment like a punch in the stomach.

Jenny's voice softened, 'I know you're only trying to protect your son's legacy and this would be a way of your family retaining the title, in name at least. It's good for tourism. Look, we don't have to come to any decisions right now. It's late, you're off to Luxembourg in the morning. We just wanted you to know the options before you go. Just think about it. We'll go back to the committee and see if we can't add a few percentage points; you take it to your financial advisors. We'll leave you the paperwork;

our people will speak to your people, we'll work something out. I'm sure you realise how very important you are to us and how hard we'll work to make this work. Please, Lady Anglicus, Dinah, just remember when you're talking to the judge in Luxembourg: if you stay invested in Faughie, we could be looking at a great future together.'

Chapter 67

Dinah left the next morning. To maximise the chances of her accepting the offer, or at least supporting independence when she met the judges, Jenny insisted that we all see her off. Standing there in a line, nicely turned out in smart clothes, smiling obediently, the casual observer might have mistaken us for Dinah's faithful staff: Walter as the butler, Jenny the housekeeper and the rest of us as below-stairs lackeys. That's what we looked like. Dinah was gracious, waving at us like the Queen of England, but determinedly non-committal on the subject of her support. Jenny put a brave face on it but from take-off her hopes seemed to be fizzling out, the fizz evaporating with every whirl of the helicopter's rotor blades. I had offered to look after Mimi while Dinah was in Luxembourg, but Dinah politely declined, taking the dog with her. Another bad omen.

Two days later Dinah wasn't greeted with the jubilatory flag-waving that Jenny and co. got when they'd come back, because Dinah didn't come back. It was reported that she had gone straight to her home in London. There was no word from her about the offer.

'Back to being an absentee landlord,' proclaimed Walter, 'the very people who sold Scotland to the English the first time around.'

That evening Walter and Brenda spent six hours on Skype with the legal team in Luxembourg trying to prevent the case from collapsing. Dinah was chief landowner, and without her support an independent Faughie wasn't judged to be viable. Walter pleaded with them: we hadn't had the referendum yet, so how could they make a decision without knowing what the people of Faughie wanted?

As I let the chickens out the next morning, Brenda told me, with tears rolling down her face, that the dream of independence was over. With Dinah's collusion, Westminster had managed to convince the world, and more importantly, Luxembourg, that Faughie was being held by a minority of lawless rebels. I sat her down and made her a coffee but I had to turn off the radio. It was full of upbeat commentators – and some Faughians – saying how delighted they were with the ruling. I didn't see anyone delighted. Westminster wasted no time. That afternoon a party of three ministers – Tobias Grunt had conveniently been replaced – requested a meeting with the committee and were helicoptered in.

'Coming to offer baubles and shiny trinkets to the natives,' said Walter's bitter tweet.

The ministers came with a 'no hard feelings, let's kiss and make up,' attitude, gracious in victory. To heal wounded pride and prevent any festering sores, they declared an amnesty on all legal and licensing infringements. Under the UK Disregard Regulations, tax revenue was discounted, and normal tax-raising powers were reinstituted. Everyone could keep the money they had made, tax-free, up to this point. When the council special committee attempted to argue, the ministers gently explained that they were not here to negotiate, they had no power to do so, they were simply delivering the message. They smiled, shook everyone's hand and left.

'I have to open this meeting with a heartfelt apology,' said Walter, standing on a table in the Caley's function suite, the only place big enough to hold everyone. 'I'm so sorry we've let you down, but, in our struggle for independence, we may have come to the end of the road.'

There was silence. Everyone had already heard it on the radio and telly of course, but until Walter said it I don't think we really believed it.

'They can't shut us down just like that,' shouted Jackie, 'if independence is what we want, what's that got to do with London or Luxembourg?'

'But Jackie,' said Walter with a humourless laugh, 'we haven't yet been able to establish that independence *is* what the majority of Faughians want.'

'It isn't!' yelled Betty Robertson to applause from some of her camp.

'To be fair, that hasn't been established yet either, Betty,' Walter replied. 'The advice we've had is that, sadly, the referendum is no longer material to the case.'

This didn't go down well.

'Mr Speaker please?'

Minding her manners this time, La Robertson asked permission and was given the floor.

'What would be the point of a referendum when the legal case has already been decided?' Betty asked in her deep-toned reasonable voice. 'All that time, effort, and money expended; what would it realistically achieve?'

There was a surprising amount of support for this point of view, and I could understand why. People were fed up with all this pointless political wrangling; they just wanted to go back to normal life. It would mean fewer meetings, that was for sure.

'Nevertheless,' Walter continued, 'the committee met again today and we have come to a decision. Whatever the legal situation, however material to the case it may or may not be, the fact remains that you voted for a chance to decide your future and we promised you a referendum. We've decided to bring forward the date of the referendum by one week and make good our promise to you. I would beseech anyone who has yet to register to vote to do so immediately. Please come to the front and we can get your details. Remember, we're not only deciding our own future here but that of future generations. It is crucial that each and every one of us takes part, whichever way you vote.' He spoke slowly and carefully to let the weight of what he was saying sink in. 'Please be aware of the consequences: if we vote No we accept the Luxembourg ruling. If we vote Yes,' and here he took a long pause, 'another Faughie is possible.'

A defiant cheer went up.

Betty Robertson and the No Campaigners remonstrated, of course, and both sides tried to drown the other out, though they seemed equally matched. One of the Claymores, Will, started thumping a bass drum to a battle-ready rhythm. Somewhere behind me a primal heeeuch split the air. I recognised that heeeuch, and turned round to see it fly from my Steven's mouth. He and Mag were doing some kind of Highland fling war dance.

All day I'd nursed the hope that this defeat might finally winkle Steven out of Inverfaughie. I'd planned a lovely dinner of roast pork to soften him up followed by home-made tablet and ice cream but that heeeuch told me everything I needed to know about Steven's plans. I shook my head and found myself simultaneously shaking my head and tapping my toe to the rhythm of the booming drum.

Chapter 68

Steven and the Claymores were still at the meeting banging the war drums, so before I started dinner I had a quick look at my emails. One of them, I couldn't believe: I had to read it three or four times to get the sense. It was from Tennyson and Cosgrove, a firm of London solicitors acting on behalf of Lady Anglicus. How did they even know my email address? They were offering me, at a reasonable price, the conversion of Harrosie from leasehold to freehold. Who knew what kind of market I'd find for it now, but still and all, I'd easily swap a successful eight-bedroomed B&B here for one in Glasgow.

I had a fleeting dilemma about the morality of taking the bribe – Dinah obviously believed I'd been working on her behalf – but I could be certain in myself that I hadn't sold out, that Jenny and Brenda had begged me to help. And anyway, the Anglicuses had made a fortune from the sweat of Robertsons through the centuries – this was a wee bit of payback. But if Steven was set on staying in Faughie, should I sell? And what about Jackie? I knew, because he'd grudgingly told me, that he was glad me and Steven were here, keeping Harrosie in the family.

Steven and the rest of them still hadn't come back from the meeting. I needed a good think and Bouncer was whining at the front door. Walkies.

The hills were a lonely place to be on your own. On the news it was always dog walkers who discovered raped and mutilated bodies. If I threw a stick for Bouncer to fetch, I always worried that he'd come back with a decomposing human hand in his mouth, so I always tried my hardest to keep up with him. I was peched out. We had been out for a good hour and a half and as I turned to walk back down the hill I almost ran into Keek cycling up the path towards me. What the hell was he doing up here? I'd never seen anyone up here with a bike before, the ground was too rough.

'Hey, keep your dog under control!' he yelled at me.

Bouncer was the most surefooted dog I knew; he'd given the bike a wide berth as he'd passed.

'I nearly came off my bike there!' Keek insisted.

I was too dumbfounded to be angry.

'What the hell are you talking about? The dog was nowhere near you.'

'That dog should be on a lead!' he screamed, one skelly eye on Bouncer, the other halfway up the hill. He was hysterical. And then he leaned in and mumbled something down the front of his anorak.

'Sorry?'

I was starting to worry. I was alone on a hillside with this nutbar.

'Tonight. Tell them tonight.'

'Ok,' I said, scuttling past him.

I wound Bouncer's lead round my fist into a knuckleduster ready to swing it into Keek's face. As I galloped down the hill I heard the bike getting closer behind me. I set my jaw and waited to be ravished. I would go down fighting.

'Sorry,' he mumbled again, 'I didn't mean tell them tonight, I meant it's happening tonight. Will you tell them? Don't use your phone. Please, Trixie?' And then he loosened his grip on the bike brakes and skited off down the uneven path, his bum lifting off the saddle with every bump.

Chapter 69

Jackie answered the door at Walter's house. He ushered me immediately into the kitchen. Walter and Jenny were at the table having a pow-wow, eager to hear what Double Agent Keek had said to me. Nobody seemed surprised when I told them.

'Good old Keek, I knew he'd come up with the goods,' said Jenny, 'too glaikit-looking to show up on their radar as a spy threat; what a secret weapon that lad has been for us.'

'It's the Bay of Pigs all over again,' said Walter, 'or Batalla de Girón, as it's more properly known, the amphibious invasion undertaken by the CIA against Cuba in 1961. We're about to witness history, as it so reliably does, repeating itself. They're coming to liberate the poor downtrodden Faughians, that is to say, Betty and her ilk, and deliver them from the tyranny of dangerous communists, that is to say, us. And, as they're not legally required to recognise our sovereignty, they'll claim it's a law-enforcement issue. Like the Bay of Pigs, they'll come by sea, in the dark, with no witnesses. Put simply, they want to get the jump on us, reassert control before we can establish a mandate for self-rule.'

'Walter, this is scary, what's going to happen?'

To my amazement, Jackie, who sat across the table from me, reached over and took my hand.

'It's ok, Trixie, there's nothing to be scared of,' he said gently.

'If the invasion is successful they'll overthrow the committee, they'll probably arrest us, but I doubt they'll actually shoot anyone, that wouldn't play well,' said Walter, not exactly reassuring me. 'But it won't be successful, we're prepared. Don't worry, there's nothing to fear.'

I burst out crying, bawling like a wean. I couldn't really work out why I was crying: probably the thought of a terrifying invasion, but it might have been a subconscious appeal to my dad. This was a side of Jackie I'd never seen, this gentle paternal side.

Jenny put the kettle on while I cried out every tear I could muster. Jackie moved to sit beside me, patting me on the back and briefly letting me cry on his shoulder.

'Sorry, Trixie,' Jenny apologised, 'we have a lot to organise. Slightly caught on the hop, we didn't expect it to be this soon.'

Suddenly everyone was bustling about, my tears forgotten.

Walter and Jackie went into the front room and I took this moment alone with Jenny to make my confession.

'Jenny, I need to explain what happened.' I blurted before I had the chance to change my mind. 'Dinah's paying me a bribe. When she was desperate to sell she asked me to nobble the committee.'

'Huh! You didn't work very hard for your money. As I remember, we had to talk you into coming with us.'

'I didn't want to do it, you know I didn't, but Dinah doesn't know that so now her lawyers have offered to sell me Harrosie freehold. I feel ...'

'Hang on, Walter has to hear this.' Jenny rushed into the living room and rushed back with Walter and Jackie.

'Tell them what you've just told me.'

I hung my head.

'Tell them, this is important. It's ok, go on.'

I was forced to admit my black burning shame all over again, this time in front of Jackie.

The three of them looked at each other across the table.

'I'm so sorry. I don't really know how it happened, I just got caught up in it, I'm so sorry I–'

Walter interrupted me, 'Do you have the money to buy it?'

Oh god, this was awkward. How could I tell them that I'd salted away every penny, that I'd spent every waking hour dreaming up ways to make more money so that I could buy my way out of Inverfaughie?

'Eh, yes, I think so.'

'Right,' said Walter, 'This is an absolute gift – well, a literal gift for you, Trixie, but it gives us just the opportunity we've been waiting for. Ho ho! The architect of her own undoing!' said Walter, rubbing his hands. 'A small blundering step for Anglicus, a giant leap out of feudalism for Faughie. This sets a precedent for us to buy the town, one property at a time.'

'If we win,' said Jenny.

'Aye, sure, if we win,' repeated Walter.

'You're not angry with me?'

'Well, all's well that ends well, I suppose,' said Jenny, somewhat grudgingly. 'Whatever happens tonight, win, lose or draw, they're going to write books about this.' She cleared her throat, always a sign that she was about to make a speech.

'We know what the past has given us and, based on hundreds of years of experience, what it'll keep on giving us. This is our chance to rip up the old heraldic rulebook, transform the way we do things around here, make our own social democracy. This is the most exciting moment in our lifetime. I don't care what anybody says about you, Trixie, och, you're selfish like most folk, and you're a bit annoying, but when it comes down to it, you're actually not a bad sort.'

Despite the selfish/annoying dig that Jenny couldn't resist, I was so relieved to hear her say this, I rushed at her like an enthusiastic dog. Another enthusiastic dog joined in and we both nearly knocked wee Jenny off her feet. I clung to her and sobbed my gratitude. I didn't deserve these people.

'We'd better make a move, Jackie,' Jenny said, as she forcibly removed my arms from around her. 'You go out the front, I'll go out the back.'

'Trixie,' said Jackie, trying to take the heat off Jenny and let her make her escape out the back way, 'you did the right thing. I'm proud of you.'

I rushed him too. I sensed his embarrassment and, trying to be a little less selfish and annoying, I released my grip on him. Jackie gathered up his stuff, put on his bicycle clips, voluntarily returned to give me a lovely hug, and then made to leave.

'Where are you going?' I asked but he didn't answer. I trotted after him, out the front door, but Walter hauled me back inside.

'What's he going to do? Be careful, Jackie!' I shouted after him.

'Shhh!' said Walter, quickly closing the door.

Bouncer jumped up and rested his head in Walter's lap as we sat at the kitchen table sipping tea.

'Why did I have to shoosh?'

'ScanEagles,' said Walter pointing his finger straight up, 'drones gathering information. Jackie's gone to make arrangements for tonight.'

'Is Steven mixed up in this?'

'Steven and Mag have volunteered to play their part.'

I felt sick. 'Please Walter, no. He's only sixteen.'

'Calm down, Trixie, he's in no danger, they're not on the front line. Stevo and Mag are very much our backroom boys, but they'll play a vital role nonetheless, absolutely vital.'

'Why, what are they doing?'

'Providing the energy to power the lights. We can get round the shortage of diesel by using Mag's water and wind turbines.'

'The lights?'

'And the cameras. For the action. Very important to capture everything, to provide a record of what's really happening here. The boys will power the generators for the Outside Broadcast Units. The world will be watching. Everyone else will film whatever they can on their phones. This revolution will be televised.'

'What revolution? Walter, what the hell are you going to do?'

'We're going to meet the invaders and resist them.'

'But how can you possibly resist them?'

'Och, not for long, just long enough to get the votes in and counted.'

'You're still going ahead with the referendum?'

'We most certainly are,' said Walter with his old chirpiness, 'and this is where you come in.'

'Oh no.'

I put my hands up.

'I don't come in anywhere.'

'Ethecom have kindly donated their Routemaster as a mobile polling station. Jan will drive. You, if you agree, will accompany him round the farms and cottages. There is an international legal precedent for this; they did it in the Falklands when they had their referendum. While we hold them off on the loch, or at least prevent them from landing for as long as we can, Jenny's cohort will set up a decoy polling operation in the village hall. Brenda and her cohort will man the real polling station, in the kitchen of the Caley. Are you with me thus far?'

'No.'

Undaunted, Walter carried on, 'It is important that you ask people to enter the bus to cast their vote, not on their doorstep and certainly not inside their homes. To strengthen the legality of the ballot, voters must voluntarily attend the polling station, do you understand?'

'But Walter ...'

'Here's a map and a list of eligible voters. Do not come back to the village until you have been round all of them. Do not use your phone. When you see the Faughie flag flying from the Caley flagpole, and only when you see the flag flying, enter the hotel kitchen from the back door. Guard that ballot box with your life.'

'No chance.'

'Ok,' he relented and switched to a less dramatic tone, 'you don't have to guard it with your life. Just make sure that you give the box only to Brenda.'

'Walter, there are two sides to this. There was a lot of grumbling at that meeting. I don't know if you noticed but people are getting fed up with this. That Luxembourg ruling knocked the stuffing out of everyone. You heard them, they're saying we don't have the skill or experience to run things and we're too small to make it on our own.'

'Ok, let's take that point by point. Point one: Lesley Riddoch tackled this in her book *Blossom*. She said that if we believe in our own capability we can rebuild from the ground up, because it can't be transformed from the top down. From here on the ground in Faughie, to quote the cliché, "the only way is up". Point two: in terms of acreage, Faughie is small, but with the technology available to us – global markets and communication and what have you – those limits are mostly in our minds. Small is beautiful, each person's vote is a greater percentage of the whole; it carries more weight. Sorry to keep coming up with quotes, Trixie, but I've just thought of another beezer: Alasdair Gray said in *Lanark*, "the vaster the social unit the less possibility of true democracy".'

'The quotes are great, Walter, honestly, I'm impressed that you can carry all that around in your head, but the bottom line is: what if people vote against independence? You've got to admit, the odds are stacked against it, there seems no point now. You can do all this running around, quote all the quotes you like, but what if the box comes back full of No votes?'

Walter stopped and thought about that for a moment as he stroked Bouncer's head. Then he smiled and shrugged. 'Maybe it will, maybe it won't. Maybes aye, maybes naw,' he said, 'that's democracy for you.'

Chapter 70

As soon as I got back to the house I collared Steven.

'Haw you,' I said, right in front of his Claymore pals, 'I want a word with you.'

His pals deserted him, melting away out of the room. The big Highland warriors that were about to face an invading force were scared of me.

'Consider yourself grounded. You're going to stay here with me and we are going to have a wee night in the house – watch a video, have a bit of family time. Why not invite Morag over to have dinner with us?'

Steven laughed and shook his head.

'You know, Trixie, I can't take you seriously when you start that disciplinarian shite.'

'You watch your mouth!'

'That's what you're worried about? My mouth?'

He shook his head again, as if I was a lost cause.

'Look, Steven, there's no use lying to me, I know what's going on,' I said.

'Well, if you know, then there's no use lying, is there?'

He had me there.

'Well, I ... och I don't know what to do!' I wailed.

'Look, I understand,' he said, as if he were the adult, 'you're just trying to do your job protecting me and it's sweet. I appreciate it.'

'Please, son, don't go, I'm scared, please.'

I burst out crying again but the tears that had been so effective with Jackie made no impact on Steven. He didn't hold my hand or let me cry on his shoulder, but at least he didn't leave the room.

'I'm sorry,' I said, once I'd got my sobbing under control. Once I realised that he wouldn't bend, 'I'm really scared about what's going to happen.'

'Go back to Glasgow. I'll be ok.'

'I'm not leaving here without you, Steven, we've been through this. I don't know what to do!'

'Well then, just do what Walter asks of you. Or not. Either way is fine. I'll still love you, you'll still be my mum.'

'But what if ...'

'Look, the worst that'll happen is that we'll be arrested.'

'But Steven,' I wailed, 'I can't get arrested; you can't get arrested, you'll have a criminal record! What about uni; what about your future?'

'I've told you, my future's here. Look, Mag's waiting for me, I need to go.'

Left with nothing else, I started crying again, not howling any more but weeping, and now he came and cuddled me.

'I'm glad you're staying, Mum,' he whispered.

*

Jan pulled the bus up outside and waited. I thought he'd come into the house and try to talk me into it at least, but he'd probably been briefed by Walter. The house was empty, the Claymores had left, tooled up to the teeth. They each gave me a hug as they left and told me not to worry; Dave promised they wouldn't do anything stupid or heroic, but it was an emotional farewell.

As soon as they left I went to the hall cupboard and rummaged around behind the boots until I found what I was looking for stuffed down a welly. Whisky. There were maybe three fingers left in the bottle that I had planked one night after an intense poker game when nobody was looking. Three fingers was too much to down in a wannie, but too little to leave. I unscrewed the lid, held the bottle to my lips and finished it in two long exhilarating slugs.

Jan left the engine running outside; the fried fish and chip smell of the recycled vegetable oil was starting to permeate the house, making my mouth water, and still he wouldn't come in. I didn't want Bouncer getting mixed up in this so I left him sleeping, found the Extra Strong Mints and grabbed my jacket.

'Don't be getting any ideas that I'm a Faughie patriot. I'm only here for Steven's sake,' I huffed, as I climbed up and hung at the driver's door.

'That's why we're all doing this, Trixie, for our children.'

'I didn't know you had kids, Jan.'

'Not yet I don't.'

I was relieved to hear him say that; it made me smile. I didn't like to think of Jan having a life beyond Faughie.

'Maybe some day,' he said, giving me a look he'd given me before. It was a look that suggested he was saying a lot more than he was saying. Which caused me to do something.

I leaned into his driver's cage and kissed him. I never even blushed. He reciprocated, thank the good lord.

'That was most unexpected, and very nice,' he said when we came up for air, 'I like a lady with good oral hygiene.'

I looked at him quizzically.

'You've used mouthwash, haven't you?' he said, tasting the remnants of my saliva in his mouth. 'I'm loving the minty-fresh flavour. Zingy.'

'Cheers,' I sighed. I shouldn't be having this good a time. 'Right, here's the map with the route Walter wants us to take. I suppose we'd better get this referendum on the road.'

I'd have squeezed in beside him, but there was no room. I had to get aboard and sit in a passenger seat and, from there, as the bus rattled along the country roads, it wasn't long before the euphoria of the snog wore off.

I was worried sick about Steven. I tried his mobile number, not to try to talk him out of it – I knew it was too late for that – but just to tell him again how much I loved him. His phone was switched off, which panicked me before I remembered that Walter had insisted upon it. I prayed that Steven, and everyone else – but most importantly Jackie and Steven – would be safe. I thought of parents whose kids had joined the army and gone to war zones – how the hell did people cope with that? How did I get myself messed up in all this, and worse: how did I manage to get Steven embroiled in it? Yeah, sure, people all around the world fought for self-determination, but it wasn't as if we were in Syria or under some other horribly repressive regime. As horribly repressive regimes went, Britain really wasn't that bad. I didn't mind it. So what was I doing here?

Jan was pulling up a narrow farm road.

'First stop, Fentons' Farm,' he shouted.

The rain soaked us through while we waited for them to open the door.

'It's ok,' I said, 'we don't need to both get wet. You wait in the bus, I'll bring people out.'

Jan grasped my hand. 'Nah, it's ok. I like getting wet,' he said through a huge grin.

Morag opened the door and let us in. She was in her jammies and slippers wearing her hair in a pony-tail, but she still managed to look beautiful. She really suited her hair up. Good genes, and, as it was just her and her dad, she was likely to inherit the dairy business. Steven had chosen his burd well.

'Hello, Mrs McNicholl, Jan. I'm sorry, Dad's in bed,' she said, 'we're up early for the milking. What did you want to see him about?'

'Oh, Morag,' I said, 'this is really important.'

Morag looked worried. And guilty. I dreaded to think what she and Steven had got up to, but that would have to wait.

'It's ok,' said Jan, 'nothing to worry about. We've had to move the referendum forward a few days. Can you ask him to come out to the bus to cast his vote, please?'

'What?' she asked, horrified, 'wake him up?'

'Well, yeah,' I said, 'he needs to come out to the bus to vote.'

Morag rolled her eyes, 'I'll try.'

A few moments later she was back downstairs.

'He says bugger off, he's trying to sleep and it's pelting down. He says come back in the morning.'

'No, but ...'

'I'm not asking him again.'

'Miss Fenton,' said Jan, oozing charm, 'I see your name here on the roll. You turned sixteen only three days ago, congratulations, an adult now, eh? Would you care to step outside and cast your vote?'

'Can I not do it tomorrow? *Don't Tell the Bride* is starting in a minute.'

'And that's all it'll take of your time, Morag, one teeny wee minute.'

'Och,' she moaned, pulling her housecoat over her head, 'what a load of fuss over nothing.'

The three of us ran together to the bus. Jan had her sign the list and gave her the voting papers. He showed her the private voting booth and she hesitated.

'I don't even know what I'm voting for,' said Morag.

'Surely you've seen the campaigns down in the village?' I said. 'You can't avoid them.'

'Aye, but what I mean is, maybe it's safer not to vote. Look what happened the last time Dad voted. We had no grazing for ages.'

'Well one thing's certain,' said Jan, 'if we don't vote for change then things won't get better and they could get worse.'

Morag had pulled open the curtain ready to enter the booth, but this stopped her in her tracks.

'Worse than having no grazing?'

We were about to lose our first and only voter so far. Walter was going to go radge. Jan joined me on the bench seat in front of the voting booth and invited Morag to sit on another seat opposite, as though we were three day-tripping pensioners, with all the time in the world.

'Morag, you're a farmer, you're running a fine business here. Let's imagine you had a cow that had voting rights.'

She smirked, 'What? A magic cow?'

I fidgeted. We really didn't have time for this.

'Not really, a normal cow, a milker, that's what you call them, isn't it?'

She nodded. *Don't Tell the Bride* must have started by now, but so far she was going along with the magic voting cow idea.

'But let's agree this cow can vote, ok?'

'Ok,' Morag reluctantly agreed.

'The cow has two choices: one, it can roam Faughie, eating what it likes, when it likes; or two, it stays in the barn and lets you decide how much you're going to feed it, ok?'

'Ok.'

'Now, no matter how much – or how little – you feed it, it still has to produce the same quantity of milk.'

'Hah, that would be magic.'

'So, it chooses option two: it stays in the barn and lets you make the decisions. How much will you feed it?'

'I get the same yield no matter what I feed it?'

'Yes.'

'Well, I feed it less then, obviously,' she said. 'It'll increase my margins. That's just good business.'

'Better for you if the cow lets you make the decision.'

'Not so good for the Faughie cow,' said Morag, laughing.

I laughed too; so did Jan before he turned serious. 'Exactly. It all depends on whether you want your calves, or your children – and I'm sure that one day you'll have very beautiful children, Morag – to stay in the barn or decide their own future, because that's what's at stake.'

Morag filled her cheeks with air and huffed out her breath. 'Ok, ok,' she said, pulling closed the curtain in the booth, 'I'll be glad when it's finished.' She yelled from behind the curtain, 'It'll be finished tomorrow, won't it?'

Suddenly one side of the sky lit up.

'One way or the other,' Jan called in agreement, 'it will be finished.'

Jan and I kneeled up on the bench and stared out of the window. The light was coming from the loch side, a bright diffuse glow that bounced off the clouds.

'Floodlights,' said Jan, 'the lookouts must have spotted activity at the mouth of the loch.'

Now we heard the slow dreadful moan of the lighthouse fog warning. Everyone in the village would be taking up their positions. This was all getting a bit too real. I knew Steven and Mag would be working to keep the generators going, powering the big lights for the cameras. I felt sick when I thought about what might happen to them. I felt the vulnerability of their young bodies to Tasers or rubber bullets or whatever. I felt *my* body vulnerable and unprotected, as though it was happening to me. I'd rather it was happening to me. I wished at that moment that I was standing beside Steven and Jackie instead of being stuck on this bus. I reached for Jan's hand.

Jenny told me ages ago that, whether I liked it or not, I was already bound to this place. Steven might end up staying in Inverfaughie all his days, Jackie almost certainly would. Steven might have a family here, Morag might end up being his wife, the mother of his children. The mother of my grandchildren. Jan and I might get it together; I was only forty, there were still plenty of eggs in my basket; I might be the mother of his children. So many ifs, buts and maybes. Maybes aye, as Walter had said, maybes naw.

Morag emerged from behind the curtain.

'Oh, is there something going on in the village? Oh god,' she moaned, 'it's not the Claymores doing one of their historical re-enactments again, is it?'

Jan looked at me and I smiled. No point in worrying her.

'Aye, I suppose you could call it that,' I said.

'I've been a good citizen, I've filled it in,' said Morag, waving her form at us, 'I'm not sure I've even done it right, but I've done it. Where do I put it?'

These last few months in Faughie had been full of upheaval. When I'd first pitched up in this wee Highland village I'd been as lonely and miserable as I'd ever been in my life; it was only in the last few weeks that things had started to change. Of course, Steven being with me and Jackie finally acknowledging me had begun the process, but it wasn't just my family that had made me feel better. It was my friends: Walter and Jenny, and Brenda and Mag, Dinah and Betty even, and Keek and Moira Henderson and Andy

Robertson and everyone who mucked in on the council and at Ethecom. And Jan. I'd been so reluctant to join Faughie Council, but now I realised that Jenny had been right: getting involved with other people had given me my accommodation licence, my means of escape, but it had also given me a reason to stay.

As the lights down at the loch side flickered, Jan and I pricked up our ears. What was happening down there now? Were the Claymores rushing with their swords aloft into bloody battle? I sincerely hoped not. I couldn't bear to think of my friends being hurt or hurting anyone. No, no amount of sword play was going to win this fight. I only hoped that the world would bear witness to our democratic procedure. The battle was now going to be won or lost by what the people of Faughie put in the ballot box.

'Aye, thank you, Morag,' I said, 'just put it in the box.'

Acknowledgements

Obviously if you've ever seen the 1949 Ealing comedy *Passport to Pimlico*, you'll know where I got the plot. I prefer to think of it not as a direct rip-off but as a 'difplag', (diffuse plagiarism) to borrow Alasdair Gray's portmanteau word. And talking of great Scottish writers and artists, books such as Andy Wightman's *The Poor Had No Lawyers*, James Robertson's *And the Land Lay Still*, Lesley Riddoch's *Blossom* as well as Anthony Baxter's documentary *You've Been Trumped* were all terrific spurs. I hope you will seek them out. They're not generally funny, in fact they might make you cry, they did me, but they are essential reading. I had invaluable help from first readers: Karen Jones, David Fernandes, Cynthia Rogerson and Alison Stroak. Sara Hunt and Jenny Brown have been brilliant as usual. David Fernandes not only read it, he also let me obsessively discuss characters and plot twists and gave me loads of help and useful ideas.

Sources

Crichton-Smith, Iain. *Consider the Lilies* Phoenix; New edition 2001. ISBN 9780753812938

Gray, Alasdair. *Lanark: A Life in Four Books*. Canongate, Edinburgh 1981. ISBN 9781847673749

Jenkins, Robin. *The Cone Gatherers* Canongate (Canons), Edinburgh 2012. ISBN 9780857862358

Passport to Pimlico. 1949 British comedy film made by Ealing Studios and starring Stanley Holloway, Margaret Rutherford and Hermione Baddeley. Directed by Henry Cornelius. Screenplay by T. E. B. Clarke

Riddoch, Lesley. *Blossom: What Scotland Needs to Flourish*. Luath, Edinburgh 2013. ISBN 9781908373694

Robertson, James. *And the Land Lay Still*. Penguin, London 2011. ISBN13: 978 0141028545

Wightman, Andy. *The Poor Had No Lawyers: Who Owns Scotland and How They Got it*. Birlinn Ltd, Edinburgh 2013. ISBN-13: 978-1780271149

You've Been Trumped http://www.youvebeentrumped.com/youvebeentrumped.com/THE_MOVIE.html

About the Author

Laura Marney tries to do a good deed every day. Occasionally bad deeds do accidentally slip in, but there you go, nobody's perfect. She is the author of five novels: *For Faughie's Sake, No Wonder I Take a Drink, Nobody Loves a Ginger Baby, Only Strange People Go to Church* and *My Best Friend Has Issues*. She also writes short stories and drama for radio and the stage. She lives in Glasgow and is a Lecturer in Creative Writing at Glasgow University.